DAYS OF WINE AND ROSES

Novels written by the author

KOREAN VENTURE

SLAVE FROM ANTIOCH

RIBALD TALES & STORIES FROM U.T.

BRING BACK THE B–47

DAYS OF WINE AND ROSES

LOCK. S

iUniverse, Inc.
New York Lincoln Shanghai

DAYS OF WINE AND ROSES

iUniverse books may be ordered through booksellers or by contacting:

iUniverse
2021 Pine Lake Road, Suite 100
Lincoln, NE 68512
www.iuniverse.com
1-800-Authors (1-800-288-4677)

ISBN: 0-595-34868-8

Printed in the United States of America

CONTENTS

▼

TRAILER PARK BLUES

FARCE

"What's the gross?" Phil Jerigan put his feet up on the worn desk with a sigh, his glance resting on the accountant.

Andrew Todd looked at the print-out he had prepared for this daily ritual. "Fifty two thousand one hundred and fifty—full. house plus SRO." His dark brows framed a lined, but otherwise expressionless face.

Jerigan studied the worn spot on the desk under his scuffed shoes. "We got one luke warm review, the rest panned the show or ignored it altogether." He shook his head as he picked up the Village Voice folded over to the quarter page ad.

Tennessee Williams theatre W 51 s t. S t

MARVELOUS MONTANA MARY in KISS ME JED I AINT TYPHOID MARY

A spicy musical revue based on an old soap opera Can a sweet from a small mining town in NW Montana find love and happiness with a rich, handsome mining engineer who buys the local saloon where she's one of the chorus line that 'moons' the audience in the black-out finale?

In the middle of the copy was the bottoms-up outline of a chorus girl wearing nothing but black high heels. The same silhouette outline on tie billboards downstairs in front of the off=Broadway theatre.

Phil Jerigan sighed. "I don't understand…."

"Anything else, you want Phil?" the deadpan Andrew asked.

He looked up sharply, "Yeah, what's the weekend advance? Go ahead I can take it." He reached for a cigarette then dropped his hand from the empty shirt-pocket. "Shit…."

Andrew put his horned rims back on, shuffling the print-outs, "Today's about three-quarters sold out and Sunday evening maybe forty percent. Both matinees are roughly fifty percent."

"OK, fine, take five."

The box-office ticket reservationist, ticket taker, money manager, pay-master, accountant, tax consultant ran a hand through his thinning hair, stuffed his glasses nervously in his jacket pocket and stepped toward the door. Jerigan's "What d'ya think, Andy?" caught him with his hand on the knob. He relaxed his grip. "If I can get back to the phones sometime this morning we might make the 'angels' happy in three or four weeks," he rasped.

"Sic'em, Andy." Phil broke his sour expression with a rough cackle.

Twenty years in the business and he thought he'd seen everything—he could tell when he had a hit, when a show would make money, when it would fold. Now he wasn't sure. The uncertainty puzzled him. Should he jump in with both feet or be ready to pack up in a half hour? He reached for the cigarettes again. "Damn!" He coughed, his hand flat on the empty shirt-pocket. If I'd known this I'd have jumped in the stock market, last year, he thought. He pressed the intercom wondering if it still worked on stage. To his surprise there was an answer, the stage-door watchman.

"Good mornin', Joe," he said raising his voice, "glad t'see somebody's on the job down there. Is Randy, the choreographer, around?"

The dusty box on the wall crackled, a message from Marconi was imminent…"Mr. Jerigan?"

"Yeah."

"He come in a few minutes ago. Y'want'im?"

"Yeah, Joe, I wanna kick his fruity balls up into his ass so he'll look the part. Send him up here."

A laugh crackled through the ancient interphone box. "Right away, Mr. Jerigan."

"You wanted to see me, Mr. Jerigan?" Sweat beaded the young man's forehead under a lock of wet, curly black hair. He was wearing warm up clothes, a towel around his neck.

Jerigan looked up. "Yeah, Randy. Take a seat. You workin' out so early?"

"Getting ready to rehearse the line."

"Good, that's what I wanted to talk to you about." He studied the young dancer, his watery eyes unblinking. "Let me get straight to the point. This young girl, the one in the center of the line, ah, Mary—is it?"

"Yes, Mary—"

"She's not a dancer. Why's she in the center on that number? Draws a lot of attention. Why not Nellie?"

Randy shifted, looking away momentarily. He wiped the towel over his face, hesitating, "She's got the best apple ass in the group and—"

"But she can't dance," Jerigan interrupted, "What's her experience?"

Randy gazed back at Phil Jerigan unblinking.

"OK, OK so we don't pay so good. Is she the best we can get?" He remembered that this was Randy's first job as a choreographer. He'd been hired because he was willing to defer part of his salary in order to get the experience and credits.

"Mr. Jerigan, the answer is yes and no. Nellie is a pro. She helps keep them together, we need her on stage, but she's a little stringy…know what I mean? Mary's fresh and bright—her enthusiasm comes across, besides…"

"She's got the best damned apple ass, etcetera," Phil broke in tiredly. "OK. Work 'em." He forced toughness into his voice.

"Yes, sir. That's what I was warming up for, they should be waiting for me on stage right now." Randy's tone was even and he met Jerigan's eyes directly.

"All right. Get to it!" Jerigan waved an arm with a spastic slap of his empty cigarette pocket. "Why'd I ever quit?"

Randy spun out of the chair. "Oh, Randy," Jerigan cut in as he was halfway though the door, "Good job last night. The audience…aah, get out o' here, 'n get that girl dancing. We can't rely on the black-out number to carry the show forever."

"Yes, sir," Randy grinned and escaped the dingy office.

Jerigan got up and went to the grimy window overlooking 51st, four stories below. Traffic pounded the slush of a late November snow. He stared, alone with his thoughts. Maybe that Randy was OK. If he could whip that bunch into shape they might survive and even make a few bucks. Randy's exasperated look was familiar—it didn't have anything to do with the pay or even Mary's apple ass. It was Britt Holmbrook III or IV, whatever.

The backer was a thirty-five percent owner of the show and Mary was his squeeze. Mr. Holmbrook had appraised Mary's ass long before anyone at the Tennessee Williams theatre had or Jerigan had lost all insight into why backers, angels, were willing to risk so much money on untested playwrights with unknown casts in off-Broadway shows. The stock market was safer, a lot safer.

With glazed eyes, he looked around the barren office, his paper strewn desk, the old 'girly' calendar on the wall. So what was his excuse for being there? Was he an old fight manager still searching for that unique fighter, a challenger, a boy with the potential, to go all the way—win a championship?. Jerigan was familiar with flops. Familiar? Hell, he could give chapter and verse, write a best selling novel, you name it. Like the washed-up stumble-bums who'd had too many fights, he'd been in the business too long. So what did that have to do with MARVELOUS MONTANA MARY or KISS ME JED I AINT TYPHIOID MARY? Stupid title, an ingénue who couldn't dance, but had a great ass, the critics had nothing good to say about it and the show had the tinniest door crack of being a box office smash—that's what. Just give me four solid weeks, he thought.

Mary Staffelbergen, Mary Staffe her stage name, stood apart from the other three girls who were excitedly comparing their reactions on opening night. Nellie hadn't come on stage yet. Mary was as excited as the other girls, but they were all New Yorkers, they talked funny and they ignored her.

"All right girls," Randy called as he came down the center aisle of the theater, "we're going to start with the number from the saloon scene. Places." He clapped his hands. "Where's Nellie?"

"Coming, Randy," her voice came from the wings.

Mary took her place in the middle as Nellie hurried into line next to her. The tinny sound of the dance hall piano began the introduction. "All right, and one, and two," Randy picked up the beat cueing them.

When they had finished, Randy walked across stage. "That's not bad for a cold start. Last night you weren't together, it was ragged. The high kicks—you've got to get your heels over your head. Let's run through it again."

After the next run-through, "Mary, you're ahead of the beat, stay with it, relax! All right once again." Randy watched with folded arms, the run-through more ragged than the last. "OK, let's try this," he ran over and took a place in the line on the other side of Mary. "Mary, feel the beat with Nellie and me when we have our arms on your shoulders. You're getting the height on your kick, it's the timing that's a little off…Hit it Nick!"

Mary frowned in concentration as she danced between Nellie and Randy, embarrassed to be singled out. At the end of the number Randy stepped out in front of the line. "That was better…now once more to nail it down then we'll get on to something else." He motioned to the piano player. "Smile! Keep it bright— this is a comedy, a farce—sell it to the audience."

After running through the other four numbers several times each, Randy called them around him. "You're better, but we still have a way to go. I'm going to skip the black-out number, do it as well as you did last night and we'll be a smash. Tonight's the night, the audience won't be filled with backer's families and friends, you've got to win them over right from the first number. Matinee, be here at one—tonight seven, warm-ups seven twenty."

As they started toward the dressing rooms, Randy caught Nellie by the arm. "Talk to her," he said under his breath with a sharp nod toward Mary's back, "we're that close."

The face in the mirror was sober to the point of breaking into tears. Nellie slid a chair close to Mary's, pushed some make-up jars out of the way, leaned on the dressing table cupping her chin in her hand and threw a long leg on a rung of Mary's chair. "Why the gloom? Isn't this what you wanted?"

"I guess so…it was such fun in rehearsal. I couldn't wait to come back the next day," Mary said.

"Honey, that's the candy coating. Three weeks is not a lot of time to put a show together, even if it is off-Broadway." She watched a tear roll down Mary's face and felt her anger rising. "Look! You got a chance to be the next Gwen Verdon or Paula Kelly or Rita Moreno."

"Who?" Mary looked up, her blue eyes glistening.

"Ten years ago, I had your ass…and I could dance," "Nellie said.

Mary blinked. "Last night Britt said we were terrific, a sure hit—"

"Look, we need something from you," Nellie bit off, "that's the unvarnished truth." She wanted to tell this sniveling nineteen year-old to forget Britt, that she was lucky to be in the right show to make it big. Nellie took a deep breath. "We need that bright, fresh appeal you bring from Pocatello."

"Pot O'Luck," Mary corrected.

"Pot O'Luck," Nellie wrenched out. "She wanted to say 'from the sticks': give this country girl an unflinching look at life.

"Relax, enjoy it.…even if you can't keep time," she said, her voice lowered. "You're reachin' the audience, they dig you, big time."

"I do? Really?" The young face sobered perhaps even brightened, Nellie wasn't sure, but she'd run out of sugar coated words.

She envied Mary Staffe on the verge of stardom and with a handsome million-aire to take care of her. How could this hick chorus girl lose? Still you couldn't buy stardom, just check Pia Zadora if you wanted proof. She'd like to tell this kid to go stuff it, the show should have been her's anyway. Instead they were all tied to Mr. Britt llolmbrook's shooting star from Pocatello—Pot O'Luck. Oh, well, that's show business.

She patted Mary's arm and got up to get her coat, Sam's corner deli wouldn't be too crowded if she hurried.

The white limo was double parked directly in front of the Tennessee Williams theatre when Mary pushed through the front doors. holding her long coat around her legs. Britt Holmbrook IV's head appeared as the smoked glass rear door window slid down.

"Hurry honey, our reservation is for 12 :30."

Mary stepped through the slush and jumped to the open door keeping one foot dry, the long coat falling away from a slim leg in warm-up tights as she did so.

Britt kissed her warmly as they pulled away from the theatre. "I got reserva-tions at Tavern On The Green," he said.

"Oh, but Britt I'm not dressed. I'm wearing my rehearsal clothes. I'm not wearing any make-up. I thought you'd get take-out and eat in the car," she pouted.

"Don't worry, no one'll see you. I'll make sure of that…you can keep your coat on…you look terrific." He looked into her eyes, leaning closer.

"Britt, please. This hasn't been a good morning."

"Mary, what's the matter? I thought you'd be on top of the world after last night."

"So did I." She looked out the smoke tinted window at the gray slush made darker by the tint.

"Honey, you were terrific. What's wrong?"

"In rehearsal, Randy personally helped me with dance steps. Then Nellie was telling me how much they needed me, like I wasn't doing enough. Oh, I don't know—it made me feel bad," she sobbed.

Britt put his arm around her. "Mary, Mary, it's OK—they're jealous, that Nellie, she wants your part. Randy's scared. He's never been anything but a chorus boy, this is his big chance. "Honey they're wrong. You carry the show…that finale is a 'show-stopper'. There you are center stage," he smacked hi s lips. "Delicious—they depend on you."

She half turned toward him. "I'm scared too—really scared now," Nellie's words coming back to her. "I don't want the show to depend on me. It's fun, I like being in the center, being naughty in the black-out and…and wiggling…just a little," she half-smiled through her tears.

"That's why…the audience loves you. They can see **you** somehow. They know who you are…. Enjoy the moment, that is what they want…why they come and why they cheer at the end. You're so honest, you're wonderful. I knew you would be." He kissed her cheek. "Don't think about the whole thing depending on you."

Phil Jerigan, in his tuxedo, stood at the back of the Tennessee Williams theatre looking over the full house as the last of the audience hurried to their seats, fifteen minutes to curtain. His brow was furrowed in deep thought as Andrew Todd slid up beside him. "Another sell-out, even some SROs," Jerigan spoke out of the side of his mouth, "we shoulda got the Mark Hellinger, five hundred seats."

"Yep, same tomorrow," Andrew said.

Phil turned toward Todd, reaching reflexively for a cigarette.

"What the hell's that you're drinkin'?"

"What d'ya think? Alka-Seltzer," Andrew said scowling before downing the rest of the bubbling glass.

"Ya got a headache?"

"No my doctor prescribed it ten, two and four instead o' Dr. Pepper." The ticket taker belched quietly behind his hand.

Phil Jerigan pulled back the starched cuff under his tuxedo. "But, it's eight now."

"I know. I've been busy, missed the two and four," Andrew said straight faced.

"A comic…you ever in vaudeville?"

"What d'ya take me for George Burns' brother?"

"With a stogy you could pass."

"Thanks, Phil. I got work t'do." Andrew turned, the dim light catching the shiny seat of his blue serge. "Try some Alka Seltzer…you need something."

"Hey, come on, Andy," Phil Jerigan rasped, "what IS the story here? Who's in town? The Shriners? The Moose? 'The Mystic Knights of the Sea? Who?"

Andrew half turned his eyes fixed on the producer's face, his dour expression unchanged. "What? Do I look like Dionne Warwick? Am I psychic? Go rent the Mark Hellinger and while you're at it I could use some help, full time."

MARK TWAIN SEZ

"Excuse me, what did he say?" The youthful man asked the man a little in front and to his left. They were standing at the outer fringes of the literary gathering after Mark Twain's lecture.

The man turned half-way toward him. "I don't know, I wasn't listening. My job is done until we go to Pretoria." He noted his questioner had a steno pad and a pencil poised to write like the reporters who covered Mr. Clemens' lectures at every stop.

"You work for him?" The young man asked as a laugh went up from the crowd around the bushy haired, white suited center of attention.

"Not exactly. I work for Harper's. I'm supposed to see that everything's OK at each stop so that Mr. Clemens is comfortable and has his needs taken care of at each hall. You a reporter?"

A chuckle. "Not exactly," the first replied, "I work for Harper's too—I'm supposed to write down the clever things he says—at least one a night, I was instructed."

"Really?" He sounded incredulous. "Why would they want to do that? Reading his books or attending his lectures would seem to be sufficient. My name's Al by the way." He turned fully toward the young man.

"Oh." he blushed, "I guess because they think he has something worthy to say," his words tumbled out, "—about almost anything. O'course, one of the junior editors said to me quite confidentially, it was because they were paying him $25,000. a year and wanted to protect their investment."

Al threw his head back, laughing heartily, causing many in the circle around Mark Twain to turn with frowning faces. The man, himself, had interrupted himself to take a deep puff on his cigar. A waggish look crept over his bewhiskered face as he stared at Al for the moment. "I don't have much truck with sayings," he continued, "Take Ben Franklin—probably as famous for his pithy sayings such as his comment on mistresses, as his government work," he grinned. "Y'all know the one 'Nothing is surer than death and taxes' or something close to that.

"I suppose that's got a lot of attention because the words strike everyone as true but to me it's downright silly, unless, of course, some reporter was asking him if he was the one seen crawling out of Madam DuBarry's French window at 3 AM one night. As a necessary diversion, I expect such a phrase might give a man some time to collect himself—think of another excuse or hope the reporters change the subject—of course, they won't—they never do with me." He paused, possibly reflecting a bit on the ridiculous scene he had suggested, "Now that I think of it, I don't know if Ben was really all that agile, but surely you take my point about sayings."

Once again anonymous, Al held out his hand. "What's yours?"

"Everyone calls me Synch—for Sinclair," he said shaking Al's hand.

"Unusual. Why did you take this job?"

He rolled his eyes looking a bit sheepish. "They promised to consider my novel—seriously this time—if I came up with something they might be able to publish based on his sayings."

"Oh, the great American novel, eh?" Al smiled, a look Sinclair had seen many times. "What's it called?"

"Main Street."

"Main Street, hmmm," he avoided the eager eyes of the young novelist, "catchy." Then without pause he asked how many quotes he had of the great one.

"Part of one…."

He smiled, "Better get busy." He turned from the group to leave. "Take care, kid. Maybe I'll see you tomorrow night,"

The pencil point broke against the pad as Sinclair, reflected on Al's reaction to his dream—getting published. Not surprising, everyone seemed to react the same. At least the publisher, Harper's, had given him a job and put him in the presence of one of the greatest authors of his time.

Mark Twain was finishing with his attentive audience. "Ladies and gentlemen it is time I bring this nonsense to an end for the evening." He looked down at the stump of his cigar then back at his worshipful audience, "I never smoke more than one cigar at a time." There was enthusiastic applause as the group reluctantly began to disperse from the salon.

The next night the audience in Pretoria was also enthusiastic. Mark Twain was discussing travel. In particular his first trip abroad on a paddle wheel steamship with a religious group traveling to the Holy land. "I suppose most people are a little intimidated when they find themselves in a foreign country. I found apparently simple words become complicated and suddenly do not sound the way they're spelled anymore. You take the Italians—this famous artist, sculptor, inventor, code maker, painter and probably a novelist too for all I know. They spell his name Vinci and pronounce it Vinchy. I've noticed this is true with many words. Foreigners always spell better than they pronounce." He paused looking out over the grand audience in Pretoria's largest theater, his face very sober, "I also learned on that voyage the serene confidence a Christian feels in four aces—no I won't go into that, many think card playing is the Devil's pastime, might even destroy the confidence some people have in American missionaries, especially those going to China."

Sinclair was writing furiously trying to keep up with Mark Twain's comments and asides. For instance, Twain's comment on language came out 'They spell it Vinci but pronounce it Vinchy, foreigners sure can spell better than they can pronounce words.'

There was a sudden laugh from the crowd cutting off part of a homily Twain was articulating: "Always do right This will gratify some people and…the rest." Since Twain was still talking about a church organization, Sinclair guessed, substituting 'astonish'. As in "…astonish the rest." He debated using 'surprise' but 'astonish' seemed more in tune with Twain's standard of hyperbole.

The man had a knack for sly jabs at religion and the way it was practiced. He was able to catch Twain's next comment verbatim. "O kind missionary, O compassionate missionary, leave China! Come home and convert these Christians!" He wrote it down uncertain what it meant or how he might use the phrase.

Now the great one had returned to the voyage itself and was remarking on the weather.

"Y'all probably haven't experienced a storm at sea but let me tell you even the old salts blanched at one I remember vividly out in the Atlantic, before we reached the Straits of Gibraltar. First the thunder came rolling over us, going by like a freight train headed for New Orleans. That didn't bother them much but they did look up. Then came another roll of the drums and the whole clash of sound like a symphony orchestra with cymbals and all playing the 1812 Overture. Those old hands were awe struck with that one, yes sir, I guarantee you. But the lightening bolt that lit up the foremast in the dark gloom of the storm as if it were a candle lit in blue flame from one end to the other sent them scurryin' for the fo'c'sle quick time, hoping the mast wouldn't get there before they did."

Scribbling as fast as he could go Sinclair wrote: 'Thunder is good, thunder is impressive, but it is lightening that does the work.' Unnoticed Al sidled up beside him and reading over his shoulder tapped the young novelist indicating he wanted the pencil and pad a moment. Puzzled, Sinclair handed them to him.

Al wrote 'He talks a lot about the weather but what's **he** done about it?' and handed the notepad and pencil back, grinning.

After a quick read, Sinclair wrote: '**Everybody** talks about the weather but **nobody** does anything about it.'

Al nodded vigorously and patted Sinclair on the back, "Now you're in gear, Synch!"

Twain continued to rail on about religion, he was saying: "The Bible has noble poetry in it, and some clever fables, and some blood-drenched history, and a wealth of obscenity; and upwards of a thousand **lies**. I might suggest this very likely—at least in part—is responsible for the way man looks at heaven. Man has imagined a heaven, and has left entirely out of it the supremest of all his delights….sexual intercourse!…His heaven is like himself; strange, interesting, astonishing, grotesque. I give you my word, it has not a single feature in it that he actually values."

Sinclair, open mouthed, lost in the picture Twain was painting with his words, belatedly wrote down. 'Man's view of heaven is surreal—no sex.' This to be followed by Twain's next, related comment on man: "Adam was but human—this explains it all. He didn't want the apple for the apples sake, he wanted it only because it was forbidden."

This inspired Sinclair to record: 'Adam is but human and wants what he can't have—Eve for example.' He was, however totally at a loss when he wrote down Twain's last comment on the subject: "I believe the Heavenly father invented man because he was disappointed in the monkey. However, upon further reflection (and considerable evidence) the human being is another disappointment and no considerable improvement on the monkey." Raised as a strict Unitarian the concept of evolution or any belief approximating evolution was rejected out of hand. Was Twain's remark intended as some reference to evolution? Sinclair wasn't sure and all the more puzzled by the irreverence and seeming lack of continuity of what the author said in his lectures.

Al winked at him, apparently caught up in Twain's comment about man versus monkey, then laughed out loud, along with most of the audience, at Twain's next comment.

Sinclair dutifully wrote down: "Man is the only animal that blushes—or needs to."

Now rolling along with his premise of man under god Twain turned the satirical light on himself, an introspective moment surprising Sinclair. "I have had a 'call' to literature, of a low order. ie humorous. It is nothing to be proud of, but it is my strongest suit….Seriously scribbling to excite the laughter of god's creatures."

For Sinclair the words were self-effacing and so humble as to make him wonder if Twain really meant them, yet he realized he was in the presence of a true man of literature, approaching greatness in his own time.

"Some people—' Twain continued, "I won't say which reporters, lest I embarrass those sitting on the front row—say I color the truth a shade or two or maybe by a whole lot. And I'm forced to admit: When I was younger I could remember anything whether it happened or not, but I'm getting old, and soon I shall remember only the latter."

Sinclair was amazed as the evening continued. If anything Twain seemed to gather momentum as if a bond formed between the speaker and his audience. They fed off each other. Thus emboldened, Twain not only successfully transitioned from travel to religion but with the aplomb of a high wire aerialist, lurched into politics.

The erstwhile reporter could only shake his head with wonder and amazement as he tried to keep pace. Twain seemed to be violating all the conventions to the great encouragement and enthusiasm of **his** audience—for surely they were accomplices now.

"As you all probably know," Twain was saying with a broad gesture, "I come from a country whose system of government is called a democracy. We have three branches in this government: the Legislative Branch, the Executive branch, and the Judicial branch all bundled together with something called politics," he chuckled dryly as the audience waited with anticipation.

"It could probably be shown by facts and figures that there is no distinctly native American criminal class except Congress.

"And, of course we have the Executive branch to deal with them and somehow govern the country—between them.

"As if this isn't enough, we have the Judicial branch as a referee. A small body of august (stern) men to interpret what the other two bodies have already done and tell them when they're not doing it right.

"Well, you can see what a mess we're in and it is by the goodness of god that in our country we have those three unspeakably precious things: freedom of speech, freedom of conscience and the prudence never to practice either of them.

"Therefore we wobble on a course that's neither straight nor predictable and we're happy with that most of the time or at least some of the time but certainly not all of the time.

"Just as Lincoln, I believe, said:'…you may fool all of the people some of the time; you may even fool some of the people all the time; but you can't fool all of the people all the time'.

"Of course all of this doesn't take place in the dark, nor are we blind, we have the Constitution as our guide. It fit's the definition of a 'classic' in literature. 'Classic' A book which people praise and don't read.

"Of course, the great unwashed public, unwashed by objectivity, that is, love to humble those people in power even the ones they voted for and elected. This tends to keep everything in balance—even better than the Supreme Court, our final arbiter of what's right and what's wrong.

"On that note, ladies and gentlemen, I better quit before someone starts taking notes and I find myself sued for slander by some politician—Lord knows if anyone would recognize slander right off, a politician would likely be at the head of the pack." He bowed to the applause, cocking an eye in Sinclair's direction.

"Good evening Synch…" Al paused looking down at the scribbled notes on the note pad page, "Did you get some good quotes this evening?"

Sinclair smiled. "I don't know how good they are, but they certainly are provocative."

"Would you like to meet him?" he nodded toward the nearby stage.

"I would indeed, but do you think it's wise? Wouldn't prudence dictate I remain in the background, given my assignment from Harper's? I assume they didn't tell him about me."

Al laughed in that open way of his, much to Sinclair's concern, "Harper's probably is afraid of him too. The old curmudgeon can be cantankerous, that's for sure…"

They were interrupted by a gravely voice, "Curmudgeon? Cantankerous? Al are you taking my name in vain again?" Mr. Clemens had crept up behind them and apparently heard the last part of Al's comment.

"No, sir, your honor," Al raised his right hand, "I was simply reminding my friend here there were a number of cantankerous curmudgeons on the Supreme Court you just mentioned." His huge grin contradicted his words.

Looking at Sinclair, Clemens said, "I don't believe we've been introduced. What's your name, young man?"

"Sinclair, sir," he blushed, "ah, Sinclair Lewis."

"I was just about to introduce you," Al broke in as they shook hands.

Clemens gave him a look, then turning back to Sinclair, "Be careful of the company you keep, young man. If it weren't for Al, I shouldn't be able to look myself in the mirror each morning. Nothing so needs reforming as other peoples' bad habits. You a reporter?" He looked down at the notepad in Sinclair's hand.

"No, sir. I'm a writer." There was almost a defiance in Sinclair's voice as Al's smile faded.

Clemens grimaced, "That's nothing to be ashamed of but be careful where you admit it out loud." With a clap on Sinclair's shoulder, he passed on to a knot of admirers still drifting near the theater stage.

As the old man strolled off to another group, Al looked back at Sinclair, obviously relieved. "On second thought, kid, I think you're right. For the present at least, it's probably not a good idea to tell him your assignment from Harper's. Are you supposed to accompany us the rest of Mr. Clemens world wide tour?"

"No, they told me once we got to Europe, Paris or London, they would send me a cable and book passage home."

"What do you think of his lectures?"

"I'm in awe—it's like trying to saddle a cross between a horse, a camel and a mule. You may get the saddle on, certain in your own mind it's facing forward, and you may even get up in the saddle, but it's a total gamble which way you're headed."

Al stared a moment, his face frozen like someone trying to count the cars in a fast moving freight train. Then shaking his head he turned away, "Kid, this is serious. You're even beginning to sound like him."

Blushing, "I'll take that as a compliment," Sinclair called after the departing figure of the tour manager. 'Is that one of his quotes?' He began leafing through his notes, uncertain.

THE CAPTAIN

By the second day out of Montego Bay, some passengers began to avoid him. Not that he noticed. Everyone being on holiday, perhaps they accepted him too readily at the start. Certainly some might be considered gullible, surely not everyone. Somewhere, there-in, lay the tip of the iceberg, the crux of events to follow.

The Filipino bartender smiled from inside the Oval bar, both white-shirted arms leaning against the bar. He had just opened for business. "Good morning, Captain. What you like, sir?"

"Heineken," he said and sat on the barstool facing the row of windows overlooking the sunny blue-green Caribbean. "What a gorgeous day, and New Year's upon us already," he said as the bartender poured the Heineken into a tall, graceful tumbler.

"Yes, sir. as you say—good day. Do you sleep well last night?"

"Oh, like the proverbial log. Yes, indeed."

Bertcham Atchinson Tanner spread his ample form over the thickly padded bar stool precisely at nine AM, as was his habit of two days, at the Oval bar in the Main Ballroom of the Regent Sea cruise ship. The bright sun reflected into his face from the choppy sea far below. He tugged the bill of his khaki, Navy billed cap slightly lower reducing its rakish angle.

"Tell me Barong, have we been pitching and tossing like this all night?" He raised his glass.

"Yes, sir. Bad night. Very bad."

"Hmmm…to paraphrase Shaw: 'He who can, does. He who cannot, goes without sleep.'" He chuckled. "Here's to sound slumber." His self-indulged chuckle had the deep rasp of a phlegm thicken throat as he took his first sip of the day. "Ahhh…"

The bartender smiled weakly and retreated to stack glasses on the far side of the bar.

BAT, as he liked to be called when he wasn't referred to as 'Captain', straightened his favorite black tie, over the long sleeved. Khaki shirt. The golden tie clasp with its twin dolphins would remind anyone of the US Navy submarine service. He had picked it up at a flea market. Early in life, he decided he wanted to be called BAT instead of Bert, as his father preferred, or Bertie, which he absolutely hated and his mother insisted on calling him as a boy. He liked the flat, no-nonsense sound produced by his initials. The romantic image of Bat Masterson that often came to mind didn't hurt either. Strangers always asked him about his name and that appealed to him as well. Especially because he didn't mind telling the whole story, often embellished with his own essence of a quote from George Bernard Shaw's Maxims for Revolutionists. The only thing in MAN AND SUPERMAN he really understood, if the truth be known.

"Good morning, BAT." Her soft voice sounded of smoke as she slid an arm around his khaki shoulder and kissed his whiskered cheek above the Vandyke.

He half turned throwing a thick-fingered hand around her slender waist. "You finally got your hair dried, eh?"

She stepped out of his grasp fluffing her short blond hair with the fingers of both hands. accenting the swell of her breasts under the simple, cotton, lilac dress. "What d'ya think?"

"Rocky, you're a knock-out," he half smiled, still pawing the air.

"Thanks." She twirled, displaying show-girl legs, "See ya."

"My roommate, you know…" BAT threw at the man three stools away who watched her indolent walk as she left the ballroom.

"Really?" The man looked away and quickly snatched his Bloody Mary, leaving the bar.

"Barong. How 'bout another beer?"

"Yes, sir, Captain, right away," he called from the far side.

"When do we get to Aruba…that is our next stop, right?"

Barong started to pour the beer into a fresh glass, his boyish face frowning in concentration. "Maybe one o'clock, I think."

"Good. Plenty of time then. Will the bar stay open while we're in port?"

"Oh, yes, sir." He set the glass in front of his sole customer and removed the empty. "You not go ashore? See Aruba?"

Bertcham Atchinson Tanner rolled his eyes at the thought. "Oh, I don't think so."

"What about roommate?" Barong grinned, gold incisors exposed.

"Oh, yes, I'm sure. Wouldn't miss it. She bought enough jewelry in Cartagena for three women. As Shaw says: 'Self-denial is not a virtue: it is only the effect of prudence on rascality'. Good thing our stay was cut short."

The bartender frowned, considering this a moment then brightened, "Probably same for Aruba," he allowed, "strong wind slow us down still."

"Yes, yes, wind can play havoc…how many times I can remember having the same problem…yes, indeed."

Barong busied himself at the other end of the bar while Captain BAT stared blankly at the row of windows overlooking sunny seas.

Only a few people passed through the cavernous ballroom. None stopped at the Oval bar. Their mid-morning interests were elsewhere, but Captain BAT stayed on, a routine he'd established their first day out of Montego Bay.

✻   ✻   ✻   ✻

"There goes that horrid man," Evie shuddered. "He accosted me in the Anchor bar last evening."

"Oh, really, Evie, he's harmless," her husband broke-in after quickly swallowing the bread he was chewing, "just wants everyone to think he's a sea captain, an 'old salt' as they say."

"I think he's funny," Ned said from across the table, "Course he was a little tipsy when he regaled me the other night with that tale of a typhoon in the South Pacific," he chuckled softly. "Tramp steamer, third mate out of the engine room, would be my guess," he added.

"Evie's right! He's disgusting," Ned's wife said with a piercing glance at her husband. "Funny?…And that woman that hovers over him," she quivered, "kissing him and all…she's a…well you know," her eyebrows knit together in distaste.

The object of their derision, Bertcham Atchinson Tanner, lurched to an adjacent table setting his Heineken down with exaggerated care while greeting his two hapless table mates who looked as if they were beginning to regret their decision to lunch in the Main Dining room instead of roughing it on the Sun deck with hamburgers and hot dogs.

"Ah, so good to see you ladies, mind if I join you?" He sat without waiting for a reply. "I see you're loading up on victuals for the strenuous trip ashore." He smiled broadly raising his glass to toast them.

Between them a twitter, lost on him as he continued loquaciously, "I myself, have decided to avoid the hot sun and stay in the shade…Seen enough of the tropical sun, I have, on my Pacific crossings. Yes, indeed.

"Either of you ever been on the Pacific?" He raised his brows, looking from one to the other, daring a response, any response.

One of them mumbled something about rough seas and fell silent. Then both excused themselves almost inaudibly while Captain BAT challenged the waiter who was trying to tactfully explain to him it might be difficult getting a steak since it wasn't on the luncheon menu. The choices were swordfish steak, fillet of haddock with chef's special sauce or spaghetti and meat sauce,

"Oh, very well *garcon*, I leave myself in your hands," he waved agreeably. "What do you recommend?"

"Sir, I believe the spaghetti is the best choice at this hour," the waiter replied with a perfectly straight face.

"Yes, of course, I bow to your wisdom," he bobbed his big head, his cap at an angle only a bosun's mate could appreciate.

"I may get sick!" Ned's wife hissed. "All we need now is for that hussy to show up in her purple bikini."

Ned caught his compatriot's eyes across the table. He had to be of the same thought, but remained silent. This was not the time to offer an opinion on the Captain's roommate, Rocky.

Evie visibly suppressed a smile. "She certainly has a gorgeous figure," she said looking at her husband who appeared to be using his water glass to hide his face before he sipped.

"I think it is significant the Captain is taking lunch, even at this late hour," Ned grinned. "Of course, it does increase his staying power—tonight we may be privileged to another tale of the South Pacific or a rhetorical quote from Shaw."

Not to be diverted, Ned's wife came back, "Well! She certainly doesn't mind displaying it…for all the men." As if Ned hadn't spoken.

Like the number you sensed but didn't bet on the roulette wheel, the card you knew you should have asked for but didn't in draw poker, the thought you avoided because it might come true, then and there—**she** sauntered into the dining room, gold high heeled slippers, a diaphanous robe bordered in gold covering a skimpy, lime green bikini.

Ned, his coffee cup suspended halfway to his mouth, his eyes tracking the insolent saunter, tried vainly to maintain his train of thought. All that came out was a whispered," Hers…I don't understand…."

Rocky smiled at the two couples as she passed then stopped at the Captain's side, bending over—just enough. She kissed his ear as he gave a slight start. "Don't turn around, our friends at the other table are eyeballing me," she said with a low, throaty laugh.

"Indeed? Why doesn't that surprise me? You wicked woman, you. Here, sit down, join me. The old maids have left." He leaned against her as he pushed the adjacent chair away from the table. "You can continue to beguile and bedazzle them here at my right hand."

She sat almost facing the adjacent foursome crossing her legs slowly giving them a languid glance.

"Shaw, you know, was very perceptive in these matters," the Captain said raising his head, eyes closed, drawing some sort of inspiration from the ether. "Ah ha, I have it—'Virtue consists not in abstaining from vice, but in not desiring it'."

"BAT," she slapped his khaki shoulder laughing aloud. "You might as well be dead!" She rocked back in her chair allowing the gold bordered robe to separate across her minimally covered breasts and legs.

"That tramp! Come on Ned, we're leaving."

Ned's eyes shifted back to his wife, "Didn't you hear her threaten him?" he whispered urgently, his face twitching with effort to remain impassive. "Surely, it's our duty to stay and bear witness." He looked across the table seeking support. "She might be planning to murder him when he gets drunk," he breathed, looking from one to the other at his table. The 'look' he got from his wife was enough. "OK.OK." Smirking, he started to rise.

Evie laughed. "Bravo, good try Ned, but Aruba calls." She put her hands together in mock applause. "Poor baby," she looked across at her husband, his back to the Captain and Rocky at the next table, "next time you can sit here. Careful don't trip over the chair when you get up.

Evie's husband grunted. Looking up at Ned, he half smiled, "Did you say 'when? When he gets drunk'?"

"Lower your voice. They'll hear you," Evie giggle

*   *   *   *

As the passengers crowded the gangway returning from their sojourn in Aruba, Captain BAT refused another Heineken. "No, my friend," he held a hand up to the bartender, striking as heroic a pose as possible on a bar stool, "as Shaw has said, and I repeat myself with your indulgence: 'Self-denial is not a virtue: it is only the effect of prudence on rascality'." To the puzzled look on Barong's face, he rattled his phlegm filled laugh and headed off for his stateroom.

Among those on the gangway returning to the Regent Sea, a dark-complexioned man of medium height and build mixed in, unnoticed and unchallenged. If any of the passengers noticed him at all they may have assumed he was one of the crew or perhaps a passenger located in another part of the ship whom they had not seen before. The purser, assailed by the anxious mob and momentarily without help, failed to get his boarding pass and he sailed with the Regent Sea three quarters of an hour later. The stow-away didn't plan to stay aboard long, a few hours at most—his confederates with their Zuni power boat would see to that.

*   *   *   *

The Anchor bar was a cozy place, room for thirty people at most. The illuminated, frosted glass, etched with fishes, mermaids and sea grass extended below and along the length of the bar. That frosty display provided the most constant illumination, a ghostly green, since the overhead lights were dimmed by the bartender as the evening progressed. More to the point, at least from Captain BAT's viewpoint, the bar stools were comfortable, black leather, captain's chairs which swiveled. They gave one a sense of security—something he needed whether he acknowledged the fact or not. This intimate little lounge was a few steps from the Main Ballroom which was especially convenient this evening because the Captain, the ship's Captain Thermapopolis, was hosting the traditional New Year's eve reception there. Full dress was *de rigueur* with the allowance that men could wear a dark suit with white shirt and bow tie if they didn't have or bring a tuxedo.

This was the cruise line's attempt to add old world romance to the cruise with a bit of class—something from the old days when formality was not only the custom, but enforced. In addition the reception provided a means for the passengers to fraternize with the ship's Captain and appreciate his position as absolute master of everything while afloat. Women loved it, men tolerated it, while Captain BAT was of two minds.

The reflection of the Captain's aura was an enhancement in which he could bathe willingly. However, wearing a tux violated his dress code. Instead, BAT was dressed **quite** simply in his Navy blue blazer, white trousers, shoes and shirt, offset by his billed white cap with the fouled anchor on the front—the counter part to his khaki, daytime cap. His only concession to the occasion was a clip-on, black, bow tie. He was easily confused for one of the ship's officers if not the Captain, a fact which openly delighted him.

"Come on BAT it's time to go through the reception line," Rocky put her hand under his arm.

The Anchor bar was empty but for the two of them. "My dear I've just filled the cup," he said, raising a full Heineken a few inches above the bar.

"BAT, you promised," she whined, putting on a pout. "I didn't buy this new dress to sit alone in the Anchor bar." She clasped her other hand around his arm, both hands tugging gently away from the bar. "Please?"

"Oh, very well," he let her pull him to his feet, mumbling, "Self sacrifice enables us to sacrifice other people without blushing."

"What was that? You sacrifice?" she laughed. "Was that one of your bits from Shaw?"

He struck a noble pose. "Ah yes my dear, an inadvertent slip of the tongue...may I say you look ravishing," he slurred.

Her long black, spaghetti strap sheath was decorated with a large sea horse in black sequins over the front and fit her figure like—well...it didn't distort any of her charms, as the Captain noted.

They proceeded through Captain Thermapopolis' receiving line without incident although Captain Thermapopolis hesitated enough to bring stares when introduced to his near mirror image with a cap cocked rakishly over his right eye For his part, BAT was the epitome of charm and brevity, stumbling over his words only when introduced to the Purser, Third Officer Smith, at the beginning of the reception line. BAT pronounced his name 'Smythe' with a not-too-subtle grin. This went unnoticed or ignored and Rocky maintained a firm grip on his arm to insure against any other possibilities.

Immediately after shaking Captain Thermapopolis' hand at the end of the receiving line, BAT peeled-off to the left heading for the port side companionway that led to the Anchor bar.

"Thank you BAT," Rocky called softly after him. He wiggled a few fingers over his shoulder without turning.

✳   ✳   ✳   ✳

"Captain BAT," he introduced himself, releasing his glass of Heineken to extend a huge paw to the unsuspecting, tuxedoed passenger next to him in the crowded Anchor bar.

"Matt Kirby.' The graying eyebrows behind the steel rims went up. "Are you the relief Captain?"

BAT's phlegm filled laugh broke through as they shook hands, "No, no, I'm retired—too many years on the Pacific."

"Really? You must have some real tales to tell." The steel rims reflected the ghostly light. "I suppose this rough weather we've been having is nothing to you."

BAT liked this man instantly. He hadn't had an opening like that since the first afternoon of the cruise. "Matter o'fact," he slurred slightly after draining his Heineken, "r'minds me o'the beginning of a typhoon in the Philippine Sea." He signaled Barong, the bartender. "What are you drinking Mr. Adams?"

"Kerby, Matthew Kerby," the man corrected. "Thanks, I've ordered. You were Captain of this vessel?"

"No. Thank god. He was thow'd overboard, but that'sss another story—"

"Mutiny?" Steel rims had a look of incredulity.

"You got it," BAT pointed a stubby finger. "Crew was c'vinced the Cap'n was nuts."

"That sounds just like THE CAIN MUTINY."

"The what?" Captain BAT blinked rapidly, covering a gassy belch with a gnarled knuckle.

"The book—Herman Wouk's, THE CAIN MUTINY."

"Oh. Yeah, 'xactly."

"That's terrible."

Captain BAT laughed his pebble filled croak, coughed and nodded sagely, "Like George Shaw says: 'The only golden rule is that there is no golden rule', 'xactly."

At that moment Mr. Kerby and his steel rims parted company as he was violently thrown to the floor—the deck—of the Anchor lounge. Captain BAT blinked, sensing some sort of visitation.

"Get over there," a Bahamas-Barbados laden voice ordered. "The rest of you—over there," he waved a sinister looking handgun toward the other end of the lounge.

There were gasps, cries and stunned looks, but no screams as the group of twenty or so, formally dressed men and women, tried to comply, bumping into each other and stumbling over chairs and small cocktail tables in their haste.

"You," he turned back to focus on Captain BAT who had barely managed to swivel away from the bar, "get your fat arse over here and take off that stupid cap—now!" The gun, a MAC-10 semi-automatic, machine pistol, menaced.

The man with the MAC-10 turned back again toward the group, "I want your jewelry, your wallets, your watches, everything of value on this table." His free hand came down on the black top of the nearest cocktail table with a resounding slap, "in fifteen seconds or I'll start shooting." He lowered the machine pistol, pointing it at them.

At last realizing what was happening and that he had just been directly threatened, Captain BAT struggled to get out of the captain's chair, reaching for his cap as he stretched his leg uncertainly for the deck. He succeeded for an instant, however the first step away from the secure chair initiated an unplanned sequence of events resulting from his body movements.

Almost in slow motion, the heel of his other foot caught the footrest of the heavy captain's chair. His cap shot into the air like a cowboy riding a bronco at the rodeo. His front foot did a stutter step trying to compensate, unsuccessfully, for the sudden shift in center of gravity.

Whether it was the heavy chair falling into the back of his legs or the failure of his rear foot to catch up with his lead foot or his state of inebriation only high speed photography, blood test and physiological analysis on the spot could determine, but BAT's considerable bulk was forcibly propelled across the five or six feet from the bar to the hijacker before either of them sensed or could arrest it. BAT sprawled awkwardly, arms flailing over the slender Bahamas-Barbados accented man who collapsed, face down, spread eagle under the designated cocktail table which wobbled from the impact of BAT's forehead as he went down. The MAC-10 fired off two rounds before it separated from the hijacker's hand

and flew in the general direction of the lounge crowd pressed against the bar to his right.

Fully three seconds of silence followed the canon sounds of the MAC-10, then, when no one seemed hurt, the group all reacted at once. In the reactive din, the bartender, Barong, it turned out, gingerly picked up, the MAC-10. The rest surged *en masse* engulfing the unconscious thief and the somnolent Captain BAT.

Following a loud belch, which went unheard, Captain BAT closed his eyes, quite content to lie on the inert form under him. In seconds he was being pulled to his feet. People were pounding his shoulders and calling him brave and a hero. He vaguely heard a friendly voice praise his quick thinking and recalled a familiar face from the table adjacent in the dining room.

She smiled at him. "Why Ned, it's our neighbor from the dining room," she gushed, "how gallant." Her shrewish face was bright with excitement.

Together, the crowd pushed, lifted and grunted his heavy, relaxed form into a captain's chair at the bar. "I'll have a Heineken," he mumbled, unheard and unheeded.

Rocky fought her way through the crush of well-wishers and wrapped a bare arm around his shoulders. "Oh BAT, are you OK?'

He turned slowly, blinking. focusing through bleary eyes. "Yes, o'course." An involuntary shiver ran through him. Then he winced in pain as he tried to lift his left arm "…'cept for my other drinkin' arm." He managed a rough cackle.

"You've got blood on your forehead." She dabbed at the cut with a cocktail napkin from the bar.

"Let's get you down to the cabin." She slipped his arm over her surprisingly broad shoulders.

"Better get the doc to look at that," someone suggested.

"Where's m'cap?" BAT slurred.

Another called out, "Bravo. Here's to Captain BAT, a brave man," There was applause and a few cheers as some of the ship' s crew arrived and took control of the would-be robber.

Ignored, Mr. Kerby searched on hands and knees for his steel rims in the ghostly, green light under the bar.

The next morning, almost nine-thirty Captain BAT slowly approached the Oval bar in the Main Ballroom, his left arm in a sling. a patch of white gauze over his right forehead forcing him to wear his khaki cap angled over the other brow.

"Ah, good morning Captain BAT, how you this morning?" Barong greeted him. "You OK?"

"Yes, fine, Barong. Moving a little slow and a little behind schedule, but still have my dependable drinking arm." He flexed his right arm.

"You big hero. Everybody, say so. Captain. Therm'popolis say you drink 'on the house' rest, of cruise. Anything you want. He started to pour the Heineken before BAT settled in his customary place, facing the bright morning sun.

"And a toast to my counterpart this glorious morning." BAT raised his glass. "As Shaw would have said: 'All scoundrelism is summed up in the phrase *Que Messieurs les Assassins commencent!*'." He took a generous swallow of beer.

"What means these words?" Barong asked, his face in a frown.

"Eh!" BAT came back from his reverie. "What does it mean?" Barong nodded.

"Pardon." he belched delicately behind his gnarled hand. "I haven't any idea."

THE DINNER PARTY

I could tell he was upset—why, exactly, I wasn't sure. I stood there in the living room trying not to appear nervous while Irene, his wife, busied herself straightening the curtains and smoothing the doilies on the club chairs and the sofa, as if they had somehow been disturbed by the storm.

I took a quick drink, more than I intended, and nearly choked.

"Ya like that, Ken?" His black brows narrowed.

"Yes," I managed, halfway between coughing and throwing up, "it's good." The brandy burned.

A harsh laugh. He stared at me, his gaze intense. "You all right? I figured you needed something strong after that."

"Fine," I croaked, "…down the wrong pipe." I gestured vaguely.

His eyes pinned me like a butterfly under glass. "Sure?"

I nodded.

"'What happened?" he pressed. We were back to the previous subject. "Where did you two get to?"

"Oh, we were right in the next room—the storm—I was scared." Irene smoothed her short print dress down, then clasped her hands behind her back, avoiding his searching gaze.

"Where's your apron?"

That's it, we're in trouble, I thought.

"My apron?" She gave a quick nervous laugh, looking-down to check.

"Yeah, you were wearing it when the power went off."

"Why, I don't know. I must have taken it off when I came out of the kitchen before we sat down to eat." Her gaze flitted around the living room.

He looked toward the food on the dining room table and back at me. "Probably cold now, the lights must have been off forty-five minutes or more." He turned to the wall clock.

Irene's eyes darted to me. She looked pale and was wringing her hands. "I'll look in the kitchen," she said.

'What was he thinking?

"Ken, what time ya got?" He stretched to reach the wall clock.

"It's ten twelve," I said, checking my wrist watch. "They weren't out so long, I remember looking at my watch at nine thirty before we sat down. That was well before the power went off."

"Really? Funny," he said, after resetting the wall clock, "it seemed longer."

I was first to look away from his penetrating stare.

"Didn't you hear me call you?" He turned as Irene scurried by headed for the bedroom.

Shortly, she returned holding up the wrinkled apron. "I found it. Imagine. It was on the floor in the bedroom." Her smile seemed forced but then that may have been my own sense of guilt.

"Didn't you hear me call you?" he repeated, arms akimbo. "I was trying to find the candles in the kitchen."

"When dear?" The smile became a concerned frown.

"During the black-out, when do you think?" He threw his arms out in frustration.

"Oh, Charles. No, I guess not. I…did you hear him Ken?"

Both of them focused on me I almost choked again. "No. There was so much thunder I couldn't hear anything. That's the most violent storm I can remember."

Charlie looked from me to Irene and back again, his face twisted into an imitation of a gargoyle. "I didn't call during the thunder claps, no one could have heard anything then. Were you both petrified?" He turned toward his wife again.

"I was scared. The thunder and lightening were so close." The apron twisted over and over in her hands. "I was holding on to the bedpost, my eyes shut tight."

Charlie looked back at me as if to say "you too?" I shrugged. "After I found my way out of the bathroom it took several lightening flashes before I saw Irene. I stumbled over a chair then reached the bed then the lights came back on."

"For forty-five minutes?"

"Oh, I don't think it was that long—it just seemed..." I let it die, the memory of Irene clinging to the 'bedpost', warm and quivering, surged through my thoughts.

"I had to move the clock up almost fifty minutes," he said. "What were you scared of? We've lost the power before." He stepped toward his wife reaching out an arm for her.

Irene glanced past him at me. "I don't know." She walked out of her husband's attempted embrace. "Let's get back to dinner. I'll heat this up won't take long." She took two of the plates off the table, the apron across one arm. "Would you bring your plate, please, Charles?"

I set the brandy snifter down. "Can I help?"

"Strange, I would have sworn it was at least forty-five minutes," Charlie mumbled, bemused.

I carried his plate out to the kitchen.

Irene busied herself with the microwave avoiding my eyes. "Why didn't you tell him something?" I whispered.

"You don't know him like I do," she came back, then in a normal voice. "This'll only take a few minutes. Would you freshen up the wine, please, Charles?"

He appeared in the kitchen doorway. "Where are the candles, anyway?"

Irene searched the counters of the small kitchen in a sweeping glance. "Oh, I forgot, they're on the table. I was going to light them when we sat down for dinner."

"That's all we have? The two of them?"

"Charles, please, I haven't tine for that now, there's a box somewhere—six originally—the long tapered, blue ones. You want to eat don't you? Did you get the wine?" She took the apron from the counter and tossed it behind the door in the laundry room.

"Funny, I found the matches. They were right in that first drawer there."

"Charles, please!"

"OK." he pulled the wine bottle out of the refrigerator and turned toward the dining room.

"Go sit down," she said to me. "I'll bring your plate as soon as it's warm."

"You all right? I whispered again.

"Yes," she said, her eyes glistening, then waved me toward the dining room.

I did as I was told.

"Might as well leave it out, now." Charlie. set the bottle on the table.

I couldn't forget the feel of Irene's warm body. Even while she was shaking, I had the sensation there was nothing between us. In thirty seconds, I was fully aroused, and embarrassed. If anything, she clutched me even closer with every clap of thunder. That slight movement brought an instant, involuntary response.

"That's good wine," Charlie broke my reverie, "don't you think?"

"What? Oh, yes." I picked up the glass holding it to the light, "Nice color."

"Color?" He laughed. "Chardonnay? That must be why they call it a white wine—right? Tell me, what d'ya think of the bouquet?" His lips were curled in a sly grin.

"The brandy was stronger—"

"—What?" His laugh roared again. "Ken, you're a real connoisseur."

I shrugged, somewhat embarrassed for my inattention, "I don't know, much about wine…it's good." I put the glass down after a sip. He refilled his glass. Until then I hadn't realized how much he'd drunk.

"Irene, what's taking so long? Ken's really getting hungry, so am I." He gave me an exaggerated wink.

I started to get up. "Maybe she needs some help."

"No, no, sit down. Irene'll get it."

"Coming," Irene said.

She brought in two plates. "I hope it's all right. I tried to heat it without over cooking the chicken."

I felt her soft breast against my shoulder as she leaned over to put the plate in front of me.

"Charles, would you light the candles, please," she hesitated a moment, still leaning over me. I glanced at Charlie, my face felt flush.

"Sure, still got those matches in my pocket, I think." He shifted to dig in his left trouser pocket, his eyes blinking slowly as if in deep thought.

"I'll be right back, my plate should be ready." Irene hurried back to the kitchen.

She returned, smoothing the short skirt down with her free hand as she set her plate on the table.

Charlie turned to her. "Ya, know, honey, maybe we ought get one of those generators so we'd have back-up power. You being so scared and all."

Irene gave me a quick look. "Is it all right? Oh, how silly go ahead and eat. Generator?

"What generator?"

"Yeah, I saw one advertised for about four thousand."

"Charles, that's awfully expensive."

"Well, you can probably get one, you know," he waved a careless hand, "enough to light a couple bulbs," he laughed, "for a lot less."

"Oh, Charles, really…go ahead and eat. The food will get cold again."

Charlie finished his wine and reached for the bottle. "What do you think, Ken? Were you scared in the bedroom with my bride, all alone in the dark?" He grinned as he refilled his glass with studied concentration.

I forced a smile hoping, he could see I caught his clumsy humor. "How often does this happen?"

"Oh, this is a first," he roared, "my wife's never been trapped in the bedroom with a stranger before—in the dark—for forty-five minutes."

"Charles!"

"I meant—"

"'ats a Gotcha." He pointed at me, his fingers fashioned as an imaginary gun.

"Do you have a lot of power outages?" I finished the thought.

"Oh, almost every month, right hon?"

"That often? I don't know, it seems longer since—"

"You should have seen her, Ken." The dirty laugh again. "I thought she was gonna rape me."

"Charles please—I was scared." Her cheeks flamed. "You know how afraid I am of thunder and lightening. I'm terrified."

"Yeah, what a night," he rolled his eyes at me, "I thought we were back on our honeymoon."

Irene hung her head over her plate. "Please. Can we talk about something else?"

"Aw, I'm embarrassin' you." Charlie got up and with a big sweep of his arms enfolded his wife in her chair knocking over her wine glass in the process.

She jumped up pulling up her skirt, trying to avoid the wine. He staggered after her, still trying to embrace her. "I'm sorry honey if I embarrassed you…. but it **was** quite a night, 'member?"

In the movement of their bodies, their feet tangled and they fell heavily on the floor.

Irene's dress went up, a flash of white like a deer suddenly alerted in a thicket. Charlie laughed.

"Charles, please," came her muffled cry, one free hand frantically clawing to pull her skirt down.

"Aw, honey, I'm sorry. Let me help you," he giggled. A big hand fumbled between her thighs.

"Stop it!" Freeing herself, Irene struggled to her feet, cheeks flaming. "Excuse me," she sobbed and fled past me to the bedroom.

I watched, stunned. What was I to say? The sight of Irene squirming on the floor trying to get her dress down revived the sense of her closeness in the bedroom while I struggled with my own sense of guilt.

Frozen in place, I could hear Irene's sobs in the next room and Charlie sat there on the rug, at the other end of the table, a bewildered smile on his face.

What could I to say? I wanted to vanish into thin air. He's drunk, I thought and somehow that surprised me. The picture of him greeting us with a brandy in hand when the lights came on ran through my head. And he was looking for candles?

Charlie crawled to his feet using Irene's overturned chair for support, then he set the chair back up. "What did I do? Why's she upset? God love her, I was trying to tell her I was sorry. He sagged over the chair. "What'd I do?" he muttered again.

After an awkward pause, I said, "I should be going, Charlie." Run, run, I was desperate to leave. "I hope Irene feels better tomorrow and please thank her for me for dinner."

"No, no Ken, don't leave, not yet." He straightened. "I gotta talk to you. I need to know what happened."

The sinking feeling in my stomach wasn't from overeating.

"Please. I gotta know somethin'," he slurred. "What would you do? This lightening thing—did she? You were with her in there, what happened?" He slumped into Irene's chair.

"I don't know what it is Charlie. Maybe something happened in her childhood…maybe if she saw a doctor…."

"I mean did she grab you in there?" His eyes were pleading, his face so serious, trying to see through the fog.

"No—nothing," I lied. "I held her hand, she was shaking so."

"Really?" His voice rose. "That's all? You swear?"

"Charlie, go to her, tell her how you feel. I've got to go."

"I do, I do…She doesn't understand," he stammered again. He looked like he was about to cry and I didn't feel too good myself.

"Charlie, I got to go. Take it easy, tomorrow's another day. Good night."

That night still haunts me. I remember the darkness and the inviting warmth of Irene pressing against me and I remember the pathetic plight of my friend Charlie. And, I wonder…

They separated a few months later, Then one night, late, in the midst of a heavy, summer thunderstorm I got a call: "Can you come over?" the voice whispered, "I'm so afraid. Please, I'm so afraid." A crack of thunder and I shivered violently, her warmth remembered, flooding my senses.

"Hang up. Using a phone is dangerous," was all I could think to say.

WAR STORY

"War is hell!"

General Sherman made his now famous observation based on the American Civil War, up-close, brief and accurate.

Lt. Col. Sam Windom's eyes lost focus after reading the classified message, his thoughts reflecting on Gen. Sherman's comment. Steck, Mr. Steckhouse, his man in Israel, was sending home a war damaged van of Soviet origin. This vehicle was captured by the Israelis while battling to retake lost ground in the Sinai desert. The van was a mobile electronic jammer intended to protect front line troops from aerial attack by aircraft using radar bombing systems. Windom had seen a picture of the vehicle in the intelligence library—an ordinary looking truck, camouflaged, boxy, easily mistaken for a furniture delivery truck.

The TWX said the Jammer would be flown out to Ft. Huachuca, Arizona. Sunday. Since it was ground based, the Army was the prime agency for Exploitation, but Air Force planes where the target of the Jammer—'we need to get in on this,' Windom thought. The ins and outs of how the jamming system worked and its effectiveness were critical to the Air Force. '…And here we are in Ohio,' he mused.

Clasping his hands behind his head, Windom gazed, unseeing, at the far wall of his office covered by a large scale map of the Middle East. A plan was forming. With their limited resources his division would have to mesh with the technical exploitation by the Army. As managers of the FTD (Foreign Technology Directorate) effort they had to take the lead. 'We have more expertise than the Army,' he thought, 'and it is vital to find out just how effective this system is.' According to what Steck told him on the phone two days ago the Jammer wasn't burned but had been hit and damaged by an Israeli shell. 'War is hell, all right—why couldn't they capture a brand new one for us?' Analysis would be a lot easier. He knew the Israelis were not above holding out prime hardware they captured to extract something they wanted from the US. Still, whatever they turned over was another piece in the fluid jig-saw puzzle of the never ending Cold War. He sighed. What was the next step?

He jumped up and in two strides reached the doorway to his small office. "Nadine," he smiled at his attractive, blonde secretary, "would you ask Major Martin to step up here, please?" He turned from the doorway as she answered, and returned to his desk. He was making an outline of what he wanted done on the margin of the yellow papered message as Major George Martin knocked on the wooden frame of the open doorway.

"You want to see me, boss?"

Windom made a motion toward one of the straight backed vinyl cushion chairs at the small table butted against his desk and shoved the message toward him. "Take a look."

The major sat with a sigh and pulled out his reading glasses, his brow wrinkled in concentration. After a short while he looked up, his eyes questioning.

"You heard about this?"

"Yes, sir…Vaguely—rumor mostly. This is the first official info I've seen." He waved the small yellow paper.

"Let's start preparing to help the Army exploit the Jammer. I've made a little list, a rough outline, there on the margin, of what I want you to do. Make some contacts and come back in a day or so with a rough plan of what's needed and how to proceed. OK?"

Martin looked at the message again for a few moments. "No problem. I can do this by this afternoon if you like."

"Good. Since it's Friday, why don't you fill me in before quitin' time and we'll head up to the Club for 'twofers' when we finish."

He laughed, "Good idea, boss, but Audry gave me a list. I gotta hit the Commissary on the way home or she's threatened to open a can of beans for supper. The cupboard is bare."

"Spoil sport, I wouldn't think of pulling rank on Audry."

Martin's plan of action was straight forward, He had assigned a Program Manager who would see the exploitation through to the final, formal report on the completed analysis of the system and exactly what sort of threat it posed. This would take about a year if the past was any indicator. To satisfy the immediate demands TWX (classified telegram) messages would be sent. These were routed to operational commands and other interested agencies detailing the exploitation as it progressed. Unofficially, the TWX served as a weekly report. Usually by the time the formal report was published, everyone had all the information they needed, although occasionally the final, formal report included significant information that couldn't be verified until all the areas of analysis had been completed, a certain synergism common to complex electronic devices.

The whole information process was a constant battle: thoroughness versus the operational commands' desperate need for facts. Operators often thought the analysts were seeking their own self satisfaction chasing every electron to the absolute end of every ganglia of wiring. Windom had been a Radar Navigator on a bomber crew in the Strategic Air Command (SAC) at one time and knew the feeling. He wanted the analysts to get the Final Reports out in less than a year while at the same time expecting them to be accurate and all inclusive. He put a lot of pressure on his Program Managers to keep after the Analysts—don't let them be side-tracked, either in completing the analysis or by turning to another project before the current effort was completed. Since the Analysts didn't work directly for him the process was somewhat akin to pushing a rope through a knot hole.

With a groan, Windom thought of higher headquarters. One Systems Command office in Intelligence was a constant thorn in his side. Too often they clashed. How would it play this time?

A few days into the next week, Windom saw George Martin in the hallway of their Quonset hut office wing, "Where are we with preparations to exploit the Jammer, George?"

"You mean, HAVE CARGO, sir?" He grinned pausing to let the nickname sink in. It was customary to get an unclassified Program nickname off the designated code list so that work on classified projects could be discussed more or less openly.

"Oh. You've got a code name—what else?"

"We're ready to move as soon as we get TDY funding. We've got two Analysts packing their bags ready to shove off Monday after we get a funding cite number—you did know all travel funds are frozen?"

Windom nodded. "Who's holding them up?"

"Guess."

Windom gritted his teeth. His look confirmed he knew which office Martin referred to. "I've got a message ready for your signature, detailing the need, justification etc." he said, "I'll bring it up soon as 'our gal Sunday',—uh, Betty." he slapped the side of his head remembering her name, "types it up—without any mistakes, of course," he added wryly, rolling his eyes.

Martin's branch had finally gotten a new secretary sent over by Personnel, after being without one for six weeks. The woman formerly in that position had retired. The new girl was an entry level stenographer.

Windom smiled knowing George Martin was afraid to send the new secretary back to Personnel fearing it would be another six weeks before he saw another candidate for the job.

"Well, we can't wait for the spring thaw to get them out there, the Army needs our help." He grinned. They both knew he was pushing the effort.

"Yes, sir. We've talked with Huachuca and they say the damage is more extensive than we thought. It's going to take some work to get the thing to work at all, even at reduced power."

"OK, George. Get that message up to me and let's get our analysts out there ASAP." He was sure the FTD analysts would be more than a positive stimulus getting the jammer to work, knowing the Army's limited capability might be driving their initial, pessimistic evaluation.

Major Martin saluted off-handedly. They both knew Systems Command posed a problem.

The problem was bigger than either suspected. Systems Command turned down their request for TDY funds using the rationale that the Army was prime on the Jammer exploitation—they were holding the limited travel funds available for Air Force 'needs'. The two analysts remained at Wright-Patterson AFB keeping track of the Army's efforts and helping as best they could with messages and phone calls.

Windom scheduled a meeting with the FTD commander after reviewing the effort with his boss including the significance of the exploitation and the need to have Air Force involvement.

Colonel Hoke, Windom's boss, accompanied Windom and Martin to the three story, brick headquarters building. "Now, Sam, let's keep it calm and cool with Col. Whentdahl—OK?"

Windom smiled, his lips pressed tightly together. They had already lost three weeks and it was clear the Army needed all the help they could get. "Yes, sir, but why these knot-heads can't—" he closed his mouth at a glance from Col. Hoke.

The meeting with Col. Whentdahl was short and sweet, as tidy administrators like to say. As the Commander put it: "Essentially, there is a real crunch on TDY money and it won't ease up until the next quarter, if then. And since funds can't be transferred from 'one pocket to the other'," the Colonel liked to use those homey euphemisms, "we simply have to curtail our travel."

"Sir, this Jammer could blast SAC right out of the sky!" Windom exploded. He was gambling on the test results of a SAC bomber running against the Jammer, once they got it operational. Desperately he tried to shock the commander into diverting funds from elsewhere—people in this organization had money, they always did—he knew it, for certain, and he was equally certain Col. Whentdahl knew as much too.

Hoke and Martin both snapped their heads around at Windom in surprise while Col. Whentdahl gazed at him steadily, a slight smile struggling across his face. "You been tangling with Col. Freedorf again?" He referred to 'that' Systems Command office.

"No, sir—we haven't spoken on this matter." Col. Whentdahl's reference to Freedorf was about the MiG-23 defection, Windom arranged—at least Whentdahl thought that was a defection. Actually the truth was—Reminded, Windom made a face. He and Col. Freedorf had had a face-to-face confrontation on that exploitation which set the whole process back about six months. Windom lost that argument too—now his own commander seemed to view him as a trouble-maker. Obviously, he wasn't going to get any support from the Commander.

There was a long silence. Windom knew it was a lost cause but desperately wanted to go on arguing, seeking some kind of opening that would get the Air Force involved in getting that Jammer ready to test as soon as possible.

At length, Col. Whentdahl said, "I appreciate your dedication, Sam," he winked at Col. Hoke. "There simply aren't any funds at this time," he finished with a slight shrug of his shoulders.

Windom collapsed into his desk chair, angry and frustrated. They just didn't get enough respect for their part of the task either at Systems Command or even right here in FTD. "There's got to be a way," he challenged Martin who had followed him back from the Commander's office. "What about the Log Air network? I was able to get to Nellis out in Las Vegas on one of their flights. They cover the whole country every night moving parts and high priority maintenance stuff from base to base."

"How do the analysts get to Ft. Huachuca from Vegas? What about per diem? These guys are all GS-12s or above, they don't live like you and me, sir."

"Hell, Steck is the one who put me on to Log Air—he flies military air whenever he can. Look in to it, maybe they go close to Huachuca."

"Yes, sir." 'Actually,' Martin reflected, 'the Log Air flights weren't too bad.' Most aircraft had a cushioned seat or two up behind the pilots in the cockpit, the rest of the airplane configured like a cargo plane with rollers and tie=down rings. Log Air was the FedEx of the Air Force. 'There's a possibility'.

Over the weeks that followed the best efforts of Windom and Martin failed to break loose any travel funds for the analysts to go to Ft. Hauchuca. To Windom it seemed the failure was in his face every three or four days.

There was some evidence the Army was making progress toward getting the Jammer system operational and that was about the only glimmer of satisfaction in the HAVE CARGO exploitation—none of it credible to direct, hands on, Air Force assistance on the project. The new quarter Col. Whentdahl mentioned in his attempt to sooth Windom did not offer any consolation, funds were still not available.

At the bar one Friday, Windom was contemplating the weekend, hoping his mind would be relieved of HAVE CARGO for awhile. His mood was dismal as he sipped the Old Fashion served by the bartender at the Officer's Club. He would allow his sour mood to dissipate with this one drink then head for home, he resolved. 'No use taking my work home.'

Unsolicited a glimmer of hope appeared from thin air. He felt a hearty clap on the shoulder and turned to see an old friend—Jimmy Lynch, now a full Colonel. After an exchange of the usual pleasantries and a freshening of the drinks, Windom learned that his friend and former associate in SAC was now a Division Chief at SAC Headquarters, working in Plans—in other words he was responsible for generating part of the EWO—Emergency War Order. Windom immediately realized Lynch had a huge responsibility and the job a stepping stone to promotion. "I'm very happy for you," Windom heard himself saying as his mind immediately registered the potential opportunity being presented him.

When Col. Lynch asked about his job, Windom began to edge into a scheme that was only now beginning to form. "Have you ever heard of HAVE CARGO?" Then he lowered his head, self-consciously, a ploy, "Of course you haven't, it's an FTD nickname. I—"

"This one of those innocuous names for a deadly project you Intel guys are cooking?" Lynch grinned.

"I suppose you've heard about the recent Egypt-Israeli war? Yom Kipur? It was in all the newspapers for a couple weeks—you do come out of your underground hole periodically—right?"

Lynch chuckled. Windom hadn't changed. "You going to tell me a war story?"

"Let's go sit over there," Windom tilted his head in the direction of an isolated table away from the bar, next to the picture window overlooking the practice putting green for the golf course. Two or three golfers were visible stroking practice putts into one of the holes cut in the lush turf.

As they settled into chairs across from each other over the small cocktail table, Windom began, "Suppose one of your crews is flying a low level training mission and on the bomb run the Radar Nav's radar scope is full of interference—so bad he can't see his target—what's the EWO Standard Operating Procedure for hitting the target?"

Lynch sobered. "As you well know, it's a non-starter—you can't bomb if you can't see the target. Even a couple megatons won't buy a target if you don't hit close enough." Their voices had descended almost to whispers and both glanced casually around to see if anyone was close enough to hear their conversation.

"We have a Soviet system which might do that to your bombers—that is we have a damaged one that's been captured from the bad guys."

"I'm sure the Command would like to have a run at that."

"You bet your sweet ass you would, however," Windom paused, ostensibly to insure no one was close enough to hear. Actually he wanted to impress his friend, bait the hook before trying to land him. "There's a fly in the ointment."

Lynch rolled his eyes, admiring Windom's story telling. "Ain't that always the way." He sipped his highball, watching Windom over the rim of his glass.

"The Army's prime." His tone terse. "There's no quarrel here, they need help—big help—the kind we can give them. But we can't." He looked at Lynch who stared back, waiting—big pause. "Now's when you're supposed to ask me why."

Lynch sighed, "Does this have a happy ending or is this going to turn out to be a shaggy dog story?" Windom's expression didn't change. "OK, OK. Why?"

"Because Systems Command, one Col. Freedorf, an Intel weenie, won't release travel funds—there's a big crunch and they're doling out quarters like they were manhole covers, to paraphrase Mike Ditka."

"The bottom line?"

"Our guys can't get to Huachuca and the Army can't get the system up and working for several more weeks so you guys can find out how to cope with it."

Lynch took a big gulp from his glass and looked out the picture window, the golfers casting long shadows in their frozen poses studying their putts. "How can I help?"

Windom smiled. At last—"Maybe if Col. Freedorf was to learn that SAC was interested in HAVE CARGO and whether or not that system was a threat to the

EWO, he might open his pockets—might even ORDER us to go out there and help the Army so that the Air Force is at last involved and they get the system up and running sooner at maybe something close to full power—the jammer was hit by an Israeli shell—and SAC could fly against it—and we'll all find out whether or not it can hurt us." He paused for breath, his spiel a torrent.

"Sam, let me buy you a drink. This has the possibility of a beautiful friendship. You say his name is Freedorf, F-R-E-E-D-O-R-F?"

"You want his office symbol, too?"

"No, I'll address the message high enough so it will filter down to him. You sure of your facts?" He frowned at Windom as he waved to the waiter.

"We need to get a couple analysts out there to speed up the process. After that we can begin to run the tests you guys need, so this system doesn't turn out to be a nasty surprise someday."

Monday morning Col. Jimmy Lynch descended into the underground, deep beneath the SAC Headquarters building. After a week at the Pentagon then forced to spend Friday evening at Wright-Patterson for some minor repairs on his aircraft, he knew there would be a mountain of paperwork waiting for him. Still it was good to be back on the job.

The morning passed quickly, a staff meeting, some notes from the panel meeting at the Pentagon dictated to his secretary, and finally he was able to hold his own staff meeting and catch up on the SIOP (Single Integrated Operational Plan) due out by 1 June. The coordination of all the nuclear strikes on the Soviet Union in case the Emergency War Order (EWO) was initiated was his responsibility. The plan included long range missiles both Air Force and Navy and SAC bombers. Cities from Khabarovsk in Siberia to Stalingrad on the Volga and more were targeted, some with several weapons. The idea was to separate the impacts of those weapons in time so that there wasn't any fratricide—the SAC bombers being the most vulnerable since they were the last over the targets in almost every case.

The meeting was well along before a young officer, new to his division, asked about the conditions which would cause a bomber crew to withhold their weapon—not release against the target. Until that moment Col. Jimmy Lynch had completely forgotten about his conversation with Sam Windom. The standard answer was if the target couldn't be identified the weapon was withheld and they went to the alternate provided they had one and could reach that target. The question was one no one really wanted to answer because the emphasis was on striking the target no matter what and all sorts of contingencies were covered for various malfunctions and problems. Now another loomed in Jimmy Lynch's mind. What if? And he had no answer—he had no data—there hadn't been any tests. No corrective action had been developed. SAC had to have an answer for **every** possibility. Windom's little 'War Story' came home to him full force.

The more he thought about it, the more Lynch hesitated, Systems Command was the coequal of his own command, Strategic Air Command, and subordinate units constantly chaffed over the heavy handedness of their parent commands—always did—always would. Certainly that was true in SAC and he had no reason to believe it was any less so in Systems Command.

As much as he liked Windom and respected his dedication, Lynch wondered if he wasn't being over dramatic. Being outspoken or emotional was often a fatal flaw even in outstanding officers. Might this be the reason Windom was not yet a full Colonel? Then the young newcomer's question about withholding a weapon during execution of the EWO came back to him. The plan was always perfect, the conflicts non-existent. However things did not always go according to plan, Murphy's Law applied. If the Soviets could jam SAC's bomber radars there was a good chance many targets would be spared, the SIOP skewed.

Working on a scratch pad, Lynch began composing. HAVE COAT? HAVE COOK? HAVE CLEW? He ran through the possibilities before finally recalling HAVE CARGO. He scratched out half the first draft. Wisely, he decided to soften the tone—the message had to be conciliatory even though SAC was the 'big stick' of Air Force Commands, he couldn't allow it to appear to be telling another Command how to run their business. Genuine concern had to be the sense of the missive and the words flowed after this mood settled into his thoughts—one of the reasons he'd been promoted, he was sure.

Having finally recalled the unclassified nickname, Jimmy Lynch left it in the revised massage for his two star to sign. That was enough horsepower, he decided and his friend Sam Windom would be suitably impressed and satisfied when he got his information copy at FTD.

Two days later the message was back on his desk with a 'See Me' scrawled across the upper right hand corner. Jimmy Lynch pondered the message and his two star boss's 'See me' trying to anticipate the General's concern and how he might reword the message and still overcome Systems Command's inertia.

Following some pleasantries with the General's secretary, a habit he'd formed, Col. Lynch was invited into the General's office. After being reminded of his note and rereading the message, the General looked up, "What's this all about, Jimmy? Catching them cold at Systems Command, it sounds like we're trying to tell them how to do their job. Why?"

Lynch decided on the direct approach. He suspected the General didn't have much respect for Systems Command, but would never let that sense appear in a message. So he emphasized the importance of finding out what the Jammer could do to SAC's bombers if it was effective. "There are signs Systems Command is dragging its feet on the exploitation of the jammer system because the Army is prime and they don't want to spend their money to help out," he concluded.

"The old Venus fly trap routine, eh?" The General smiled up at him as he reached for his desk pen.

"Yes, sir, something like that." Jimmy Lynch hadn't the vaguest idea what the 'old Venus Fly trap routine' was but he made a mental note for future reference.

As he turned to leave, the General said, "If this backfires, it's your ass, Jimmy—capish?" Then he laughed.

"Yes, sir." Was it ever otherwise?

Monday morning. Windom hated Mondays. Staff meetings, drivel and usually a flock of trivial messages to wade through. Everyone at higher headquarters seemed to get diaherra of the pen Friday afternoon. He sighed and decided to get as many read as possible before the 08:00 staff meeting with Col. Hoke. The third message down, stamped priority, got his attention.

Quickly scanning the text, he let out a 'whoop' and dashed out of his office past the startled Nadine and headed down the hall. "George!" He burst into the second office on the right rousing everyone inside. "Get those analysts on the way to Ft. Huachuca! We got a fund cite and have been ORDERED to help the Army—ya got that, ORDERED?"

Martin smiled, trying to catch the yellow TWX as it floated off the edge of his desk while at the same time fumbling for his reading glasses on desk.

Windom's ecstasy was short lived. At the staff meeting he learned that he and Col. Hoke had an appointment with Col. Whentdahl at 09:00.

Col. Hoke cocked his head to the side, "What are we in for this time, Sam?" Then threw up his hands at Windom's puckish grin.

Col. Whentdahl was frowning over a message when Col, Hoke and Windom entered his office—a contrived pose Windom was sure. The Colonel looked at Windom for a long minute, keeping them both standing in front of his desk as if making up his mind about something. Then he shoved the TWX at Windom, "You seen this?"

Windom anticipated seeing the message from Systems Command, instead it was from SAC. The TWX was addressed to Systems Command, info to FTD. Apparently Jimmy Lynch had lived up to his promise. Then he read the line that included HAVE CARGO—the finger pointed directly at him. Jimmy Lynch had missed the point about that being the FTD nickname, not the Army's. He looked up to meet Col. Whentdahl's piercing stare.

"Col. Freedorf at Systems Command was embarrassed and I'm embarrassed that an outside Command felt it necessary to prod—hell shove—us to do our job. Did you know about this?"

Windom wanted to point out they had finally gotten the necessary release of travel funds to do their job on an important threat to the U.S. but he realized that would be like throwing gasoline on a small house fire. "I ran into a friend from SAC and told him we had a piece of Soviet equipment that could threaten SAC's bombers. Naturally, he was—"

"And you had to give him the unclassified nickname too, so Systems Command could jump down our throat? Bad enough you even discussed this with an outsider, you had to go and hang yourself and us along with you. Thank god I'm retiring in July—your next boss won't be so tolerant. Get out of here, the sight of you gives me heartburn."

Col. Hoke wasn't too happy either and made some corrosive comments as they walked back to their cluster of Quonsets half a mile from the Headquarters building. He finished with a clap on the shoulder, "You better get it right, Sam, you need a success story pronto."

Back in his office Windom found the SAC message in the pile he hadn't gotten to before the staff meeting. Aside from mentioning HAVE CARGO, the message was innocuous, a mere expression of concern and interest in participating in any test of the jammer system as soon as it was operable. By noontime everything was under control and Martin assured him the analysts would be on the plane to Arizona the following day. Another Monday brought back to normal, he thought—wrong.

Late that afternoon as he was picking up his cap to go home, Major Martin stuck his head in the office. "Boss, I've got some late breaking news you'll be interested to hear."

Windom sighed and threw his cap in the IN box, "No blind fold, no last cigarette, let me have it—straight."

"One of my guys just got off the horn with 'Jerry, Terry and Mary' (his continuing reference to Col. Freedorf's office) they say rumor has it the Colonel's got his orders—"

"Good, I'll drink to that. Care to join me at the Club?"

"There's more—don't you want to know where he's going?"

Visions of relief, "I don't care as long as he's out of my hair." He looked at Martin in disbelief as the Major's smile broaden. "Here?" He croaked.

"That's what the guys in 'Jerry, Terry and Mary' are saying. They send their condolences. For what it's worth they think you have balls."

"Ah, faint praise from afar. That and twenty-five cents will get me a coffee at McDonald's"

"Apparently, Col. Freedorf put on quite a show when he came back from his boss's office with that SAC TWX in hand." Martin chuckled. "His office is going to be under repair for the rest of the week, they say."

Over the next two weeks considerable progress was made getting the captured Soviet Jammer system repaired and ready to test. The FTD analysts were able to provide the Army a great deal of help and sent back progress reports each week. Soon, it became apparent that the damage from the Israeli shell would limit the function of the jammer to about one third it's normal operating power—the prime reason being that two of the three huge magnetrons in the system had been smashed, there being no comparable tubes in the American electronic industry or anywhere in the military. Windom's efforts and concerns appeared to be so much hyperbola, surely the system wouldn't have much effect on Sacs aircraft at one third power—the system's range alone would be severely reduced.

Windom dutifully reported what progress there was at Col. Hoke's staff meetings and braced for the crowning function when SAC ran a bomber against it at low level, The simulated bombing run would approximate SAC's wartime mission.

"Are our guys going to be in the van when SAC sends the bomber against the Jammer?" Windom looked at Martin.

"They tell me one of them is going to be at the controls when the bomber makes its run," Martin replied. "Should be a pretty good test—proof of the pudding, no doubt."

The test came on a Monday which offered no encouragement to Windom, however, he reflected, the time difference would at least postpone the results until late afternoon and the 'morning miseries', as he referred to them, would be over. He was jittery all day as if anticipating a heavy weight title fight or waiting for the opening kickoff to the Super Bowl—Major Martin was supposed to be in contact with the analysts as soon as the test was completed.

By four in the afternoon Windom had run out of 'busy work' and against his resolve not to hassle Martin, stormed down the hall to the Major's office. Martin looked up as he appeared in the doorway.

"Sorry, no word, sir—but we've been told CINC SAC has classified the results Top Secret—something's definitely made an impact." There was a hint of a smile as their eyes met.

Windom controlled his excitement. "Are we talking <u>THE</u> CINC SAC as in the Commander IN Chief of the whole Strategic Air Command? The one out in Omaha, Nebraska that General LeMay used to command?" He was beginning to bubble from within.

They both were losing control of their smiles and beginning to laugh, "One and the same, sir."

"I wonder," Windom tried to control himself unsuccessfully, "I wonder—why—" he laughed, "why—he would—do—a thing, a thing—like that?" His laugh now bordered on hysterical,

"I don't know—Must be something—something—went wrong, sir." George Martin put his head down on his arms on the desk, his whole frame shaking with laughter. The other three officers in the office, Martin's branch, starred quizzically, faint smiles on their faces wanting to join in if only they knew why.

Windom waved helplessly and started to turn for his office, "Well. George," he sobbed, unable to control himself "let me know—if—if there's any further development." And he laughed all the way back to his office, waving feebly at Nadine as he passed her desk. "I'm OK—don't—don't need a doctor. Take—take—the rest of the day—the day—off." And went into his office, tears running down his cheeks.

The calm was shattered by the telephone on his desk—Nadine had left long ago. He jerked in his chair with the sudden sound, almost as if he'd been in a deep trance. He answered on the third ring. "Colonel Windom."

"Pad'ner, I owe you one—the drinks are on me next time. Got any more war stories?"

"Tell me what happen, Jimmy."

"Can't talk, orders—but you were right. My General thinks the sun rises and sets right here in my office. Thanks—see ya."

Sam Windom lowered the phone slowly and sat back for a long minute. Then he reached for the overseas cap he'd tossed in the IN basket. 'General Sherman are you listening?' As he got up to leave he wondered if the general ever made any observations about bureaucracy.

LETTER TO A FRIEND EN LOS ESTADOS UNIDOS

…so I'm going down this super highway at 95, no traffic (two disabled cars in 100 kilometers) and ahead I see a huge gate and toll booth. Uh-oh, I knew this was too good to be true.

Sixty-one thousand pesos! Now I know why no one uses the super highway (or why those cars were disabled).

Then it cost another sixteen thousand to get off thirty kilometers later to take the high road to Chichen Itza, capital of the ancient Mayan empire. I had a hard time maintaining my composure, the day having already been blighted by other events which ate up the morning and delayed our departure from Cancun.

Hold on, I gotta tell you the beginning—it's classic tourist, I hate to admit.

"Hey, *senor*, what you looking for?" That's the way it began.

I'm with a female friend, a scholar, who after a brief discussion agreed to split the cost of a rental car to visit the 'Mayan ruins within a couple hundred 'clicks'. She's doing research for her Masters' thesis, she says. I look at her then back at this young guy hanging out of a kiosk behind us in the Carcol mall. "Oh, just locating the Budget Rental Car place—gotta be here first thing in the mornin'," I answer. (The mall is a 'glitzy' place designed for Americans to spend money.)

"What kind of deal, they give you?" he asks.

I hesitate, wary, but what the hell. "A hundred and fourteen for three days, tax, mileage and insurance included for a VW beetle," I rattle off, exaggerating a bit.

"I can do better," he says, modestly.

I wink at my newly acquired companion so she can see I'm an intelligent man of the world. "Show me." (I'm wise to this approach. The travel office guy told us all about these street vendors on the ride in from the *aero puerto*—air port.)

"I can do it for ninety," he says without a blink, after some quick pencil work on a hand pad, he just happens to have handy. (A nice touch, I must admit.)

The deal was twenty down (his) and we had to go to the Sun Palace hotel for a free breakfast and a promotional talk the next morning. The limo would pick us up at eight. Then we could go on our way in the beetle. Couple hours tops, he says.

"Deal."

Aside from breakfast, were I recouped a good chunk of my twenty bucks, the highlight of the morning was when they started around the room asking the invited guests (couples, had to be couples) where they would they would like to spend their dream vacation. Each couple was at a table in a very comfortable meeting room with their guide/chaperon/baby sitter. There were 'oohs' and ahs and applause (led by the guide/chaperon/baby sitter) from the assembled group as each couple announced their choice.

The idea was to build enthusiasm to buy rental sharing at various places around the world also known as a 'come-on'.

I was sickened. Progressively, each couple named a more exotic place to vacation—until they got to me. I was last and getting impatient to get on the road.

Without consulting my 'wife' of an hour and a half (part of the deal without benefit of ceremony), I allowed as how I was dying to go to the Club Med on the Gaza Strip in Palestine—when it was completed, of course.

The reaction—well, it was different. No one applauded or cheered. A vague sort of sigh, maybe a small groan, seeped out as the fifty or so people in the group caught up with their visual images. I'm sure they could visualize a beautiful, sandy beach, on the warm, blue Mediterranean, surrounded by barbed wire, outlined in anti-personnel mines, with watch-towers whose guards alertly scanned the boundaries, Uzis slung over their shoulders for immediate use.

From there it was all downhill. First, they replaced our pleasant little Mexican girl—who said she'd been on the job for ten days—with a thirtyish, balding American entrepreneur (read salesman). His tent collapsed when my ersatz wife asked him in a rather blunt manner, how much these 'vacation points' they were offering, cost—as in: how much is one point? He immediately took on a surprised, offended look which I interpreted as, 'if you have to ask, you can't afford it.' (I considered proposing to her on the spot.) Besides, I don't think he liked my 'dream' vacation. Kept a straight, vinegar jug, face the whole time.

Anyway, the guy jumped up from our table and held a hurried conference with a couple other business suits who had been eyeing us ever since my exotic vacation wish. Then he turned back and politely informed us he didn't think they could help us. We were directed to an office on the mezzanine to get our voucher (for the VW).

When we got there some other tourist was arguing with the lady behind the desk and I could see my twenty bucks flying out the window. After some convoluted financing that I still don't quite understand, we were directed to the next hotel along the strip to actually meet the rental agent and get our car.

Outside, the morning heat rising, we walked to the road, Kukulcan, then left past the broad front of a hotel construction site, then left again, up a winding drive to the imposing entrance of the next hotel. Maybe three hundred yards all told.

My 'wife' was fanning herself fiercely when we found the car rental agent behind a small counter concealed behind some large, potted palms in the lobby. Somehow it all worked out. He had the keys to our VW. After almost three hours of breakfast, promotion, hiking and form filling, we were on our way in the unairconditioned 'Beetle', under a hot sun.

We took a right out of the impressive hotel drive and headed north toward Cancun to get off hotel island and onto the road to Chichen Itza. Alas the detailed map we had been given was very vague as to which route lead to Volladolid, nearest town to the old Mayan capital. There were several to Merida. In fact, over the next three days, I must have seen hundreds of signs to Merida—you can get there from anywhere, but I still don't know where or what it is.

I had all I could handle with the stick shift, traffic, kids, chickens and traffic lights so I had to rely on the 'wife' to read the street signs. Not that that was much help. I was hoping she might be able to match one with a name on the detailed map. If the street looked wide enough and there wasn't a car, dog or pig in the way I turned every time I heard a familiar sounding name.

For a short, golden period I was transposed without benefit of Aladin's Lamp, I was back in the time of marital bliss—yelling at the wife and expecting her to actually be of some help. (Amazing how quickly old habits return.) She tried to get out and walk home twice. She thought better of it when she almost flatten a moped driver the first time she opened her door suddenly. The other time, I'm ashamed to say, I sped up trying to beat a Mexican taxi to the right lane before reaching a traffic light. I would have beat him too, except he blew his horn and I hesitated, checking my mirror, and lost that precious second I needed. I still feel bad about that. You know I don't bluff that easily at home. Only then did I hear her faint "I give up" and the door slam.

Chichen Itza was marvelous. I hurried around taking pictures of the place in the failing light which should heighten the drama of my shots (got a lot of imposing silhouettes). Needless to say, we spent about a third of the time the place deserves. Our worst day among the ruins I have to admit.

Going home we decided against the toll road, 180 (after all we were splitting expenses) and I found myself on the old road, 80, which was two lane, black top except for the last twenty or thirty kilometers. (I was thinking old route 66, all the way.) All the rest of the traffic was on it too.

As in the US, Mexican truckers drive at night. So from twilight till 9:30 PM or thereabouts, I battled headlights, high beams, shoulder high beams, visibility and sharp, gut wrenching, surprise speed bumps.

Let me tell you, they really know how to build speed bumps in Mexico. There's the big asphalt ones which look like small mountains and aren't really too bad at slow speed. They're a lot like those in the US. Then there are the ones you can't see, like an unimproved railroad crossing in rural West Virginia. A sharp impact and a quick drop at any speed. The third type, the innocuous looking yellow, cup-shaped ones that are individually laid across the road in a string, are far the worst. I clench my teeth just thinking about them for they rattle your teeth at any speed. There is no easy way over them. (When NAFTA gets in full swing look for the company that makes these and invest heavily.)

With some uncanny foresight, each little hamlet you pass through has at least two speed bumps, one entering and one leaving—adios, ouch! They are extremely effective especially if you're not expecting them. After I hit the first one, I knew I'd met my match especially in that Beetle. Now I know what those signs that looked like a top down view of Marilyn Monroe meant. Usually there are three of them, one at 300m, one at 150m and one at the actual location of the speed bump. The last one, for some reason, was always the one I had the most difficulty seeing in the dark.

The signs in the smaller villages we passed through were old and the one at the speed bump itself was a dirty red brown with only a little white showing behind the M M symbol.

Without fail a large portion of the local population (well maybe eight or ten people) of these hamlets stand or sit on their bicycles around the speed bumps, waiting and watching along with their dogs and chickens. I don't know whether they are waiting for the laughs or the scrap metal. That would probably make a good thesis subject for some graduate student who wanted to vacation in Mexico at government expense (assuming he got a grant).

Back in Cancun again the challenge was to find hotel island. I had a better idea which way to go, right? Wrong. All I knew was I had to turn right somewhere, loop through Cancun and get on the causeway to hotel island—find Kukulcan road. None of the streets looked promising and, to make it more difficult, Kukulcan was not labeled on the map. Actually the street's called Coba in town, but I didn't know that then. (I thought they only did things like that in Charlotte.)

Since it's December, everywhere I look all I can see is Christmas trees, big ones with colored lights. Good land mark I think, getting back to map reading, but no, there's one at every circle. They all look the same at night.

Oh, did I forget to mention the circles? Just like D.C. you get on'em, you can't get off—you go around till you see the street you want and dive for it. If your lucky you're in the right lane when you need to be so you can make the turn before someone hits you or maybe only blows his horn when you cut him off. It's a wonderful system really—you can keep going around as many times as you like till you find the street you want.

Tulum avenue is the main street which connects the three circles of Cancun— I know each of them intimately—but don't ask me any of the names of the streets coming into them. Coba is one, I know, but I haven't a clue which circle it comes into and goes out of as the elusive Kukulcan. The logical one is the southern most, but since I'm not sure where I am when I see the first Christmas tree, I don't know whether or not it's the southern-most circle. Confusing? I guess.

Men never stop and ask directions, right? That's the common complaint I hear all the time. I stopped. I asked for directions.

"Ya go down about six blocks to the next circle, go around and off to the left," he says in pretty good English after the first fellow I stop calls him over.

No luck. My 'wife', soul mate that she is, has tolerantly ignored my colorful language (after all she's been married four times previously) but she can't read the signs.

"They're all going by too fast," she says.

I can't see them either, the Mexicans cleverly put them wherever they have space left over from the other signs. The traffic, which is still heavy, blinds me as well.

After following the directions if I'm closer to Kukulcan, I don't know it. I pull over again. This time the place looks like either the entry to an apartment building or a warehouse (see I'm getting punchy). Again, I'm in luck. The second guy *espeaka da inglese.*

"See that car turning (across the median)? Go that way, maybe seven, eight blocks. You see big FORD sign ahead—you go *a la direcha,* right, yes, that's it, to right. Is Kukulcan—hotels. I thank him profusely. (If it hadn't been for the wife, I would have kissed his hand.)

With the big FORD dealership sign in front of me I turn right and behold—hotels. Hotels to the left of me, hotels to the right of me, it even looks familiar at night—kilo 3 or 4 and there's the Kin-ha, home at last. They know me too. shout out my room number and they open the gate so I can put-put right into an open parking space. The last pigeon has returned.

Now why did she go off like that? "See you in the morning," she says. That's it. Women!

Su Amigo,
Charlie Strange

PS I know you're dying to hear more about my great Mexican getaway, but when you've seen one Mac Donald's, you've seen them all—ruins aren't far behind. I won't keep you in suspense any longer—yes Wendy's is here, so is KFC, TGI Friday's, Hard Rock Cafe, Burger King, Denny's and several I can't remember. It's impossible to get homesick, even if you're trying.

PPS Don't worry about me running out of funds. I found out there are two kinds of currency floating around—Pesos and Nuevo Pesos. Divide the former by 1000 to get the latter. Thus my toll wasn't so bad even if it was a lot more than it was worth.

BOND, JAMES BOND

"Hello, Mr. Cartwright, my name is James Bond, I understand you're a property owner with a septic tank,"

Was I imagining this? Did he say James Bond? The words came from the phone so smoothly, so matter-of-factly, I wasn't sure I heard correctly. "Yes," I said, almost an after thought.

"We're offering an Easter special," he continued, while I had visions of his namesake reporting to 'M', his controller, in that easy Scottish brogue, "…good through Lent. We'll pump out your system and flush your septic field before those hot heavy summer months are upon us."

I managed another yes. FROM RUSSIA WITH LOVE, GOLDFINGER, DIAMONDS ARE FOREVER, THUNDERBALL, YOU ONLY LIVE TWICE, Sean Connery, Roger Moore and the others in exotic settings, women falling all over them as they steadfastly pursued the evil SPECTRE amidst explosions, violence and mayhem set to the pulsating Bond theme music in a hundred variations. Incredible.

"…our slogan," Bond was saying, "Why be a drudge? Let us pump your sludge."

The cold war was over. Spies were out of work. The CIA was frantically searching for a new mission, a new chief. The latest nominee had quit. "Washington has gone haywire," he said according to the Washington Post. Heading the CIA apparently was no longer a 'plum' worth the fight.

And Bond, James Bond, wanted to pump my sludge. The world had turned upside-down.

I couldn't resist. "What did you say your name was?" He'd probably heard that from every prospect he called—'not THE James Bond?'

"James Bond," he replied stoically.

'Bond, JAMES Bond, I heard him say in that familiar way. 'Stirred not shaken' or was it shaken not stirred?' And the sludge?

Was it 'sucked not pumped' or perhaps 'pumped not sucked'? Did his secretary look like Ursula Andress or Jill St. John?

"Mr. Cartwright?" I heard the voice, accent in place, impatient.

"Yes, sorry," I said. He was looking at me now over the Walther Pk-38, deadly serious, his eyes fixed on mine, ready for any tricks, any deception. "Tell me some more about your service." I wanted to hear that voice again.

"Well, Mr. Cartwright, I'm sure you're aware a clogged, backed-up septic field can be a health hazard. Frequently, there is a large, odorous, swamp-like spot somewhere on your lawn as well. Classic symptoms of a septic system gone berserk."

"Berserk?' Yes, that was Bond speak all right. I could see myself as 'M', taking Bond's report and narrowing the options. This was a tough one, draconian measures were in order. "Terms? What terms, Mr. Bond?" I gave it my best imitation of the unimpressed 'M'.

"As I said this is an Easter special good through Lent. Half price. Why be a drudge? Let us pump your sludge."

Clever, but I didn't just fall off the turnip truck yesterday (or the day before for that matter). "How much?"

Now Bond was at the roulette wheel in the casino at Monte Carlo, 'thirteen black' I heard him say. "We can do it for five hundred."

"Dollars!"

"Perhaps a little less if the combined run of your fields is under a thousand feet," came the urbane reply. "Does your soil 'perk'?"

'Perk'? I looked over at the coffee pot—it was drip. Out the window the grass was quite green—perky? I'd only been in North Carolina a year and in the house maybe six months. 'Perk'? Does my soil 'perk'? I wasn't sure about this. "Don't you know?" I countered.

There was a dry chuckle. Bond and his reassuring smile into the phone, I visualized. "In your area it's variable. There are several different strata of clay, some more permeable than others."

He was suave, all right. I knew as much as I did before the question. I capitulated. "OK, when can you be here?"

"Mr. Cartwright, my team will be there first thing tomorrow morning."

As I put down the phone I could see Bond resignedly going to meet with 'Q' and the necessary pre-mission briefing on the latest exotic gadgets to enhance his mission. His expression reflected boredom but his mind, ever alert, missed nothing in the patronizing description offered by 'Q'.

There was the hand held water pressure gun which generated 2000 psi for 5 seconds to flush his way out of a tight squeeze (literally). The device neatly folded into the sleeve of his coveralls, virtually invisible to the casual observer. 'Q' was particularly emphatic describing the emergency augur for drilling through packed clay and loose rock to reach an impacted septic run. The device fitted into a little leather pouch along with the high torque electric motor and strapped around the ankle—left ankle that is, since the right ankle was reserved for the electronic locator, 'Q's pride and joy. James frowned at another device, which pointed, like a divining rod, at the mole-like tunnels, runs, leading to the septic fields. "In case your main sensor should give out," 'Q' offered in reaction to the 007 look. Then, of course, there was the standard stuff like the thin wire, wrist extractor with claw that allowed Bond to extricate himself from a tight situation by catching onto an object up to two hundred feet away simply by pressing the activating stem of his wrist watch. 'Q' was adamant that 007 put the watch on then an there and cautioned that Her Majesty's government had a lot of pounds sterling invested in these special devices and that he, 007, should be conservative in their usage and insure their safe return whenever possible.

The usual routine and Bond's expression of boredom only deepened as 'Q' continued to lecture in his dry, headmaster manner.

I wasn't particularly surprised when the rainbow colored tank truck pulled into my drive as I cleared the breakfast dishes, but I wasn't prepared for the septic tank crew, the Honey Dippers. A blonde, a redhead and a brunette hopped from the vehicle, Honey Dippers in bright red letters across the shoulders on the back of their formfitting, white coveralls. I set the dishes down with a clatter, silverware bouncing to the floor, and hastened out the kitchen door to greet them. I was intercepted by an average sized, balding man with a pointed, graying, Van Dyke beard and sharp, snapping brown eyes. He was wearing blue coveralls.

"Mr. Cartwright? Good morning," he said crisply, extending his hand.

There was no mistaking that voice. It was Bond, JAMES Bond.

"Yes, good morning." I took his hand, my eyes leaving the Honey Dippers for an instant as they bent to their tasks. I heard his chuckle.

"The Honey Dippers will hook up the hose to the truck so we can pump you out while I locate your tank and trace the runs to your septic fields."

I looked back at Bond. He was smiling, a tooth missing on the upper right side. "You…you have a female crew?" I stammered.

"Oh yes. They're quite capable you know." He followed my gaze as the blonde and the redhead snapped two sections of four inch hose together while the brunette connected the other end to the tank coupling at the back of the truck. "Each honey dipper is a specialist in septic tank resuscitation, haven't broken a nail in over a year," he confided, smiling, reassuringly.

"Inspiring," I breathed as the blonde straightened and gave me a glance.

"Come along, Mr. Cartwright," Bond commanded, "show me your soil collection drain."

He turned toward the back of the house.

"My what?"

"The plumbing…under the house. You have a crawl space, I believe."

"Oh, yes,…that." I caught up to him and led him to the small door to the crawl space.

He pull out a large flashlight (torch, I reminded myself) and stuck his head into the dark gloom under the house. He twisted halfway inside the small opening, playing the flashlight beam across floor joists, heating ducts, crisscrossing water pipes, seeking the larger pipes of the drainage system. "Ah, there it is," I heard him breathe to himself. He backed out and stood up.

Bond looked up at me with those steady brown eyes. "We're in luck, Mr. Cartwright. You have a very straightforward system." He turned slightly.

The blonde, redhead and brunette had quietly slipped behind us and fallen in rank, facing us, at parade rest, the open ended sludge hose on the ground in front of them. "Eunice, my shovel, please."

Before he had quite finished, the blonde came to attention, did a smart right turn and set off, quick-time, for the truck. He turned back to me his gaze penetrating. "That's all, Mr. Cartwright. We can take it from here. Thank you very much."

I was dismissed. I wanted to be part of the team—especially after passing the fluid Eunice on her way back with Bond's shovel.

She reminded me of someone—one of the women Bond had to 'conquer'—in line of duty, of course. Who was it?

Pussy Galore. Her name came to me as I slammed the kitchen door in my disappointment.

The bad girl in GOLDFINGER. Who could forget the judo wrestling match 007 had with Pussy, played by Honor Blackman, in the hayloft? I looked out the window; Eunice's coveralls even fit like Pussy Galore's riding breeches. 'Damn.'

Some fifteen feet from the back of the house, Bond was already clearing away the dirt on top of the septic tank, a piece of concrete about four inches under the lawn. The redhead was moving the carefully rolled sod to one side. The other two were bringing the bulky hose to pump it out. Soon the brunette had the pump on the tank truck roaring at full speed.

When next I looked out the window, Bond had all but disappeared into the septic tank; all I could see were his blue coverall legs protruding from a hole.

There was Bond semi-conscious in a huge oil pipeline under construction in DIAMONDS ARE FOREVER, a menacing automatic arc welding machine approaching in the rhythmic blue-white light, welding each pipe segment together, closer and closer. What would he do? How would he escape being buried alive? Electrocuted? Multiple catastrophes awaited him.

Bond climbed out of my septic tank, seemingly unsullied. He brushed at a couple imaginary spots that yielded a puff of dust while he issued unheard instructions to the Honey Dippers. He appeared completely unruffled.

*   *   *   *

As he folded my $500. check and put it in the breast pocket of his blue coveralls, Bond said, "Thank you, very much, Mr. Cartwright," the clipped accent precise. Then he grinned broadly; the gap-toothed transformation suddenly startling.

As he was turning for the kitchen door, he said, "Now, if y'all have any trouble, be sure an' give us a call—hear?"

I stared, speechless, at the departing apparition of Buck Henry, balding comic from the Hee-Haw gang of TV fame.

CASANOVA JONES
(A BASEBALL STORY)

My world turned upside-down after the Yankees lost the World Series. I remember because I had tickets to game seven in New York. Vicky Mayfield promised to go with me. We were going to take in a couple Broadway shows while we were there as well. My golden chance to get next to her and those damned Yankees had to go and lose game six and the Series.

You see Vicky's crazy about baseball. She catches for a women's fast-pitch softball team. They won their league championship last year. Boy can she hit. I don't mean with a bat—oh, she can do that too—I mean with her hands.

Just to give you an idea, one evening a few weeks before the Series, we're cuddling on the sofa and I gave her a little squeeze and she looked at me, like maybe she liked that. So I got in a little closer and tried again, a little more in hand, if you know what I mean. Boy, her left is like lightening and the thunder of her right shatters your senses. I saw stars.

"Oh, did I hurt you," she says in a surprised voice, as if the two loud smacks weren't still echoing around the room. "I'm sorry. I'm so reflexive it scares me sometimes." She should be on the receivin' end. Then she gave me a kiss. Not a consolation kiss—a long, tender, torchy kiss, full of future promise. I felt like smoke was comin' out o'my ears. The only thing—I couldn't tell if the one-two or the smoldering kiss caused the sensation—ya know? Either way, I was on fire.

After that, I thought, 'Well, goin' to the World Series, here's my chance to impress her and maybe really get to her. I still think she'll go all the way, I have to work up to it a little smoother, take my time and learn to bring my guard up faster. I could see where going to New York would setup a lot of possibilities—know what I mean?

My friends all think I'm sleeping with her. They think because we had to spend the night together in a motel room coming back from Atlanta one time that she's hot for me. Around the office I get called Casanova—well, not to my face. After all I'm their supervisor but I'm wise to them. Rumors and gossip are what they are and snickers around the water cooler don't bother me. I have to maintain a certain presence, I'm sure you understand—dignity. I couldn't tell them what actually happened that night at the motel any more than I could let them find out luscious Vicky may not as wild about me as they believe. And so far she hasn't betrayed me whenever they're around. Cocktail parties, she's always warm and affectionate with me and she'll tell the gang a baseball story from one of her games. Like the time she tagged some gal right on the rump as she was sliding home and saved the game. Only she didn't exactly tag her on the rump. They roared at that one and I could see a couple of the guys nodding sagely—"Ol' Casanova's got something there, —puttin' that body on him…."

Now, let me tell you, Vicky is not one of those muscle-bound, built-like-a-stick athletes who looks more like a jock than a female, no sir. She's got everything where it belongs and in sufficient quantity to cause heads to turn whether she's wearing a dress or slacks or whatever. Tall for a catcher, she can rifle a ball down to second well enough to discourage most runners from trying to steal. And her eyes, hazel under soft brown hair, well I guess you can tell I'm gone on the woman.

Thing is, I need to convert, that's the problem. Basic attraction has never been a problem for me. I see a girl and if I'm interested things seem to happen without applying too much thought to the situation. Always has been that way. Other guys ask me how I do it and I give them what they want to hear but the truth is I don't really know—chemistry I guess. I let them think what they want because I'm already working on the next stage—how do I keep them from getting bored and dropping me. At least I think that's what happens. I'm not sure so I may be working on the wrong problem—what a terrible thought. Since I attract females so easily no one notices I'm also getting dropped a lot. I don't say much about this to my friends, I sort of steer them the way they want to go.

Self consciously, I tell myself there are truths, half-truths and untruths (also known as lies). I've never told them an untruth but I'm sorry to say I've told a lot of half-truths and not as many truths as I'd like. In fact I've just about reached the conclusion that most people are dealing in half-truth most of the time. If they're not intentionally coloring a story to make themselves look better, they're avoiding a particular fact because it might embarrass them. And that's the folks that aren't doing anything illegal or shady to begin with. This is disturbing to me but I don't think it relates directly to my problem of holding a girlfriend and I definitely want to hold on to Vicky—in all ways possible—to be clear. Know what I mean?

I can be as suave as the next guy. I know when to order a beer rather than a cocktail and vice versa, however I have trouble when we get to the stage of who leads who, or is it whom?,into the bedroom. After Vicky slapped the bejesus out of me that night, then laid a hot kiss on me I was more confused than ever. What does she want? At that point I could not have told the lady whether I wanted mustard on my hot dog or not—to use a ball park cliché. Are you following me here?

I want this gal the worst way but I wouldn't tell anyone it was about sex. I'd say something like how much I like to be with her and how much fun we have together and what a great personality she has (and she does) but sex, no, I wouldn't admit that. See what I mean about half-truths? Somebody asks me what Vicky means to me I'd most likely say she's a good friend. I might even lean on 'good' a little bit. If pressed I might say she's my girlfriend—hoping she's not around to contradict me if she's of a mind. But would I say we're lovers? Not on your life—let'em think what they like, my lips are sealed. Give'em that Mona Lisa smile like they've hit on the truth and I'm being noble, protecting my lover's reputation.

The other day is a case in point. I'm waiting for Vicky outside the locker room after they've won a hard fought game 2-0. I'm standing there not paying much attention, thinking about what I'll order for dinner and how I won't have much time with Vicky afterwards because I have to work tomorrow and it's already seven o'clock. Then I hear this voice nearby say something. I keep on day dreaming trying to figure how I might get through dinner quicker—like get Chinese take-out and go to Vicky's house to eat. The voice says 'Hi' up close and personal. With a start I focus on Wendy, almost nose to nose.

Now Wendy is a cute blond, a pitcher. In fact she's the winning pitcher who just pumped a shutout against one of the league's leading teams. "Congratulations," I manage, putting aside thoughts of eating sweet and sour chicken with chopsticks for the moment.

"Vicky asked me to entertain you…. She's going to be awhile."

I thought a minute and stuck my hands in my pockets. I was hungry and the evening was slipping away fast. "Is she going to be out anytime soon? What's she doing?"

She shrugged and smiled a very winning smile. Next thing I knew we were going to dinner. I must have said something I probably shouldn't have. You know how that happens sometimes. She took my arm and we took off for the Steak and Ale not far away. And we both had our fill of each.

Of course, she had thrown a shutout and we drank to that—several times. As I said she was a good looking blonde and what an arm! Her 'riser' is almost unhitable. At her place she took off the long sleeved blouse she was wearing and I massaged her arm with two or three scented oils she said she always used after pitching a game. They play seven innings. What an arm! She said it was nice having someone else massage her since she couldn't reach all the right muscles by herself.

I was about fifteen minutes late for work next morning and forgot my tie so I got a little ribbing from a couple people but I took that in stride. Besides I brought a dozen doughnuts from Krispy Kreme still warm and it was Thursday, which is dress down day for most people. (I have to admit, as a part of management, it's not supposed to apply to me.)

After a while I get a call from Vicky. I could tell she was a little put out, you know? There's a change of voice tone—more matter-of-fact, that I can pick up right away. I guess that's because I've had so much experience. "What happened last night?" she asks, trying to sound normal, but I can sense something here.

The warning sign goes up in my head so I said, "Oh, Wendy and I grabbed a bite and I took her home." True. See I'm being' careful here, I got a feeling maybe I screwed up somewhere—like after I massaged Wendy's arm.

"Did she tell you I'd be out in about fifteen, since I had an interview with the local paper?"

Uh-oh, I didn't remember Wendy saying anything about her bein' out in fifteen, "Ah, I thought I was supposed to go with her, something about entertaining me…" As soon as I let that last bit out I knew I'd slipped. Somehow, out loud, those words didn't sound right—know what I mean? I shoulda blamed Wendy. 'No she didn't say that. She said, you said…' Well, you get the idea. See what I mean about truth and half-truth? What's a guy to do? When to use one and not the other can be tricky. I didn't want to hurt her feelin's. You know?

Well, before I can recover I realize I'm talkin' to myself. I look around and things are kind of still in the office there, like everybody's about to enter the funeral home to view the body of a dear, departed friend, so I couldn't call Vicky back right then. Besides I needed some time to think. I was at a crossroads, one of those places I seem to have experienced before—like when you don't see the lights or hear the bell at one of those Railroad crossings without a gate. At that point, I probably would have driven right though the gate too.

Maybe after I sleep on it, I think, then maybe something will come to me. Maybe Vicky will relax a bit. Next day, I give her a call. She's not mad she says, but her tone isn't exactly warm—more like she's talkin' with the umpire about that last called ball—technical, that's the word.

I'm getting' a little desperate—I can see the situation is slippin' away—I gotta do something. "How about Chinese take-out and I get a film at Blockbusters for tonight?" I knew she didn't have a game, this bein' Friday. To my surprise she says OK and I'm all set for seven o'clock at her place. Things are looking' up. There is life after death.

The rest of the day I'm walking a couple inches off the floor around the office. Everybody is all smiles and I'm having a good day. Of course, I'm thinking about Vicky, anticipating the coming evening together. For the first time I realize how much she means to me—I've never felt like this before. I was always too cool—are you following me here? I mean, I really need her and I'm upset if something doesn't sit right with her—something I may have done or caused to happen. Sort of, I'm upset if she's upset.

Guys in the office are giving me funny looks almost like that commercial where everybody's asking the guy if he's lost weight or got a haircut or inherited a million bucks—turns out he's started using Viagra or one of those other 'jump your mate today' pills and he's feelin' good 'cause he got some last night—baloney. This is real. I can't shake the feelin' cause it's runnin' right through me. You understand? I should be a song writer.

After work I'm thinking about what movie to get at Blockbuster. I realize this: whatever I pick might make a difference, a big difference—you follow me?. This is an important night. I'm up to bat with the bases loaded,—well maybe the winning run on third, at least—and there's two outs, bottom of the ninth. The game is in my hands and I'm hopin' luscious Vicky will be—soon.

You know what I picked? You'd never guess—A League Of Their Own. Is that inspired or what? I did consider Field Of Dreams—you know "…if you build it they will come"? Naaa, too impersonal, I said to myself. Then, of course, there's the Chinese take-out. I'm on pretty firm ground here—I know what Vicky likes and I can get two different meals so we can each have a little of both. She loves sweet and sour chicken and I'm hooked on Moo Goo Gai Pan. How could I go wrong? This is the way I wanted it after the game the other night when

Wendy distracted me—actually lied to me. I can see clearly now, I'm on the right track at last.

Right at seven on the dot I arrive, a bag full of Chinese take-out in one hand and the Blockbuster video in the other, my heart light as a feather. She really looks cute in her torn shorts, bare feet and faded baseball jersey—she kisses me on both cheeks after opening the front door, then leads me to the kitchen to serve up our Chinese dinner.

There we are sittin' on the sofa each with our tray full of Chinese and the titles to A League Of Their Own comin' up on the TV screen—man this is heaven. I'm thinking I'll remember this night for a long time. Vicky hasn't mentioned the other night—the Wendy excursion—and seems like her old self. Can you imagine this? I'm looking forward to cuddling with Vicky near the end of the movie after we've opened our fortune cookies and got the lap trays out of the way.

If those guys in the office thought I was high on Viagra today, wait till they see me Monday. They can talk all they want to, I don't care. I got what I want right here—and that's the truth.

I'm almost finished my Moo Goo Gi Pan, at least all I can eat right now, when I notice Vicky's plate is still pretty full, she's not eating like she usually does. And, of course, we haven't been talkin' much cause we're eating and the movie's rolling so, until now, I don't think much about it—seems normal to me. "How's the Sweet And Sour?" I ask looking over at her. "Is it OK?"

She nods kinda like she's havin' trouble swallowing, "Fine."

We watch the movie for a few more minutes and I'm beginning to get this odd feeling, kind of a prickly feelin' up my spine which increases when it gets to the back of my neck—a clammy tingle. You know? I'm havin' trouble describing this moment 'cause I can't remember feeling this way before, ever, but it's a lousy feeling and I think I'm picking up these vibes from Vicky—weird.

At this point she presses the hold button on the remote and in that deadly, silent moment, I know something bad is about to happen if it hasn't already. I see a tear roll down her cheek.

"What is it? What's the matter? Are you sick? Something wrong with the sweet and sour?" I'm all useless questions trying to postpone what, I don't know.

Now my stomach is starting to send signals too. I'm thinking, 'Maybe it's food poisoning.' I've never had my body turn on me so fast. You can imagine! Then for no reason, I desperately want this to be food poisoning, knowing somehow it isn't—it's much worse.

Vicky slides the tray off her lap and carefully sets it on the rug away from the sofa, then slides her shapely leg up on the cushion as she turns toward me "I have to tell you something—I can't be dishonest with you."

Oh god! Truth!

Then she takes a deep breath and wipes the tear away from her cheek while I sit there starring at her—frozen numb.

"I really feel bad but I can't hide this any longer. I've never felt so miserable and happy at the same time." She breaks eye contact, looking down to collect herself, I suppose.

Meanwhile, I'm holding my breath as if I'm going for the underwater championship of my hometown or something—totally crazy, man.

"I'm engaged," she blurts out, crying big tears and smiling at the same time.

I exhale—someone just hit me in the gut—hard—a monster blow. I have a thousand questions yet I can't think of anything to say. I want to grab her and hold her and pretend I didn't hear what she just said or maybe that she didn't say those words. Then I want to run out of her living room and not let anyone see my face or have to say anything to anybody I might meet. I'm embarrassed. I'm stunned. My face shows everything I'm feeling, I'm certain, and I can't do anything about it. So I sit there totally dumb, watching her cry and laugh at the same time—almost hysterical.

"When you weren't there after the game the other night, I was mad," she says, the words pouring from her in a torrent. "Then Larry comes along and asks if I have a way home and have I eaten. He's all alone too. So we go to a Hardy's and talk over a burger and a milkshake—not like his newspaper interview about the team, but person to person, heart to heart. I feel like I can talk about anything with him. I tell him about you and how uncertain I am about you and he says he recently got a 'Dear John' letter from this TV reporter who got promoted to working for the station in New York covering baseball next season in Yankee Stadium and at the Mets games among other sports events. We talked till the place closed then sat in his car and talked till three. I saw him again the next night and he asked me to marry him—I'm in love."

"This happened so fast, my head is swimming but I can't help it—things just happened," she gushed, as my heart sank to somewhere around my knee caps. 'Things', all sorts of 'things' are running through my head—like that 'thing' about the rest of the night after three AM.

Suddenly, I'm scrambling to get out of the deep sofa, legs and arms flying in all directions, my gut is about to rebel and I barely make it to the bathroom—Moo Goo Gi Pan everywhere.

After I clean up the mess on her bathroom floor, we say goodnight, sort of. I don't remember what I said, all I remember is Vicky in those faded, tattered blue shorts saying she was sorry and how 'things' just happened, leaving me more depressed than before. I was deep breathing all the way home—I couldn't get enough oxygen—hyper-whatever it's called.

I get home and pour myself a stiff drink—straight—rare for me. I choke on the first swallow and set the glass on the kitchen counter. 'Damn, I forgot the video.' Truth—the thought stabs my brain like a white hot knife in butter—truth. Vicky told the truth. I heave a sigh thinking I'm going to be sick again.

Ya know—sometimes truth really hurts.

I really hate those damn Yankees—and that's the truth.

THE JEWELS OF
KINGDOM
EXCELSIOR

Edgar Allan held the bottle up to the candle light—almost half gone. The night was long and sleepless, one of many when he turned to his writing for comfort. Sleepless in Baltimore, he grimaced then laughed aloud, this story was going to be different—amusing—something his readers would find humorous. Why? Why did no one like his stories of wit and humor? It annoyed him that only his serious stories were popular—he could write humor too, his stories didn't have to be macabre, and he would surely prove it—even if he only amused himself.

Once he had an opening line, he knew his muse would begin to tell the story. He thought of his opening line to the *Pit And The Pendulum*: "I was sick, sick unto death with that long agony..." No that's too deadly. Maybe the *Masque Of The Red Death*: "The Red Death had long devastated the country...." No that wouldn't do—not subtle enough, not for humor. Then he turned to *The Fall Of The House Of Usher*: "During the whole of the dull, dark and soundless day...." That was closer. With an idea for a first line, he picked up his pen, took another small sip from the bottle and began scratching across the coarse paper with a mirthless laugh, his juices starting to flow—

Despair hung over the castle like a mantle of gloom, deep and dark and unrelenting as a plague. The dark miasma of the scandalous trial filtered through its darkest labyrinths and into the deepest crannies. Everywhere among the maidens in the depths of the great hall a sense of doom prevailed—an anticipated preview to the King's impending pronouncement of judgment. Their wait was short.

"Off with his gonads, Castrate him!" the king roared, his voice echoing hollow down the great hall followed by the sound of whispered sighs echoing in return from somewhere deep in its depths. (These superb acoustics from the design by Sir Christopher Wrent himself, before he changed his name and became famous.)

The tall, robust prisoner looked up, his face pale, his jaw slack, a study in shock. Recovering slightly, he croaked in a barely audible voice, "Sire, Yer Majesty would take the most magnificent jewels of the kingdom?…er, your pardon, sire, excluding yer worship's, of course."

The king glowered down from his glittering, golden throne. The audacity of this man angered him. "The most magnificent in the kingdom say ye? An extravagant and wholly unsupported claim to be sure." The man's innocent boast was unbelievable. He decided to toy with this upstart—humiliate him, crush him before enforcing the sentence. "What proof have ye to offer for such a claim?" He laughed behind his hand, in an aside to his lord privy counselor who took no notice.

"I have the sworn testament of two of the fairest maids in the kingdom, yer grace."

"What?" The answer surprised him and he took a few moments to compose himself. "Maids ye say? A contradiction, I say. How could they be maids, as ye claim—under the circumstances?"

'Yes, Sire, 'tis a valid point ye make—perhaps they be waitresses in disguise. None the less, yer grace, I have their sworn testament," the prisoner continued, his hopes aroused by the king's rumored reputation for fairness.

The king turned to the wizened man at his right hand. "Lord Privy Counselor, what do ye make of this?"

The king's counselor, opened his eyes in surprise then closed them, as if in deep thought or returning to deep slumber—which could not be determined—then opened his mouth to speak, hesitated, then leaned over and whispered something in the king's ear. The king nodded, then nodded again and finally a third time as the privy counselor stepped back and appeared to resume his slumber, stuffing each hand into the wide cuff of the opposite sleeve.

"So ye have proof have ye?"

The condemned man nodded.

"Produce it, We say—this claim to have the most magnificent balls in the kingdom—except for mine, er. Ours, of course."

Without hesitation, the sturdy man drew a sheepskin from his left boot and held it out to the king who waved it to the Privy Counselor who accepted the document without appearing to wake.

"Read it,' the king commanded, "aloud."

The counselor unrolled the skin and held it up as if to read a proclamation, cleared his throat and began, "Under the sign of three balls—be it here known to all people that Adrian—"

"Oh! Sorry your worship, wrong parchment—that's me loan." The rangy supplicant reached into his other boot and withdrew another sheepskin., "I…I use them to keep me feet warm," he reacted to the king's look of disbelief and exchanged parchments with the lord privy counselor.

The counselor began to mumble his way through the text, 'the wereas's' and 'where fors'—mostly entertaining himself, since no one in the assemblage could make out what he said except near the end, a phrase "…big as goose eggs…."

As he finished, the counselor looked toward the king, whose face betrayed his reaction to this astounding claim, "Yes, m'Lord he's right it's a valid document. The maids…er sluts, both verify his claim with their mark and it's official with the seal of Maker's Mark—not the equal of Crown Royal, I'd wager, but respectable, you must agree, sire." The lord privy counselor held the sheepskin in front of the king, his dirty thumbnail under the Maker's Mark seal.

"Goose eggs! Goose eggs?" the king's voice trembled with disbelief.

"Right here your worship," the lord privy counselor juggled the parchment to move his thumb under the extravagant phrase.

The king sputtered under his breath and mumbled something to his counselor who muttered back in turn, his wrinkled face broken in an open smile and nodding firmly.

The king addressed the sturdy man called Adrian, standing in front of him, "Even without challenge to this document—some might say it's a forgery—you are charged with attempting to impregnate several ladies of the court. Incredible as the charge is, this is a serious matter. and severe punishment seems appropriate. What say ye?"

Another faint sound of sighs floating from hidden recesses in the vast great hall.

The big man swallowed hard, his face still ashen, "Sire, I cannot deny the charge. I was only trying to be fair…generous…of service…fulfilling a need. I had no idea court maidens were any the less discreet than those beyond the castle walls."

"Discreet!" the king roared, his voice trembling with emotion and filling the great hall with his indignation. "Ye would denigrate me ladies after usurping my…er, our prerogative?"

"Your pardon, sire…I had no idea…"

Before the enraged king could say more, the lord privy counselor, now fully awake as a result of the king's most recent bellow, leaned over and whispered in the monarch's ear.

As he listened the king's eyes grew wide and he couldn't help mouthing some of the lord privy counselor's words, a hint of the lurid thoughts passing through his simple brain, "Eh…contest, ye say? Nightly what? Royal family…credit? Glory of the Kingdom?"

Pausing to collect his thoughts the king looked the robust young man over—deciding. His intent to humiliate the prisoner seemed to have failed and he wasn't sure making him a capon was adequate punishment. On the other hand the lord privy counselor had shocked him with suggestions of a different sort, a tournament never before seen in the kingdom or any other kingdom he was certain. Although he had difficulty visualizing the benefits suggested by his counselor, in fairness he was willing to ponder the suggestions for a day or two. "I am considering an alternate punishment—"

More whispered sighs through the hall. "Oh, thank ye, yer grace—"

The king held up a hand, his smile sinister. All the sighing stopped. "Perhaps ye best wait 'til ye hear what the alternative is before ye rejoice." He looked around aware of everyone's full attention, a first. "I'm considering substituting yer head for yer gonads—we'll pickel them afterwards and display them prominently, next to the jewels of the kingdom—ha, ha," then his tone darkened, "as a warning to other would be Casanovas. That's if they prove to match yer 'maids' claims—goose eggs indeed!"

The prisoner, Adrian, hung his head, silent, flickering hope extinguished, his bold argument unsuccessful and now apparently facing death by the axe-man executioner.

"We will give ye, me…er, our final decision on the morrow after the cock crows," the king concluded.

Once more there was a sound through the great hall not unlike a gentle zephyr passing through a lonely willow tree at midnight, the sense of insufferable doom pervaded the assemblage as surely as the sun was under a cloud at that moment, the dim light in the great hall darkening perceptibly.

The Lord Privy Counselor nodded his approval, satisfied there would be a spectacle no matter which of his suggestions the king decided to follow. Things had been too dull around the court for too long.

*   *   *   *

A spear of light pierced the dungeon through the long, narrow embrasure high on the wall above his head. Adrian unrolled the small scroll that he found under the wooden spoon next to the bowl of warm porridge on his breakfast tray. He didn't read too well but without light he couldn't read at all. With nervous hands he tried to center the shaft of light on the scroll, heedless of the guards who might appear at any time.

At that moment he heard the chilling sound of a rooster crowing from somewhere outside the castle walls. His hands shook, his fate would soon to be announced by the King. He began to read.

> 'stay where ye are
> and remain above par
> Er tonite's North star
> twinkles from afar
> Ye be called to the bar
> of the maiden's har…'

Har? Har? Har—what? The scroll was incredibly hard to read twisting his hands in the narrow beam of light. And as an ex-Fool, Adrian thought the rhyme was, if anything, worse than the unsteady light. As his old Fool coach used to harangue him, "make it sing—If there's no swing there ain't no zing." Adrian lost that apprenticeship when his tights split while he was learning to juggle—trying to keep his tutor from being hit on the head by one of the iron training balls he was tossing. So much for his brief exposure in entertainment.

Refocusing on the message, he read the rhyme again trying to make some sense of it. Then he thought of finding the scroll under the spoon for his porridge,. If the message was supposed to be private, putting it under a wooden spoon certainly didn't hide it.—everyone in the guardroom must have spied it. That might explain why the Dungeon Master himself slid the breakfast tray, under his cell door, chuckling and cheerfully calling to him: "*Bon Appetite*!" A fool's errand. Was the message intended to trap him?

Holding the thin parchment to the light again he noticed something he'd ignored on the first reading.

There was scribbling on the reverse side of the message. Someone had failed to scratch it out in recycling the parchment. Once again he read, angling the scroll to the capricious light.

'There's a maiden outside the bar
Who's portal be set ajar
'er tonite's North Star
twinkles from afar
That ye might s__ _'

The last word was blotted out by a huge ink spot. He twisted and turned the parchment in the sunlit shaft but could not learn the last word except he thought it began with an S. It was a mystery, all insolvable, nor could he grapple with the shadowy fancies that crowded upon him as he pondered the two fragmented verses.

＊　　　＊　　　＊　　　＊

Poe put the pen down and cracked his stiff knuckles. This humorous twist is a bit challenging, he thought, and as always I'm having trouble with the women. They do get in the way sometimes. Perhaps I can make those rhymes, seemingly from the court ladies, be something the Lord Privy Counselor dreamed up, a ploy to get the protagonist to try an escape. He sighed, dipped the pen in the ink-well—

＊　　　＊　　　＊　　　＊

Adrian tried to swallow but the oak block was rough against his throat, uncomfortable. Not for long—his doom was nigh. He heard the hooded executioner, the axe-man, take a deep breath as he raised the huge blade high over his head. Acorn size was now the measure of Adrian's shriveled scrotum, his fear palpable. Then came the sigh as the axe-man released his breath in a mighty chop—the hollow sound as the blade bit into the oak block, the crowd below the platform cheering. He felt nothing. Was death so easy? Was he already at heaven's gate? Why was he hearing all these sounds? The axe man had missed! Belatedly Adrian struggled, trying to relieve the uncomfortable kneeling position—an awkward effort with his arms tied behind him.

"Stay down boy, if ye know what's good fer ye." A big hand shoved him back down. A rough cloth was thrown over his shoulders and head as he half-rolled off the chopping block. He felt something sticky oozing through the cloth. "That's it, laddie, flop 'round a bit—like a chicken—good!" The husky whisper. "Not too much! Ah, the crowd likes 'at…" He paused, "Ye done this afore?"

Shaken and uncertain, Adrian said nothing as the executioner rolled and pushed his big frame into the donkey cart filled with straw. "Be better if we had a little more cow's blood." The words grunted in the effort to get him into the cart. The donkey brayed and started to move. "Ho! Ho! silly jackass, not yet."

There was still a lot of crowd noise as the citizens of the kingdom started to disperse and wend their way to their miserable hovels.

"Now be very still, me lad—just a bit more, we'll have ye away from here…And I'll have me reward in pocket, har, har, har," he slobbered.

Adrian wondered how the crowd had been deceived? Whose head was in the basket?

Meanwhile in his dimly lit bed chambers the King was discussing the situation with his Lord Privy Counselor. "Yer sure the executioner will miss and this braggart will keep his head?"

"I'd wager on it, m'Lord. Remember last year when it took him two chops to dispatch that wretched fellow with the crooked neck? Besides I assured him, yer Majesty would give him a golden Floretine florin when the task was properly done and Adrian carted away safely."

"Really?" The King's eyebrows shot up. "Was that really necessary? I mean, really…"

"Sire, our executioner is getting along in years and he has a touch of this new thing the court physician refers to as 'attention something'." He gazed upward momentarily, "Attention distraction, that's the phrase, I believe. Do ye not recall, Majesty? Remember?"

"Oh, yes, yes," the king replied, recalling only the potion the court doctor brewed for several ladies of the court when they fainted during the sentencing of Adrian. "Now let's discuss this challenge, this tourney ye suggested. Ye actually want me to 'joust', for want of a better term, with this 'goose egg' fellow in the bed chambers of the ladies of the court?" He spoke forgetting his resolve to use the royal 'we'.

"Sire, I realize it's a difficult task, night after night, bed after bed, maiden after maiden, but someone has to do it—there will be two of you. Yer Majesty wouldn't want one of the court jesters as yer substitute would ye?" The lord privy counselor concealed a sly look, noting the king was already showing some embarrassment. "Surely this braggart must be exposed for what he is—a foolish, fumbling, fornicating, fraud, unable to meet the test when the gauntlet is thrown down."

In desperation, the counselor added the challenge to his Majesty's manliness.

The king raised his chin, his eyes slowly ascending to the religious icon over the head of his canopied bed; his own epiphany. "Counselor, Ye be right! We must uphold the honor of my…er our father, Henry VIII," he intoned solemnly, "…But is it necessary we diddle the whole lot? That might take thirty days or so—there's so many of them—even with this imposter helping—every night."

The counselor sighed, he'd been through this with the king before. He was so forgetful, even inattentive at times. "Remember Majesty, the Plague?"

"The Plague?' he shivered with the reminder, "That was 18 or 20 years ago."

"Precisely, m'Lord,—remember how it took so many male children and spared the females? That horrible scourge was about the time of the great soap scandal—that witch who convinced all the court ladies soap was a magical panacea guaranteed to assure them of a man in matrimony—the one yer father, his Majesty, Henry VIII, god rest his soul, had beheaded after he got in the tub with her…? Remember?"

The king scratched through his chin whiskers. 'So that was what happened, lo those many years ago.' "Ye forget Counselor, we were only nine years of age at the time Yer predecessor sent us to my chambers so I…er we, wouldn't be struck blind at the sight of some mystical event, never explained to the prince in waiting."

The counselor looked at the ceiling as if searching for devine guidance. "Yer Majesty, this is why there are so many females in court. There is a need to populate the kingdom—with males—future warriors—even an army to ward off King Harold over the mountain."

"Yes, yes, we understand. There seems to be no end to the labors ye would put us through for the kingdom. But what about this fellow with the 'goose eggs'? I want to boil him in oil."

"Sire, our premise is to challenge his boast! Not so? Prove him a fanciful, fiddling, fornicating fraud. Since he has officially been executed and is in hiding, all his women—those that become pregnant—can be counted as the King's offspring in addition to those yer Majesty actually impregnates—it's a win, win situation with no risk to yer majesty's manly reputation, the crown jewels, if I may be so bold." The lord privy counselor was trying to be patient, tempering his words. "The kingdom grows stronger and yer Majesty, can put this braggart in his place, however ye choose, including yer Majesty's original sentence. Remember—display jewels of the kingdom?" The counselor's look bespoke his craftiness.

"And we can offset Harold's challenge from over the mountain in a few years."

"Precisely, m' Lord—brilliant perception, brilliant—King Harold has long coveted thy kingdom." At last the light had penetrated even into this dim brain.

$$* \qquad * \qquad * \qquad *$$

Poe stopped to stretch. Now I've got'em—no place to go but for the ugly, rotten outcome, the twist of fate, the outrageous conclusion, the hilarious fate of the high and mighty, the revelation of hypocrisy and low cunning—

$$* \qquad * \qquad * \qquad *$$

As he diligently performed his nightly tasks, resting most of every day and eating a special diet prescribed by the court physician, the king reflected on the ancient family he represented, darkly and secretly noted for a peculiar instability of temperament that reoccurred with every fourth or fifth issue, and carefully hidden from public disclosure lest the court become aware and demand a new successor to the throne taken from the nobles of the kingdom. He shuddered with the thought of his younger brother long committed to the asylum by his father, Henry VIII. Even his privy counselor seemed unaware of the possibilities but Henry IX knew he must beware his counselor's betrayal.

And so it came to pass nine months and a few days after the King's reluctant acquiescence to the Lord Privy Counselor's grand scheme, the first of the court ladies went into labor and delivered the first offspring. There was rejoicing throughout the tiny Kingdom of Excelsior and the serfs were given a day off by royal decree so they could join in celebrating this joyous occasion. "Let'em eat cake," the king proclaimed to his counselor, "we'll soon have an army."

The lord privy counselor winked aside, "My congratulations sire, truly yours are the jewels of Kingdom Excelsior.

Babies began to accumulate in the Armory which had been set aside and long prepared for their arrival (there being no army). For almost forty days as the ladies of the court welped their offspring the kingdom celebrated; mead was soon in short supply and the royal bee keeper was confined in the stocks for watering down the honey. Never had there been such celebration among the peasants and never had there been such consternation and hand wringing among the officials of the kingdom. With each birth. King Henry IX's mood descended the depths, deeper and deeper, sinking ever closer to the cesspool of despondency. This would not do.

He summoned the court physician and the lord privy counselor. Turning first to the physician, "You know about these things, how do you explain this?"

"Yer Majesty, there are aspects of nature which none of us know fully, but when the moon is in the seventh house and Jupiter aligns with Mars then—"

"Silence, you nincompoop. Gibberish, nothing but gibberish."

"Ye," he pointed at the frail, trembling lord privy counselor, "ye suggested this. What say ye now?"

"Sire, I can only offer my underestimation of your Majesty's virility. Long has it been known that virile men produce mostly—"

"What? Get out of my sight the both of you."

In utter frustration and self-righteous anger, the king himself issued a proclamation: on the 10th day after the last issue. The stark, shocking message couldn't have been more unexpected than the King's abdication from his throne. It was proclaimed: There would be a double header in King Henry VIII Courtyard on the first day of Lent. The executioner would detach the heads of two men high in the councils of the kingdom—one widely known, the other a stranger, unknown except by title although a few (all court maidens) swore his face was vaguely familiar. The Lord Privy Counselor was to be beheaded for gross malfeasance in office, one count, and high treason, two counts:—undermining the monarch's authority;—advice prejudicial to good order and the future stability of the kingdom. In addition, the newly nominated head of the future army, Commander Nairda, was to be beheaded for disservice to the king as a suspected agent of a foreign kingdom, three counts: fornication unbecoming an officer; unreliable sperm in the act of fornication; fornication resulting in the future debasement of the Kingdom of Excelsior. As a footnote to King Henry IX's proclamation, a special dispensation was included for the executioner—he was allowed three strokes with his axe to accomplish each execution.

The king remained in seclusion dealing with affairs of state.

All the ladies of the court had delivered girl babies, but for one, the one the King himself apparently had impregnated, at least according to the condemned lord privy counselor. There were even three sets of twins—the sexual imbalance of the kingdom was worse than ever.

With the great tapestries that formed the shades to the royal bedroom casement drawn, the bedroom was full of gloom, dark but for a single candle as the king moaned, holding his head and his physician applied another chicken and rice poultice to draw out his pain. King Harold, from over the mountain, was rumored to be massing his army and King Henry IX anticipated an ultimatum any day. The more immediate crisis had been an emergency call for more wet nurses to feed the hungry offspring resulting from the great tourney—forever after to be remembered as Henry the IX's great, fornicating mistake or more simply, The Forn-up.

*   *   *   *

"…and they all lived miserably ever after." In the small, dimly lit room there followed the harsh sound of what might pass for a laugh. The moon briefly shone through the ragged curtains at the window. *The J.O.K.E.* was finished. He had found his muse, now he could go all night. Chokes and scrapping sounds issued from his throat as Poe reached for the bottle again.

The warmth flowing through him, he moved the candlelabra closer, picked up his pen again and turned to his incomplete short story, *The System of Doctor Tarr and Professor Fether,* a story about radical treatment of patients in a French lunatic asylum during the eighteeth century—another humorous story.

GROWING PAINS

Eric raced down Devon Drive, free at last. He had his catcher's mitt and an old, grass-stained baseball. The fresh spring day promised to get warmer, perfect for a workout.

His buddy, Brad pushed open the glass storm door. "You finally get done?"

Eric smiled, "Yeah".

Brad pushed the door shut behind him, his glove hanging from his other wrist, a half eaten an apple in hand. He took a big bite. "What took you so long?" he mumbled through the mouthful. "You said you were almost done sweeping when I was up there an hour ago."

He stopped at the bottom of the brick steps to look at Eric directly.

"Well, I was," Eric shrugged. "When I told my dad I was finished, he checked the garage and I wasn't." He grinned feeling clever.

Brad continued to stare, a smirk pulling at the corners of his mouth.

"Man—how was I to know he was going to pull all those tools out o'the corner and move t'tire?"

Brad laughed, wiping his mouth with a sleeve. "C'mon. let's go 'round back and start throwin'."

Walking over the lush green grass, Eric thought of the first team practice Thursday, really just a meeting. His dad almost always spent the first day getting to know the players and seeing who could run and throw and hit.

He wanted to pitch but he knew his dad was always worried about having a catcher although he spent a lot of time with the pitchers. Throwing hard was important, he said, but if you couldn't find the plate it didn't matter how hard you threw.

They spread out and started throwing easily back and forth. Brad took another big bite and tossed the apple core aside. After a dozen throws Brad waved Eric back. "Get ready for my 'flamer'."

"Throw a couple more first, get loose."

Brad frowned. The next one stung Eric's hand. He tossed it back with a relaxed motion.

Again Brad's throw had a sting to it. Eric threw the ball back a little harder, noticing the sly look on Brad's face.

"You chicken?" he grinned, again waving Eric to move back.

"No." Eric answered, moving back. "Don't throw your arm out before we even start the season." He crouched down, holding the mitt as a target.

Brad leaned forward then rocked back, kicking his left leg high to stride forward releasing the ball with an exaggerated motion. Eric smothered the ball in the grass diving to his left.

"I got that from TV—Great Pitchers of the Century", Brad said. "A guy named Juan Marichal pitched for the San Francisco Giants. He's one of the greatest—all time. That's his motion—neat, huh?"

"Just throw, Brad."

The next one was high. The one after higher still, hitting the neighbor's board fence with a sharp thump, thirty feet behind Eric. As he jogged back to get the ball, Eric noticed Col. Bishop, his arms folded, standing inside the glass storm door to the kitchen, watching them

He threw a fly ball back to Brad and walked back to take his position.

Brad raised his glove without having to move. "He's under the ball to make the final putout of the game. Yesss!" Brad made a nice catch of the high fly.

"All right, put it in here. Pitch to the target." Eric crouched down.

Brad threw the next two without his big exaggerated wind up. "Did that last one heat you up?" He grinned, leaning in as if to take the sign.

Eric smiled back. "Naw, they don't hurt if y'catch'em right," he said, ignoring the tingling sensation in his left hand.

Brad went into his Juan Marichal wind up again. "The high kick, the throw—"

The ball whistled into the grass in front of Eric and skipped. Too late, he saw it was going to hit him in the face. He flipped up the glove and ducked his head. The sound was like a cement truck running into a wall. The ball caromed off the top of his head and angled crazily across the grass. He started to rise, "C'mon Brad, throw—" The bright day faded into a gray haze, he sensed rather than felt he was turning right slowly, the wetness of the grass in his face, the peculiar sweetness of its smell.

He focused on Col. Bishop, felt his hand on his chest holding him down. "It's all right son, stay down," he said. Turning, "Brad, get me some ice cubes and that dish towel hanging on the frig door."

"OK, Dad." Eric heard him pound across the lawn toward the back door.

"How you feelin'?" Col. Bishop looked down, his hand still resting lightly on Eric's chest.

"Fine, sir."

The concerned lines in the Colonel's face relaxed as he laughed. He ran a hand over his mixed gray crew cut and pushed his aviator glasses up the bridge of his nose with a finger. "You took a pretty good pop. That was a nasty skip." He felt the egg swelling on the top of Eric's head carefully. "You want to try sitting up?"

"Yes. sir."

Brad arrived with a bowl of ice cubes and the dishtowel. He leaned over, after handing them to his father, both hands on his knees, "You OK Eric?" He grinned seeing his friend was all right. "I thought you were a catcher."

"I KNEW you weren't a pitcher," Eric managed before Col. Bishop tied the ice filled dish towel under his chin.

"Eric's a good catcher," Col. Bishop turned toward Brad. "If you hadn't been show boatin'…is your dad at home, Eric?" He turned back.

"Yes, sir. I think so."

"Good." He stood up. "We'll walk you home. He might want to take you out to the Base Emergency room just to be on the safe side."

After the discussion between Col. Bishop and his father, Eric was allowed to watch what was left of Saturday morning cartoons with his sister, Chris, a year younger. The dishtowel remained in place which made the top of his head both wet and numb. His father said it couldn't hurt to leave it on and they'd wait awhile before deciding whether to go out to the emergency room, especially since Eric said he felt OK. His mom gave him some paper towels to keep the cold trickle of water from going down his neck.

The grownups had left the room when Chris burst into laughter. It wasn't the cartoons, a commercial was running, Eric looked at her blankly. "What?"

"If you could see how silly you look with that stupid pink and white dish towel around your head and dirty neck. You look like an 'immigrunt'," she giggled, her brown eyes glistening.

Eric turned soberly back to the TV, apparently unaffected by his sister's taunt. "The word is 'immigrant'," he said finally.

"Is not," she said brimming with mirth.

"You don't even know what an 'immigrant' is," he challenged without looking away from the TV.

"Do too," she came back.

He turned toward her. "OK, where'd you see the word?"

"In my history book. There was a picture of all these women with big scarves tied over their heads—just like you," she giggled. "Immigrunt."

Eric turned back to the cartoon, a look of disgust on his face. Then, without looking, he grabbed her, reaching back with one hand and in an instant was tickling her with both hands.

She screamed, laughing. "Eric's an immigrunt" She tried to get at his ribs. They rolled laughing and fell with a thump on the floor, Eric more or less on top. "Stop, you immigrunt, you're dripping all over me," Chris yelled, unable to stop laughing.

"All right that's enough." Their mother appeared from the kitchen. "Get up off the floor."

Then, unable to maintain her stern voice, she smiled, "I guess you're feeling better," she looked at Eric, as Chris stopped screaming. "Are you hungry? How would you like waffles for lunch?"

"Would I! Yes, I'm starved."

"Me too," Chris broke in.

"Dumb question. All right, give me that towel and go wash your hands and face—with soap—and dry off."

After a satisfying lunch Eric stood in the living room looking out the picture window.

The trees had started to leaf and the Nebraska sky was a bright blue, the weather forecast had said the temperature might reach the middle sixties. Chris walked byond the front yard and made a face at him passing down Devon. Then, Brad came into view coming up the street.

"Hey Dad, can I go out?" he called out.

He heard his father's muffled answered from somewhere down in the basement as he pushed the storm door open for Brad, "C'mon in."

"How ya feelin'? Can you come out?" Brad stuffed the rest of an Oreo cookie in his mouth.

"Just a sec, I'll ask my dad."

As he turned his father came out of the kitchen and walked over to him, throwing an arm around his shoulder. "Hello, Brad. How do you feel, Son?"

"Fine. I'm OK."

His father touched the lump on the top of Eric's head causing him to wince. "Do you have a headache?" He turned Eric, both hands on his shoulders, and stooped to look into his eyes.

"Nope."

"Do you feel sick to your stomach?"

"Nope." And they both laughed remembering Eric had eaten three waffles, scrambled eggs and four strips of bacon with a big glass of milk for lunch followed by a handful of fig Newtons when his mother refused to give him the last of her waffle. His father straightened, sliding an arm around his son. "What do you think, Brad?"

Brad grinned. "Aw, Eric's tough. He's OK."

"You really goin' out for pitcher?" Eric asked Brad.

Brad looked slyly at Eric's dad. "I don't think so—probably third base. C'mon, let's go down t'the gully."

"Eric looked up at his dad. "Can I?"

His father smiled. "OK. But take it easy—if you start to feel bad—. "His voice trailed off, the boys were headed toward Eric's room.

"Let's get my bow," Eric said.

The gully was high with last fall's dried grass, new growth green at its base. The low area behind the houses across Devon from Eric's house was scrub growth and some Mulberry trees among the sapling maples and assorted softwoods. Many houses on that side of the street had fast growing Lombardy poplars on their property borders, some screening the gully from view.

They played here often. The ramshackle boards they had nailed together into a rough shelter around the base of one of the few mature trees was their club house. Otherwise there were no structures until the back yards of the houses on Freeman Drive, almost a hundred yards across the gully.

As soon as they entered their private domain, Eric and Brad took turns shooting arrows at cans and pieces of paper ten to twenty yards away.

"Man, this is really neat," Brad said, "it goes right where you aim. Watch this." He raised the bow, drawing the arrow back.

Eric slapped his arm, "Brad, if you stick that arrow up in a tree you're gonna hafta go get it. I only got two arrows."

"Yeah, OK." He lowered his sights and let go at a sampling in front of them. The arrow went between a narrow fork in the tree and lodged in the dirt thirty feet beyond. "Wow, did you see that? I only pulled the drawstring back halfway."

"You mean you were trying to miss?" Eric grabbed the bow from Brad's hand and fitted the other arrow. He drew back carefully, one eye closed. With a swish and quick thud the arrow hit the small sapling a couple inches below the fork. Eric looked at Brad with a satisfied smile. "Now, that's the way you're s'posed to do it."

"Yeah, right, Robin Hood. Now let's see YOU get the arrow out o'the tree," Brad laughed, running to get the other arrow.

Eric tugged on the shaft. The blunt tip of the arrow was buried in the green sapling.

Despite his best efforts the arrow wouldn't budge. "Hey, Brad, gimme a hand."

Brad pushed him aside. "Let me try." He pulled with both hands without a hint of success.

"Why'd you have to shoot it so hard?" he glared at Eric. "It's really stuck."

"Maybe if we both try." Eric moved closer and put his hands behind Brad's. They pulled hard. Nothing. Again they tried, putting their feet against the small sapling. Both slipped off the shaft and fell to the ground laughing. "Man! Eric, why'd you do that?"

"I was tryin' to hit it."

"Maybe if we work it up an' down, we can loosen it," Brad suggested. They got to their feet and grabbed the reluctant shaft again.

"Now on my count of three, OK?" Brad said.

He counted. They wiggled the shaft. Nothing. It was fully stuck.

Brad looked on the other side of the sapling. "Did it go all the way through?" He felt up and down the skin of the tree.

"Let's try again." Eric said and grabbed the shaft closest to the smooth bark of the sapling.

Again they tried to move the shaft. "Careful...don't..." There was a sickening sound.

They let go together, each dropping his hands, looking at the other. The arrow sagged at a slight angle, the shaft cracked. "I told you to be careful," Eric scolded.

"Sorry. I was trying to get it out." Brad gave Eric a mournful look. "You shouldn't have shot it so hard."

There was a long silence as they stared at the sagging arrow shaft, each of them touching it lightly, as if it might heal itself somehow, a symbol of their helplessness.

Brad handed Eric the remaining arrow. "Let's go see if Tripp is home."

"OK." They set off together arms over each other's shoulders, the sun warming their backs, a light breeze in their faces.

Tripp's house faced on Freeman drive on the far side of the gully. They passed a budding mock cherry in his back yard and walked up to the back door. There was no bell. Eric knocked on the storm door. Petty soon their friend appeared at the door.

"Hey, Tripp, can you come out?'

He poked his blonde head around the storm door. 'Wait 'til I get my jacket."

"Aw, y'don't need a jacket," Brad said. "it's warm out." Tripp disappeared and reappeared wearing the brown parka he'd worn all winter.

"Good grief, Tripp, you expecting a blizzard?" Brad laughed.

"I'll wear it open." He made a helpless movement with his hands, "My mom said I had to wear it. She doesn't want me to catch cold." He looked from Eric to Brad with a look that begged for understanding. "Whatcha got there, Eric?"

"A sixty pound pull bow. A friend of my dad's gave it to me,"

"Yeah. You should see the sixty pounds he put into a tree," Brad chuckled. They took turns telling Tripp about the arrow Eric shot into the sapling as the three of then strolled aimlessly among the daffodils blooming in Tripp's back yard. Eric kicked at a toadstool.

"How far will it shoot?" Tripp asked.

Eric and Brad looked at each other. "I don't know," Eric answered slowly, "pretty far, I bet."

"Probably half way 'cross the gully," Brad offered.

Eric raised the bow, the arrow notched, "More 'an half way, I'll bet." He drew the bow back.

"Wait! Not here," Tripp cried suddenly. "Up there." He led the way toward Freeman Drive between houses. There were no windows in that end of his house and the neighbor's house was screened by the ever present row of Lombardy poplars.

"Yeah," Brad said, "good thinking. This is perfect." He faced back toward the gully,

"Plenty o'room. He looked back at Eric who was holding the bow pointed down "You want me to do it? Here, gimme the bow."

"No. I'll do it." Eric raised the bow carefully, making sure Tripp and Brad were to the side. The back of the houses facing Devon were far across the gully with its tangle of weeds and scrub growth. Rows of poplars hid some from view. He raised the bow above the far tree line, aiming at nothing in particular and pulled the bowstring back as far as he could and let go with a sharp 'twang'.

"Wow, look at that thing go," Tripp exclaimed.

"Awesome," Brad said, whistling through his teeth. "Man, you got all o'that one, Eric."

Eric had a self-satisfied smile on his face, the bow still extended as if posing for a William Tell poster. "Yeah. That one was harder than the one I put in the tree—a lot harder."

They walked in the direction of the arrow's flight into the gully. "Way to go, buddy."

Brad clapped him on the back.

"I'm impressed," Tripp added, his big coat flopping against his sides, striding through the brush to keep up with Brad and Eric.

Halfway across they spread out, searching, taking very deliberate strides. Tripp took off his parka and tucked it under one arm. Searching side to side, he walked to Eric's left while Brad covered to the right.

"I don't see it," Brad offered. "You think it came this far?"

"Positive," Eric said.

Tripp turned, walking backyards, sighting back to the launch spot. "Are we on the right line?" He stumbled and fell into a scrub tree which kept him upright.

"That's our right fielder," Brad chirped.

Eric laughed, "You can't hide Tripp, the ball will still find'im,".

Tripp turned around. "Whoa, that was close," he said with a nervous laugh.

They continued the search, their anxiety growing as they approached the edge of the gully and the backyards of the houses on Devon. They could hear voices. "Where could that thing be?" Eric mumbled, more to himself than the others.

Ambling along in their total absorption to find the arrow they almost stumbled upon Mr. Draper, his wife and Kirsten, their daughter, in their backyard looking up at an arrow stuck in the back siding of their house about eight feet off the ground. Only the poplars saved them from being seen.

"Uh oh." Eric's hushed whisper froze them near the corner of the Draper's property. They exchanged blank looks.

"I have t'go home," Tripp broke the silence, turning for the other side of the gully.

Eric and Brad watched him dumbly. "Maybe we ought to go down a few houses before going out to Devon," Brad suggested quietly. They turned and walked along the weedy fringe of the gully. Eric held the bow along his side away from the Draper's house, one end digging into his armpit.

That night, at dinner, Eric sat next to Chris, his two older sisters next to their father and mother at the oval dining room table. He concealed his expression as his mother brought out the Brussels sprouts. Chris hated them too, in fact they were both sure their mother was the only one who liked them, even with the cheese sauce which barely reduced the gag factor.

"Oh, boy, Brussels sprouts," Chris said with a big grin. Eric's big sisters both turned immediately to look a Chris. Then they saw Eric's quick gargoyle expression and laughed.

"They're very nutritious," their mother said tartly, returning to the kitchen for the roast.

As his father was serving, Eric said, "That's enough," as he spooned four of the cabbage-like balls on his plate.

Smiling, his father glanced from the plate to Eric, "We have plenty," and served him two more while Chris dug him in the ribs, "besides a few more vitamins couldn't hurt." He passed the plate to Eric's older sister who passed it to Chris with a big smile.

"For you dear brother Eric," Chris exaggerated.

"Thanks," Eric said, trying unsuccessfully to reach Chris with an elbow.

"Your mom made Pineapple upside-down cake today," his father announced, as if to reinforce the rule of the house: eat all your dinner, especially the vegetables or you don't get dessert. And his dad always set a good example, even though he admitted he refused to eat cooked carrots when he was a boy and when asked about Brussels sprouts said he'd never had them as a child.

Eric ate one of the little balls, smothering it with the cheese sauce. He looked at Chris's plate, she only had three left. There was a suspicious bulge in her napkin. She smiled sweetly at him, noticing his attention. "Gee, Eric, you've still got five Brussels sprouts left—don't you like Mom's cooking?"

Even their mother laughed, Chris was so obvious. Eric forked in another of the dark green balls and almost gagged—not enough cheese sauce. "Mmmm, they're really good," he said making a face. His two older sisters were crying they laughed so hard.

Somehow Chris now only had one left on her plate.

"How did you make out with the bow today?" his father asked, making conversation.

"Oh, fine." He looked at Chris's bulging napkin then up at her. Her mouth was pressed into a thin line, her dark eyes brimming with mischief.

"What did you shoot at?" his father continued.

Eric took a big gulp of milk and shuddered.

"You all right?" There was alarm in his mother's voice.

"Yeah, Eric. You all right?" Chris managed to convey a hidden meaning with her look.

Immediately he sensed she knew about the arrow stuck in the back of Draper's house.

"I'm fine," he said. "That milk's cold."

"What did you shoot at?" His father repeated.

The chill, without the shudder, ran through him again. "Oh, stuff—papers an' a can. One arrow stuck in a tree. We couldn't get it out." His stomach tensed. One more question. That would be it. He'd probably be spending the next week in his room, no TV, no dessert or worse.

Through the chilling thoughts of his imagination, he heard his father asking his oldest sister about her school work. She was terrible in math. Recovering, Eric quickly scanned the table and managed to scrape two of the offensive Brussels spouts into his napkin—one to go. A messy business, but it was better than gagging on them. Chris wouldn't tell, she had a napkin full and, he was almost sure, Susan and Robyn probably did too. They never get caught. He almost laughed. In fact, he would have laughed if he hadn't been so intent on not getting caught.

He pictured the four of them standing in line after dinner waiting to pitch their napkins, full of Brussels sprouts, into the waste paper basket under the kitchen sink. Wouldn't Mom love that.

✳   ✳   ✳   ✳

Tucked in bed, he put his arms around his mom. "Good night, Eric. Sleep tight."

"G'night, Mom, thanks for the Pineapple upside-down cake, it was great."

His father hugged him. "Good night son, see you in the morning."

"G'night, Dad."

Dreamily, he drifted into sleep thinking about the arrow stuck in the back of the Draper's house. He saw himself on the end of a big rope from a hovering helicopter pulling the feathered arrow out with one mighty heave. Then, remembering the arrow stuck in the green sapling, he pictured Brad holding his dad's step-ladder steady while Eric attacked the embedded arrow with his dad's

Vise-grips. All this at mid-night after they had each slipped out of their houses and quietly met in the middle of Devon.

As he slipped confidently back into his house, arrow in hand, there was Chris, standing in the hallway right in front of his bedroom door, arms folded, with that look on her face. "I'm going to tell Daddy," she whined, "unless…."

He woke with a shiver, his hair wet with sweat, the covers twisted around him so that his left arm was asleep. He sat up in bed shaking his arm until sharp needles of returning feeling flashed up and down the whole length as if he'd stuck his finger in an electric socket.

Then rubbing it with his other hand he yawned and settled down, sleepy, Tomorrow was another day.

THE CRITIQUE OR WHAT ARE FRIENDS FOR?

"I don't know, Mike," he paused breaking eye contact, "it's a little slow. I mean the story doesn't move—very much." He looked at his feet, the ants were busy, traveling in and out of a crack in the asphalt driveway.

"Ned. Did you read it all the way through?"

"Yes, of course, but…"

"That's OK, I know you're not a writer. Just tell me what you think You don't have to sugar coat it—go ahead, I can take it."

Ned cleared his throat, searching for words, wishing he hadn't agreed to read the story, GLJNS AND BUTTER, in the first place. Now he had to come up with something. Something that wouldn't hurt his friend's feelings or be too revealing of his own. "Well, don't take this the wrong way cause you really write good, but well," he paused, "like I said it's a little slow, the characters—"

"Slow?" Mike Smith, H. Harold Ruskin, his chosen pen name, exploded. "Y'already said that—you mean pace?"

Aroused. Ned fired back, "It's…it's boring." He knew immediately, watching Mike's face sag, he had selected the wrong word. If he'd chosen "uninteresting", his first thought after "slow", that might have worked better.

However, he underestimated the author, H. Harold Ruskin. Except for the momentary pain inflicted by the word "boring", the author had a ready, quite

rational, response. "I realize you're not my primary audience. I can even understand how an in-flight emergency with a live bomb and an engine fire might not
have enough dramatic tension to be considered fast-paced by some readers." He
hesitated. the desperate images of his story vivid to his mind—the aircrew on the
verge of panic while the pilot radios the Control Room for help. Then, breaking
out of his brooding silence he said, "Maybe this is when I need to tell the reader
about the heroic, wounded navigator bleeding to death while he figures out the
heading home, blood all over his chart." Mike shook his head sadly—such an
obvious oversight.

"Oh, no!" Ned cried, alarmed by Mike's reaction. "That's not it," he said trying to lower his voice back to normal. Live bomb? Fire? Wounded navigator?
"There's something else, perhaps a little more—"

"Sex! I knew it! And I was trying so hard..." Mike pounded his fist into the
other palm, his eyes glowing with the sudden vision of another scene. "The story
needs sexing up. I'm trying to be too unconventional. Whoever heard of no sex in
a man's story?"

"Good grief," Ned exhaled. "I had trouble staying interested. I really don't
know what else to say, GUNS AND BUTTER is bor—"

"I got it!" he cut Ned off. H. Harold Ruskin hadn't been listening too carefully. "I could have the Commander kick his wav into the Command Post—
those are his boys up there, he can't fart around with ringing the buzzer and
showing his classified ID badge to get in. He's a man of action. 'Course I'd have
to have women working-on the Command Post team wouldn't I? Wouldn't be
too far fetched, would it?"

Ned was resigned. "Well, Mike, the action, the characters don't seem very
strong. What are their wants? Their needs? Maybe you could have a female Controller if—"

There was a loud smack, "Oh, that's it!" Mike slapped his forehead. "I make
the Commander a woman. Shoulda thought o'that—perfect nowadays, what
with women working everywhere.

"Instead of kicking the Command Post door down, like the guy does, she
kicks it down to get at the Controllers—sex. That would boost the story—you're
right Ned—tension, need to build more tension. And if she was an old hag that
would add to the tension—who's got to take care of her tonight? Which one of
the team is going to be stuck with her? They draw straws—take turns. Good twist
huh? All those readers out there looking for sex—not so appealing now, eh?
How's that for tension? You want tension, buddy, you got it."

Ned looked at his friend Mike, aka H. Harold Ruskin. Was this the gentle, reasonable, thoughtful man he'd come to know as his best friend? Such passion, such vehemence. "You really think that would work?" He ran a hand through his hair wishing they could get back to "boring" and "uninteresting".

"I mean your story with the airplane in trouble—an armed bomb and an engine fire is really pretty exciting but it doesn't come across when you tell the story from the efforts in the Control Room."

Mike gaped at his friend for a moment. This wasn't going at all the way he anticipated. "Yeah we talked about that in my Creative Writing class. They called it POV for Point Of View. See I wanted all my readers to know how much I admire fliers—you know, like in those old war movies, COMMAND DECISION and 12 O'CLOCK HIGH—only updated. The action was in the air but the guys on the ground were sweatin' too and **they** had to make the decision, give the orders, tell'em what to do."

Ned swallowed hard remembering the dull three and a half pages of terse conversation between one of the controllers and the plane on radio. About half the radio talk wiped out by static which always occurred when the pilot was trying to tell the controller his status. Other than blow his iiose and scribble doodles on a writing pad, the controller did nothing throughout the whole scene. No mention of the engine fire because of the static. How would having a female commander smash down the door looking for sex advance the scene? He started to chuckle as a stray thought suddenly crossed his mind, something out of the Three Stooges.

"What?" Mike demanded. "What's so funny?"

Ned's mind raced, if he told Mike what he was really thinking, no telling what might happen. Instead he offered: "Maybe you need a little humor to off-set this deadly peril. What if one of the controllers is over in the comer pukin' because he stayed out all night drinking or something. You know a light touch—contrast."

"Hey—that's a good idea." Mike poked a finger into Ned's chest with another burst of enthusiasm—but then the brightness in Mike's face faded almost as quickly as it had risen. "Naaa, wouldn't work—this is serious stuff, even puttin' the dames in the story is a little over the top." He smiled at some afterthought perhaps visualizing yet another scene. "I could have the female commander shackin' up with one of the controllers on the sly while leadin' one of the others on thinkin' he's gonna get to her tonight. That could offset the serious stuff a little, maybe even has some humor potential. But then that would ruin the idea of her being a bitch—lose all that tension we talked about. I tell you Ned, this creative writing is really tough."

Ned shook his head sympathetically, thinking he was out of the woods, at last. Certainly he was out of suggestions. Relieved, he turned, about to offer some excuse to go back home. Talking about GUNS AND BUTTER somehow upset the image he had of his friend Mike. Creative writing had turned him into a zealot, an aggressive fanatic.

"Tell you what, Ned." Mike threw an arm across Ned's shoulders falling in step with him, "let me work on GUNS AND BUTTER tonight and I'll bring you a new draft tomorrow morning. I gotta have it ready for class tomorrow night, "You know, you really have a knack for this. Really you do."

HARLEY JONES: HOW I MADE COLONEL THE HARD WAY

We buried Harley last Tuesday on a crisp, clear day full of brightness and hope. The bugler blew taps and the firing squad fired the last volleys as he was laid to rest, his homely grin stilled, the man forgotten like the mighty Strategic Air Command that spawned him. 'Mission accomplished, we don't need you anymore.'

He never made General. Yet his story of how he made Colonel was fresh in my mind. A story that still gave me a chuckle as I headed down the hill.

We met by chance that day in the Pentagon not so long ago. Our paths had diverged six years before when his career seemed doomed. SAC was the dominant Air Force command then and he was going to Training Command—a demotion, everybody said. At the time, I had mixed feelings.

My personal beacon was gone, but my crew and I had advanced one step since a top crew had essentially been disbanded. Why would he take such an assignment? Even volunteer as was rumored? He had the best 50-8 training record, especially in bombing and navigation, of any crew in the Wing for three quarters running. This accomplishment would get him a 'spot' promotion any time now, Why?

When I asked him that as we sat down for a cup of coffee in the Pentagon cafeteria, he simply grinned and looked down into the depths of his black coffee as if expecting to see tea leaves. "Not a difficult choice." he said softly.

I waited. I didn't want it to sound like envy, even if it was. Let him tell it his way, I reminded myself.

"Remember, back then, Frank Guzeman and Bill Trane were thick as thieves and Ralph had just come down with the mumps for crissakes—we were ahead of everybody.' He took a big swallow of coffee.

I remembered Guzeman was Chief of Standboard and Trane was our Operations officer. Between them they ran the squadron. Ralph was Harley's radar-navigator and the prime reason for the crew's success. He had a bombing CEA (Circular Error Average) under 800', best of 45 crews in the Wing. My radar—navigator was at about 1300'.

Harley went on, "One day Trane called me in and said there was a levy for a pilot, an Aircraft Commander, to go to Training Command and he was submitting my name." Harley's big hands surrounded the coffee mug like he was about to strangle it. "No way, Jose," I said, "we're about to make Select crew. Soon as Ralph is back on flying status, another good quarter and we get spotted."

I could understand his anger. We all wanted a 'spot' promotion. Not only did it mean a bigger paycheck right now, the real kicker, if you held the 'spot' a while, you made temporary promotion sooner. The temporary was for keeps, only Air Force could take it away from you while SAC could remove a spot as quickly as they gave it to you—one bad quarter and gone!

"Trane told me it wouldn't happen, he'd see to that." Harley looked up at me with a look that assumed I understood Trane's threat. I didn't, but I knew what a dirty deal that would be. I also knew Guzeman, as Chief Of Standardization was very jealous of his position and any potential threat, which Harley surely must have represented. Guzeman was sitting on a 'spot' promotion like a nervous hen.

In view of this setback. how had Harley been so successful? Now it wasn't my envy so such as surprise—was he that good? We were Captains when he left the squadron, now he was a full Colonel while I was still waiting to put on my Oak leaves having been promoted to Lieutenant Colonel only a month before—a big difference.

"Probably my SAC training," Harley shrugged in response to my question. "I made Major shortly after going to Training Command and LC two years later. I didn't stay in Training Command long. After a year, I realized the time had come to move on so I took a shot in the dark. I volunteered for a job in the Pentagon. I knew I was taking a big chance. And it was. They made me the Bombing and Gunnery ranges monitor/liaison for the USAF with a chance to fly SAMS about once a month to keep my sanity."

I must have looked incredulous. Special Air Missions (SAMS) pilots flew the big wheels around—like the President, the Vice President, the Secretary of State and other distinguished government people.

He waved a hand and flashed that big, ugly grin. "No. no, not what you're thinking. I flew people you never heard of, but it was fun and I did get a few neat trips. My Pentagon job was routine, even boring at times. Yet, when I saw the way the guys in the Strategic Division had it down in the basement, I was glad I had a boring. routine. sort of unimportant job on the third floor."

I thought Harley was being modest, nobody in the Pentagon had it easy. Still, what he said about the Strategic Division, SAC's Pentagon advocate in effect, rang true. I knew from personal experience. Those guys, action officers they were called, were treated like flunkies and always under pressure.

Harley was looking around now, like maybe he had some place to go and felt a little uneasy. "So, with this little rinky-dink job you had. as you put it, how DID you make Colonel?' I blurted. I hid my embarrassment as best I could, hoping my words didn't smack too much of envy. But what had he done? Where did that rumor about Hawaii and days on Waikiki beach fit in?

He stared at me a long moment, his face hard to read. "I had no plan," he sounded almost apologetic. "No idea what led to what, I took the job almost on impulse. I'm not sure now I would have volunteered had I known everything from the start."

Was he sandbagging me? The rumor said he got promoted for some fat-cat deal flying to Hawaii. His expression gave no clue.

"Maybe I was getting bored again," he continued, "maybe I should have tried to move on, I don't know. See, they had this secret mission. The circular said they needed a C-130 jet qualified pilot to take on a hazardous mission which might last a couple weeks, with international impact. I wasn't particularly interested, they always salt those things with 'come-ons'. I figured the Job was resupplying some half-assed, rag-tag CIA operation in Africa, Central or South America. I didn't want any part of that. If they wanted to cut orders, I'd go. but I wasn't about to volunteer. I passed and thought that was the end of it."

After a long pause, rolling his empty coffee mug between his hands. Harley continued, "About a week later I got called into my boss's office about some paper I'd written. I answered his questions. Then I realized that my paper had nothing to de with why he called me into his office." Harley was no longer looking for an excuse to leave# his eyes reflected the surprise of the sudden shift, reliving the feeling.

"Why hadn't I volunteered for the secret mission, my boss asked?" Harley grunted, still confronting his boss. "I said something about the busiest time of the year for the gunnery ranges coming up and I thought I ought to be there. Which was true even if I was stalling, and my boss knew it."

Harley went on to tell me that his boss tried the patriotic approach after denying Harley's worst fears about some CIA mission in the third world. Then he pointed out that there were only two people in the division qualified and the other guy had three children. Finally, after all else had failed, Harley's boss played his ace, as they say. A canny grin spread across Harley's face as he recounted that part, "He mentioned promotion—the magic word."

I chuckled. At last I was about to get the answer. But Harley wouldn't be hurried.

"At first he was vague, only a hint. Something about how this would be a vivid, colorful contrast to my routine job—not very hard to visualize. When I pressed, he allowed as how 'other' departments of government were interested in the successful completion of the mission, namely the State Department." Harley made a face and laughed. "Everything I'd ever heard about working with or for the State Department left me nauseous. My boss laughed too, he knew the score, still he said it would look awfully good on my Efficiency Report, talking 'contrast' again. Finally, I threw up my hands—what the hell—OK I'll do it, I told him.

"Later, I found out how desperate they were. The mission was a UN deal that nobody knew much about, only that State stood to gain a lot, some kind of trade-off they wouldn't talk about and they were anxious to get someone committed to the project. In addition to the other stuff they needed somebody a little naive—me—who would be the fall guy if it went sour. Apparently, that way they could somehow wash their hands of it and look the other way." Now Harley's face looked tight, even perhaps a little sorry for himself. "Like they say, NEVER volunteer."

When it seemed he wasn't going to continue. I said, "Well, what was the job? What did they want you to do?" His vagueness and philosophizing had me strung out, No mention of Hawaii, nothing. Here he was a full Colonel and I made Lieutenant Colonel barely a month ago. No matter, you couldn't rush Harley.

"If I tell you. I have to kill you first," he grinned.

He was maddening—a shaggy dog story.

"OK, OK," he held up his hands in mock surrender. My 'remember me, I knew you when' look finally penetrated his smoke screen. "Remember, you asked for it."

I continued to stare at him. What the hell, I'd been in SAC too, professionalism was our watchword.

"Three or four guys, from other divisions in the Pentagon, turned the mission down after volunteering and learning the details—they were all buried in dead-end jobs and had to take polygraph tests every six months to make sure they didn't tell anybody about the mission." Harley shuddered as if a sudden chill blast had caught him without a coat. "None of them ever got promoted again either—I checked." He looked at me, his blue eyes penetrating, his face a mask.

"By the time they got to me, they had pared the details down to a precious few. A week after talking to ay boss, I was on a small tropical island in the Marshalls group in the South Pacific with a C-130. I was to pick up this native tribe and transport them to another island. My copilot and the crew chief were to be told nothing and to have nothing to do with the natives, as if they were both quarantined." His formal tone almost made it sound like he was reading from his orders.

"I was told to wear modified protective clothing from the first contact. I thought that was because we were going to take them to Bikini atoll. I was wrong. Oh, how wrong I was! And that was only the beginning. the tip of the iceberg."

Harley's eyes focused somewhere over my head as he, at last, began the story I wanted to hear. As Harley told it, the native chief. Idago, refused to go to Bikini. The mere mention of that atoll made his eyes grow large, rolling back into his head while he started trebling and went into a panic bordering on an epileptic fit. Plus, he was mad as hell. Harley said he was authorized to take the tribe to Enewetok if Idago preferred. The Chief insisted he could only change his position after a spiritual consultation with the gods or ancestral spirits, Harley wasn't sure which, by the light of a full moon. Harley's problems seemed to be multiplying.

First of all. the moon was only in its first quarter when they arrived, The really big discovery, however, was the tribe was a colony of lepers—active, open sore lepers with missing fingers and toes and horrible looking deformities. Harley had barely heard of leprosy. He had no idea what caused it, how contagious it was or what he was supposed to do when the Chief refused to go to Bikini atoll.

"I really felt like I had been HAD, big time." Harley focused back on me, his gaze steady. "We barely had enough room in the airplane for the whole tribe and we had to get off on a the short runway with a full load. And those weren't even the major problems.

"No wonder Idago looked surprised when I shook hands with him. I thought it was because I was wearing rubber gloves and the funny looking coveralls. He's the one who told me about the leprosy, not the State Department. That was when I realized what all that liquid, yellow-green soap they loaded in the airplane was for, and why they gave us protective clothing. Believe me I scrubbed everything, and I mean 'everything'," he raised his eyebrows for emphasis, "with a scrubbing brush—at least three times.

"After a day or so, when the Chief had calmed down, we sat down and talked. He said Enewetok was unsatisfactory, he wanted to go to Hawaii. Idago was a pretty savvy guy. Now it was my turn to get upset,

"These people with their runny sores and horrible deformities wanted to go to beautiful Hawaii? I could imagine the Hawaiian board of tourism's reaction to that idea. Idago said there was an island, Molokai, that had an active leper colony. Father Damien, long ago. had changed the island from a refuge to an active treatment location. Idago thought that would be best for his people.

"He convinced me. Besides, I wasn't anxious to spend another three weeks or so waiting for the full moon with nothing to do but shower with the yellow-green soap.

"That night we cranked-up one engine and got on the horn to the point of contact I was given within the State Department. Luckily, our C-130 Hercules was one of the SAMS aircraft with satellite communications.

"First, the guy wanted to know why I was contacting them when I had been specifically briefed to do so only in an emergency. Then I got hell for not taking the tribe to Bikini or at least Enewetok. Finally, he couldn't authorize going to Hawaii—out of the question, he said. When I insisted, he said he'd have to consult higher authority and he didn't want to do that because the issue was so sensitive and his superiors were too busy. Besides nobody cared about Idago and his tribe anyway. Moving them was supposed to keep World Health at the UN happy or some 'bleeding heart' female in the State Department, he didn't know or care which."

Harley broke his poker-faced account with a huge grin. "I told the State Department 'weenie' all that was fine go ahead and consult with his superiors, as long as he didn't have to wait for the next full moon—I'd call back the next day whatever that was in Washington."

As Harley was telling me this, I knew the State Dept. was going to insist on Bikini or Enewetok. so I was a little surprised when Harley got so vehement about their reaction. He continued to argued. The State Dept. 'weenie', as he referred to him, said Harley's mission was to take the tribe to Bikini, not remake policy. Harley challenged whether the guy had even asked his superiors which, of course, only made the situation worse.

There he was, stuck, the chief wouldn't go and the State Department wouldn't budge. The full moon was three weeks away and after almost a week in virtual quarantine, the copilot and crew chief were anxious—an understatement at best. There was no one to turn to. Harley had to solve the problem.

As he said, 'maybe it was his SAC training'.

"I told the Chief everything would be OK. We got'em all aboard the Hercules," he continued. 'The airplane was full with their baggage an' all. We had a 5,000' strip for take off. Might be a little tight so I got up to full power and let it stabilize for thirty seconds before releasing the brakes. The Herc lifted, no sweat, at the end of the runway and I kept her low till we gained some air speed before starting the climb and heading northeast.

"An hour out I called Hickham tower.

"You took the lepers to Hawaii?" I was beginning to understand were that rumor I had heard fit.

"I didn't say anything about lepers." he grinned. "until ground control started to park me up near the passenger terminal. Then I told them my passengers had no passports and maybe they should park us in a remote area until I could get with Customs and Immigration and the Health people. The radio really got quiet when I mentioned my final destination, after we cleared customs.

"Without further question, they directed me to a remote parking stub and told me to standby. Shortly after that I was instructed to keep the aircraft buttoned up. It got pretty hot inside until the Customs wagon pulled up alongside about an hour later. They were some kind of pissed. Refused to come aboard. Said they had no protective clothing."

Harley managed to talk Customs into letting him take his passengers to Molokai. Hickham gave him enough gas to make the round trip, the whole business to be reviewed when he returned to Hickham. The situation teetered between the locals determination to bring higher authority into the discussion and Harley pointing out that, the threat from the lepers was minimized by getting then to Molokai as soon as possible. He was lucky. The local Customs Agent was a practical man, secure in his job, who realized that one potential leper, Harley, was easier to deal with than 40 confirmed lepers. Besides he was going to retire in a year.

Harley thought he was home free. "I landed at Molokai. Idago, was overjoyed. 'You one fine man, Mr. Harley,' he said as we said goodbye. 'Hope gloves work for you.' I must have done a double take because he said. 'Gloves not help you, one small pin hole—poof, see you in a year,' he grinned.

"I tell you I haven't felt like that since the ninth grade when Belinda Graham told me she missed her period. I was certain that old rubber I stole out of my big brother's dresser drawer was to blame.

"I hadn't touched Idago since that first handshake but I went in the ops building at Molokai pronto and scrubbed down with that yellow-green stuff right out of the sink. Then I flew back to Hickham."

"At least you accomplished your mission," I smiled at him. "Your boss must have been happy."

"Oh, yeah," he looked glum. "He was happy all right. When I asked him for a week on the beach because we'd finished early, he said no. There was a big flap over one of the gunnery ranges—some airline pilot reported a fighter made a pass at the airliner near the range. My boss said he was up to his ass in alligators. The next day when I called back and told him the next development, he darn near exploded—"

Being familiar with the Pentagon and its weekly panics, I almost laughed. The memory was funny in a masochistic sort of way. "So what DID happen?"

"First of all, I had to take a physical. That was OK and I didn't have leprosy, however, the doc said I had to stay there and get checked every day for a month—that was the incubation period. I could do anything, go anywhere as long as I didn't leave Hawaii.

"Secondly, that State Department 'weenie' got someone to jump on my boss. See, he wasn't told what the exact mission was, nothing about the lepers or that I decided on my own to fly them to Hawaii.

"Now he was really mad when I told him I had to stay there another month. What could I do? I went to the beach figuring I'd be cashiered when I got back anyway." Harley's expression seemed to match the forlorn prophecy of his words.

"So you completed the mission, pissed-off the State Department and your boss, and were 'punished' by having to stay in Hawaii for a month—"

"With the threat of getting leprosy," Harley broke in defensively, "don't forget that." Harley's hangdog expression certainly dampened my thinly veiled enthusiasm. "I tell you, I didn't much enjoy that enforced 'vacation'. After the docs told me how horrible the disease was and what happened to a victim, I didn't get much fun out of Waikiki. I spent a lot of time in the shower with that yellow-green, liquid soap.

"The copilot and crew chief were pissed too at first. Immigration wasn't satisfied that they had had no contact with any of the tribe. They had to stay in Hawaii for a month too." Harley heaved a sigh.

I couldn't imagine either of then being too upset with a month 'stuck' in Hawaii,

"Then I had to put the aircraft through decontamination, nuclear decontamination, there wasn't one for leprosy—so we did it twice. The second time, I insisted they use the yellow-green stuff." He looked matter-of-fact, his voice a monotone reciting the details now. "Well, it couldn't get any worse unless I got leprosy. Then as the Chief said, 'see you in a year'.

"Time dragged. I showered three, sometimes four times a day scrubbing with the yellow-green soap. I cleaned under my finger nails, under my toe nails. I took vitamins. I even took enemas." Harley looked at me straight-faced, daring me to laugh.

"Finally. the time came when we could go home. We all had beautiful tans; the doctor had given us a clean bill of health and the furor had died down about my bringing the tribe to Hawaii. I figured they had my discharge or court martial papers all drawn up and I'd be looking for a new job in a week or being measured for a striped suit at Leavenworth.

"The lull was agonizing. Something had happened, for sure.

"The day after I got back, I went into the office. My boss was cordial, treated me the same as before I accepted the mission. That was the first surprise, later in the day, we all got called over to the White House and had a private meeting with the President and some woman from the State Department. She apparently had a lot of clout. The President hung a medal around my neck, even shook my hand—I wondered if he knew about Idago and the rest. Anyway, I was treated like a hero and a few days later I was informed the President signed the order making me a full Colonel, a most unusual procedure.

"That's it. That's how I made Colonel—" parenthetically he added. "the hard way." A little smile played around his mouth. As if in the recounting, a month on the beach at Waikiki didn't sound so hard to bear, almost a contradiction to his statement.

So the rumor was partly true. "Why was the mission so important?" I asked. "Why was it such a big issue?"

He shrugged. "No one ever told me. What d'ya think?"

All I could do was shake my head. I guess no one wants to get leprosy, still—. Well maybe it was rougher than the rumor made it out.

As I walked down the hill from Arlington cemetery, I remembered Harley told me he found out later the woman from the State Department in the President's office that day was Madeleine Albright, US ambassador to the UN at the time. Recently, I learned that some land developer of Chinese extraction, named Wang or Hwang, the one rumored to be a big campaign contributor to the President, is now building a big resort on the island where Harley picked up Chief Idago and his tribe. Yesterday. I read in the Washington Post that a big bank from Hong Kong is considering setting up shop on the same island as a hedge against the Chinese takeover in July. Another Tahiti, they're calling the place, I wonder what Harley would say about these deals?

Haven't seen anything yet about Chief Idago or his tribe.

A DAY AT THE BEACH

There was a gentle breeze to moderate the hot sun, but glare off the sand and ocean demanded a hat or sunglasses or both.

"Look at that woman," my tall, dark-haired companion, Carla, said, "it's a good thing she has on that long dress. I wouldn't dare come to the beach in a bathing suit looking like that."

Before she had finished speaking, the woman started to pull the long muu-muu-like dress up over her head revealing a large lumpy body stuffed into a one piece bathing suit with a floral design, something like white gardenias on a dark blue background.

"Apparently it doesn't bother her," I answered. "I guess the bikini isn't dry yet."

Her sunglasses turned to me momentarily then," You think you're kidding, look over there." She was too polite to point with her hand as her nose weather vaned to my right.

Ripples of fat flowed over the substantial bottom of a two piece suited figure seated in the sand in front of her grandchildren.

Swiveling, I was distracted—lilac patches, honey colored skin, lots of it. My head snapped back immediately after inspecting Clara's subject. My eyes focused—ten o'clock level—lock on!

Right in front of me, less than twenty feet away, a full-bodied woman got out of her chair and delicately pulled the violet cloth edges of her high cut suit away from her lovely derriere. Not so subtle curves filled out and defined the minimum coverage and straight, smooth legs extending from it. As she turned slightly to say something to her grizzled companion, two triangular patches stretched to bursting like sails filled by a gale caught my eyes. She glanced at me, blue eyes under sandy-red hair, cut short and softly waved. A little belly bulged as she bent over.

"I wouldn't dare wear that either," Carla said, following my glance and reacting to my open mouth.

I had to smile, giving away my thoughts. I tried to cover by sounding objective. "She certainly seems at ease, "I offered, as the patches thrust forward, the woman straightening to an erect posture. Stunning.

Apparently, she and the grizzled one agreed she had some mission to perform. She started to walk toward the condo behind us, her head up, her shoulders back and a slight smile playing across her face. Her profile was a picture perfect posture advertisement and then some. The scraggly-haired, graying man with the stump of his cigar under a reddish, mixed mustache shifted it to the other side of his mouth and folded the paper he was reading, without glancing up. Yesterday's stock market closing?

Turning back to Clara, I visualized her wearing the purple patches. Tall and leggy, with pale skin. even a little fleshy, she would certainly command some attention. Her greatest flaw was a little pot belly which I happened to like, but probably wouldn't look well in a high cut two-piecer. Certainly no one could hide even the slightest flaw in such a suit. I chuckled thinking of the dilemma it presented. With the small triangular patches there was no choice about wearing the bottom above the pot or below.

The lady we were observing had a little belly too. At my age that was sexy in a mature woman, but women tend to compare themselves to when they were twenty with a flat belly. I don't. I like to think I accept them and enjoy them as they are. The best thing to be said for the lady in lilac was she wasn't self conscious wearing her tiny triangular patches. In fact, my impression was she was rather proud of those knockers and didn't feel she needed to apologize for the rest of her look either. They were large, firm and jutted out precipitously. And in my reverie, I think she enjoyed having men's eyes follow her. She wasn't a young woman—all the more reason for her pride. Perhaps she was an exhibitionist.

"Why the laugh?" Carla queried.

"Oh, I was just thinking how modest you are."

"Me modest? Oh! Look That man doesn't have any clothes on!"

Reluctantly, I dragged my eyes from purple patches to behold hairy, muscular loins and the sturdy torso of a man with his back to us, some ten yards away, and nothing but a string in his butt. Exhibitionist? Nudist? What?

Were we at the wrong beach—me in my boxer trunks and my female companion in a dark blue one piece suit? This must be some place in California, not Myrtle Beach, S.C. He bent over to do something, exposing what little coverage he had along with the hairy legs and torso.

"He's wearing a thong," my friend announced.

I rolled my eyes (behind the shades), "Yes. I think I can make it out."

"Would you wear something like that?" She turned toward me.

"Oh, sure, why not?" I answered glibly, without hesitating, hiding my envy of the hairy one.

"You would?" Incredulous.

"Yeah, with the lights out and the bathroom door closed."

She laughed. A sound I'd come to love. "You'd look better without it."

A young girl about sixteen crossed in front of us, her firm flesh appealing. "Now, she looks good in a bikini."

"Yes," I acknowledged, "Youth will be served, but look over there. What do you say to that?"

She twisted to look at three girls, teenagers. all wearing bikinis, walking away from us. One was heavy set, but firm, the other two were slender like the one who had passed in front of us a moment or two before.

"She's too big to be wearing such a skimpy suit, even with that little fringe—really no more than a ruffle."

"I give her extra points for a nice tan," I smiled back. baiting her a little.

"I don't have a tan. Do I lose points?"

"You make up for it in other ways."

"I do? What?"

"Intangibles." The best answer I could come up with, the sudden shift in conversation catching me off-guard.

Nice even teeth smiled in my face, the sunglasses concealed her eyes. "Name two."

"A beautiful smile and muscles," I managed, hoping she wouldn't press the question further.

"Muscles?" she tilted her head slightly as if that didn't connect.

I smiled a lazy smile. "Yeah…think about it." I wanted to get back to our study of other figures on the beach. personalizing it made me uncomfortable. For example. I couldn't compare with Thong man's physique, regardless of how ridiculous I thought he appeared on this beach where most were more modestly suited. If every man there had worn a Thong that day conservatively I estimated, he would have won the Charles Atlas look alike award, hands down.

She opened her book after a sidelong glance, apparently satisfied. Soon we were joined by Bill and Johnnie. our hosts for the three day sojourn at the beach. "Hey. what's happening?" Bill giggled as if he had overheard our conversation.

We pointed out Thong-man who was conveniently doing a reprise.

"Is that legal?" Johnnie took a discoverer's stance, shielding her eyes with a hand at the brim of her straw hat.

Bill laughed.

I started to describe lilac patches lady, primarily for Bill's benefit, when Ms. posture perfect entered our line of sight, returning from the huge condo fronting the beach behind us.

We watched in silence, Johnnie with her mouth slightly agape, Carla smiling behind her sun glasses and Bill looking bemused.

When she had returned to her beach chair in front of us and given old cigar face several quick pecks, giving us a full frontal view as she bent over, Bill said: "Someone told her that was attractive."

His words penetrated my stupor like a lightening flash. 'Damn, I wish I'd said that.' The moral high ground after a close inspection of the bronzed flesh paraded and exhibited in front of us. There was certainly nothing I could ad, no moral indignation gripped me. I had been too bedazzled to even grab my camera. Now was not the time to say something stupid, but I tried. "He's cute too."

The girls both laughed, relieving my anxiety.

Johnnie in an undertone," Do you suppose he's her husband?"

Bill looked at me, considered the possibilities, the smoked glasses conveniently hiding his eyes. The man's total absorption in his newspaper was husband-like, but the total disparity between his looks and hers didn't make her seem very wifey. "Naaa," we said in unison.

That got their attention.

"Why not? How do you know?" Johnnie demanded

It was our turn to laugh. "I'm betting she's a paid companion," was Bill's answer.

"If she was his wife, old cigar butt get's one peck, tops," I agreed. "A little reassurance and 'here I am back already', but this woman, she's selling too strong. All that kissy-kissy says 'look how sexy I am, pay me some attention you lucky pig'."

"Makes sense to me," Bill nodded, solemn as a Supreme Court judge.

"That certainly is skimpy. Would you want your wife wearing that?" Carla asked.

"I rest my case," I said, avoiding a direct answer to the question.

"I don't think so," came Bill's exaggerated drawled. He smiled at Johnnie, who looked shapely in a brown one piece suit with bronzed metallic stripes diagonally across the front.

The issue apparently settled, we settled back to our books as the sun glared down on Bill and Johnnie while Carla and I hugged the shade offered by the beach umbrella.

"Probably aren't her's anyway* Johnnie muttered, looking down at the open paperback.

I had to ask "How can you tell?"

She looked up, as if it was obvious. "They don't look natural."

"Oh." I tried to make it sound like that explained everything.

"They're too big," she amplified.

"I don't know," Bill mused, as if totally unbiased, "They could be...."

"Oh, Bill, **honestly**," Johnnie turned on him, "come back to earth, **you** want to believe—like it's the tooth fairy."

"Well, yeah, you're probably right," Bill admitted with an impish grin. "Maybe that's why he's studying the stock market—fixing 'boobs' is expensive."

"My word, look," Johnnie gasped in awed tones suddenly losing interest in the discussion of those magnificent breasts in front of us.

Everyone twisted to follow her gaze. Thong-man was adjusting his blanket again, this time standing in profile.

We watched in stupefied silence.

"That's the biggest…ah, thong I've ever seen," I breathed aloud, spellbound.

The sudden burst of laughter confirmed we were all puzzling the same question. What did he have stuffed in that thing beside the 'family jewels'? It stuck out from his body as if he were packing his wallet and a couple rolls of quarters.

Bill recovered first with: "That says it all for me—absolutely the biggest thong I've ever seen. You suppose it's all real?

The two girls giggled, but slyly offered no comment. Neither would rise to Bill's bait.

Had someone told Thong-man 'big is beautiful'? I pondered the question while wondering who said 'less is more' and how he would resolve this paradox.

TRAILER PARK BLUES

For the next six stories, the title suggests the nature of living in the urban, upscale trailer park known as Shady Acres.

JAKE

"She wants you—" he cocked an eye, his face full of sour grapes. "I don't care what you have to do to satisfy her—get your butt over to Sylvia's pronto!" Harrigan, the graying, bald manager of the Shady Acres mobile home trailer park gave Jake a meaningful look. Jake stared back at the sallow face for a few seconds then turned and left the office. Harrigan's look told him all he needed to know and especially all Harrigan didn't want to know.

Jake knew Harrigan had a jealous wife, a shrew in his opinion, who dominated Harrigan. And Jake was his buffer, his alibi, if ever he needed one.

The manager's mobile home was the nearest to the field stone and wrought iron gated entry on Hibiscus Road. As Jake stepped off the steps into the spring sunshine he looked across the narrow street. The landscape guy was unloading his big mower from the small hitch behind his 1/2 ton pick up. 'At least I don't have to cut the grass,' he thought.

Standing there watching the landscape guy, his thoughts turned to the job at hand. Sylvia was a heavyset lady somewhere in her early fifties with enormous breasts and a penchant for finding ways to display them whenever he was around to fix whatever she needed fixing, real or imagined. He had stayed away since the time she seduced him. His jaws clenched at the thought. Fool! It wasn't possible but it happened.

The saving grace was Sylvia's trailer was on the opposite side of the park from his and he didn't have to see her everyday as he might if she lived closer. On that fateful day she actually unzipped his fly and went to work on him while he was on his back, under the sink, working on the clogged drain trap. What she did with her hands and mouth were magic. Actually she was a pretty tight fit when he rode her—after the preliminaries. Never-the-less he was ashamed of himself and a little haunted by the event.

He glanced up; Harrigan was at the window of his office, hands on hips, glaring at him. Hitching up his jeans, he stepped down the sidewalk toward Sylvia's. He waved at the guy cranking up the big mower as he turned the corner at Petunia Lane across the end of the manager's trailer heading toward Floral Avenue. The coolness of the morning made the exposed parts of his arms and shoulders tingle—one of the reasons he preferred sleeveless undershirts.

Tight pussy and those big tits, his thoughts drifted back. 'What was it, three weeks now?' He caught himself. Was it all physical? Was that what counted? The woman was built like a two-hole bowling ball. 'What the hell is wrong with you? What's your excuse? Your cover-up? Is this part of your so-called people research to develop characters for your novel? Would she really be an interesting character? Can you find or even imagine anyone like her in a Dickens novel? How about Oliver Twist? No that's Fagan, the pickpocket. A Tale of Two Cities? Great Expectations? There's one—a play on words. You must be sick.' For the next ten minutes the battle raged within him as he strolled half-heartedly toward his showdown at Sylvia's trailer, at once thinking of sex and repelled by the woman's grossness. Yes it was physical he admitted to himself, feeling guilty.

Reaching 629 Floral Avenue, he took a deep breath before walking up the sidewalk to the three step, wooden, porch-like entry. He was going to be businesslike. He was going to avoid any hint of sex. He was going to be in control—especially of himself—banishing all thoughts of a tight pussy and other such eroticism.

She greeted him at the door in a full length, black leotard with a lime green sash tied loosely around her ample middle. The first things he noticed were those stereophonic nipples. One pointed north the other south. They seemed to stare at him from opposite sides of the moon—like Senator Jessie Helms in a political cartoon. Jake laughed. He couldn't help it. "Yes, ma'am, what can I do for you today?" he half giggled through the slight opening of the glass storm door she held with a bare foot. "Mr. Harrigan says you have a problem," he continued, checking his sneakers to avoid staring at those big knobs.

She smiled, her round face reflecting little warmth. "In the bathroom. The toilet—it's stopped up. Almost overflowed this morning." She frowned, as he continued to grin. "Where's your tools?"

"I need to take a look, first," he said controlling himself at last.

"C'mon in," she said, using her foot to push the storm door open further.

He followed her. The crack of her ass was as well defined as her large nipples. Her walk was slow and seemed affected in a way he could not define but was amused. Each cheek alternately bunched up tightly like a big clenched fist then released into a triple sized jiggle of femininity as she moved. He was lost in wonder—they actually made leotards this big. Obviously she wore nothing underneath and he reminded himself again not to check her crotch. This brief thought was interrupted as she pivoted like a ballerina in front of the bathroom, facing him and throwing an arm out toward the open door, the light already on. 'Incredible.'

The stench hit him as he reached the door and he could see wastes floating almost at the rim of the bowl. "When did it clog?"

She folded her arms across her chest lifting those big breasts as if that was a stupid question. "Last night," she said emphatically. "Didn't you get my call?"

He started to ask if she'd used it this morning and/or during the night, but thought better of it. At least he'd worn more traditional work clothes, jeans, sneakers and sleeveless undershirt, than he normally did. "Do you have a plunger?"

"A what?"

"A plumber's helper."

"Right behind the door," was her tired response, "I already tried that—three times—got the floor all wet."

With the level inside the toilet bowl, Jake could see the result would be the same if he tried to use the plunger again. He would have to dip some of that mass of human corruption out first. "Do you have any empty cans or pails from the garbage?"

Without a word she did another pirouette, bringing a grin to Jake's unshaven face. She disappeared in the direction of the kitchen. And returned quickly. "How 'bout this," she held out a Campbell's soup can.

Jake looked at the can and back up at Sylvia, incredulous, his heavy brows knit together in a dark frown. She grinned at him and pulled her other hand from behind her back with an empty, 3# margarine tub. "That's better," he sighed.

There was still a problem. The empty margarine tub might be OK as a dipper but he immediately realized he needed a larger container. To reduce the level would probably take two or three dippers of the margarine tub to get the level down far enough to use the plunger. He knew she would complain bitterly to Harrigan if he got any of that slop on the floor as she admitted she had. "Do you have a galvanized bucket? Even a large plastic or metal wastepaper basket will do."

She put her fists on her broad hips, her lips pursed in a thin line. "Bucket—wastepaper can? Why do you think I asked you where your tools were? I'm not a plumber."

Neither am I, Jake wanted to answer, reminding himself that he was only supposed to work part time as the general maintenance man of the trailer park. Instead he waited a few seconds, remembering his vow to control himself, albeit toward a different concern. "Do you have a galvanized bucket?" he repeated.

With a slight thrust of her pelvis and a smirk she said, "Well if you ask me nice like that, I'd have to say yes."

Reflexively he looked down with her movement and quickly looked away. "Would you get it for me, please?" He was on the verge of holding his nose and this cat and mouse game was delaying things.

Another dance step turn and she went to get the bucket as he turned on the ventilator fan. He squeezed his eyes shut to erase the mental snapshot of the subtle curves covered by the black leotard over Sylvia's most feminine parts. When he opened them she was holding out the bucket.

He took it and quickly turned to the task at hand. The stench, as he dipped, focused his thoughts on the job. To his relief, Sylvia watched without comment.

As soon as he had lowered the bowl to a safe level he began pumping with the plunger. Almost immediately the clog cleared and the toilet flushed properly. Then he repeated the process dumping the contents of the galvanized bucket as well. After two flushes the toilet was clear.

"I believe it's OK now," he turned to her, "I'll rinse these under the outside faucet," he raised the bucket with the plunger inside in one hand and the margarine tub in the other. "Everything should be back to normal," he smiled politely.

"Jake, you're a real handyman," she smiled broadly, flattening against the doorjamb forcing him to turn sideways to leave the bathroom. She stuck out her chest and he felt those big boobs slide across him—that tingling sensation beginning down below. Then he was clear and almost racing for the storm door.

Half way down the side of the trailer, he found the outside spigot and rinsed the bucket, plunger and margarine tub thoroughly, his hands as well.

'This is turning out easier than I thought,' he congratulated himself as he headed back to the entry to give Sylvia the rinsed tools of his success before leaving. He tapped on the glass of the storm door.

She appeared shortly and pushed the storm door open again with her bare foot. "Thank you so much, Jake. You're a doll." She accepted the bucket, margarine tub and plunger. "Come in and have a cup of coffee, I just brewed a fresh pot." She smiled, pushing the storm door wider with her foot. "I'd sort of like to express my appreciation more fully." She made a slight inward movement with her elbows, lifting her breasts noticeably.

"That's very kind of you, Sylvia, but ah…" he licked his lips, "Harrigan is after me to get over to the recreation area and check the pool before the pool maintenance guy comes to start the new season. Maybe next time," he said, locked on to her eyes.

"Well, you know, you're welcome anytime, Jake," she smiled. Then she made that subtle, little movement again. Without thinking, he looked down. This time his mental Polaroid was even more graphic because of the bright sunshine splashing all around the doorway. Tempting. He stumbled down the steps without opening his eyes until after the final step.

He crossed Floral at a slight angle to Daisy Lane, walking toward the recreation area in the center of the park complex since he was almost certain Sylvia was still standing in her doorway watching him. Heaving a big sigh, he ran a hand through his straight black hair. What an odd situation. Maybe Sylvia wasn't totally responsible for their sexual encounter. He'd managed to avoid her this time yet he admitted to himself he was weak and certainly she was full of hints, begging to be taken. And he'd lied to her.

Harrigan hadn't said anything about the pool except that the pool maintenance guy was coming today. Jake decided he'd pull the tarp off to save him some time, perhaps salving his own conscience a little bit.

One of the reasons he had agreed to do part time maintenance for having a free trailer at Shady Acres was the recreation area. Most trailer parks didn't provide a recreation area. If anything, they might have a children's play area with swings and a teeter-totter. Shady Acres was not only more secure than those other parks but the recreation area provided something for adults as well. The children's playground was at the far end of the complex, perhaps another perk for adults without children.

In addition to the main, living-sitting room, the clubhouse included a meeting room, which tenants could schedule and a den-like room with two pool tables, a Ping-Pong table and a couple sofas and arm chairs. There were lots of windows and the building was bright and cheerful surrounded by three huge oaks.

Off the game room in back was a fifty-foot pool with a small building at the opposite end that included 'his' and 'her' change areas. The deck was concrete with a moderate amount of deck furniture for sunbathing or just sitting and reading. The whole pool area was surrounded by a redwood, woven board fence which was overlapped in such a way as to allow free access from each of the four directions, yet still blocked off the wind and offered a certain amount of privacy from the streets and other buildings.

Jake didn't have to pay the $250 a year fee each tenant, actually each trailer lot, was charged to maintain the recreation area. He enjoyed both the billiard table and the swimming. Not a country club but as close as a man of his means was likely to have unless…. unless he hit it big as an author.

'Perhaps, after I pull that tarp, I'll play a game of pool before I go back home to work on that magazine story,' he thought. He was working on a humorous story for LAUGH magazine about a fat lady stuck in a bathtub. "Certainly no one like Sylvia," he chuckled to himself, "but maybe I can work in a malfunctioning toilet."

Entering the Clubhouse from the bright sun, he almost collided with a tall, well-dressed woman about to leave. "Oh, excuse me ma'am." He extended both hands to catch her. "Are you OK?" He held her upright by the waist momentarily then quickly dropped his hands. She had a firm, slender body, and was half a head shorter than he. "That sun is so bright—" he stopped, his eyes refocused on the woman in a tan business suit. Her deep auburn hair was piled on her head, a very feminine contrast to the efficient cut of her suit and the single copper, roadrunner brooch on her lapel.

She was smiling now—her initial annoyance fleeting—a brilliant smile.

Jake realized she must be the new tenant about four trailers above his on Hyacinth—in place less than a week. "My name is Jake and I help tenants with…well almost anything," he finished with a shrug. "So if you need anything, let me know."

She actually looked him up and down like an officer inspecting the troops. "I'm Mamie Romaine," she offered her hand, her brown eyes crinkling in a genuine smile. "And I just might take you up on that. Some times I have to conduct business in my trailer at night—"

"What IS your business?" Jake interrupted—his first thought improper—surly she wasn't a madam. Then he thought of his limited time, 3 to 4 hours a day, no mention of night work. Too late, he thought 'Why did you have to open your mouth anyway?'

"I'm a realtor. What did you think?" She arched a thin brow, her expression knowing.

"I didn't think anything ah…I was surprised…I don't do much night work." He tried to recover.

"Well, I don't require much. I might need your signature as a witness when I close a deal and possibly I might need you to convince whoever I'm with that we have Security in Shady Acres readily available—a little 'let's pretend'. You understand?" Again the knowing look. "You look like you can handle yourself OK," she added.

Jake looked down, noticing the good legs and slim ankles standing on dark tan pumps as he reflected on her words. This wasn't what Harrigan was giving him a free trailer and utilities to do but he was flattered, except for the part about security. "Do you often have clients who need to be reminded of Security close at hand?" He didn't grin although he was tempted.

She laughed out loud, a very engaging laugh. "You're pretty quick." She gave him a light tap on the shoulder. "I certainly hope not, but working alone and at odd hours…it pays to think of everything."

"Touché," he murmured. 'Smart gal, professional.'

"So can I call you when I need you?" she smiled that smile again, cocking her head to the side a little.

Charmed, Jake agreed and gave Ms. Romaine his number.

Jake didn't play pool after all. After wrestling the heavy blue tarp off the swimming pool he headed home. Seated at his computer he stared at the screen, a single line across the third page of his story, his thoughts elsewhere. He wasn't thinking about the petulant curve of Sylvia's lips showing through her leotard that had seduced him once before, no, his thoughts were on Ms. Mamie Romaine—the realtor.

This was the kind of woman he wanted to associate with, to date. She had some class and striking good looks. Perhaps close to his own age, he guessed. As a stockbroker he'd been around that type woman frequently, although he'd made no conquests or dated anyone on a steady basis. But it was nice spending free hours with an intelligent woman, someone with a little education and a worldly outlook—someone who could hold a conversation and appreciated a little wit. He missed that. Something he had not factored into his decision to take a year out to see if he could really become a serious writer.

The basic advice to all free spirits in the world, 'Don't give up your day job' haunted him. Still, he had done some planning. He had put aside enough to last him a year and with the break Harrington had given him doing part time maintenance for rent and utilities, his savings might cover a year and a half if he was careful. There wasn't any allowance for entertainment or dating.

With a sigh Jake came back to the almost blank screen that had hypnotized him into this reverie. If he could continue to sell short stories that was at least a start. Not enough to live on but a foot in the door of getting published, establishing some kind of credentials.

'Let's see now: why is this broad stuck in the tub and how do I get all that ectoplasm in motion to get her out of the porcelain fat trap? Does this happen every week? Or does she take a bath more often than that? What about candles? Is she one of those freaks who lights a whole bunch of scented candles to really turn a bath into an event as they promise in those women's magazines? What if she sets the whole place on fire and is stuck there in the tub? Who'll call 911? What do the firemen say when they find her stuck in the tub? At least it's a way out.'

Over the next two weeks things were slow. Harrigan called him over to the office once for a job and he helped clean the swimming pool so it would be ready as soon as the weather was warm enough. Fortunately, he hadn't been called to do anything for Sylvia and Jake was able to get a lot done on THE FAT LADY'S DILEMMA.

Twice he had been called by Ms Romaine to come over to her trailer. The first time he put on a nice sports shirt and even a little cologne. The trip took all of fifteen minutes. She had him sign a couple places on a bill of sale and that was it; he was back in his own trailer before the evening news was over. That was a let down. Ms. Romaine was wearing one of her business suits and had been cordial but businesslike. The client was an older man, not particularly well dressed, who left immediately after Jake. In fact, outside, Jake gave him directions how to drive back to his own part of town from Shady Acres.

The second time was a little more encouraging. Much as before, he'd witnessed some papers related to the sale of a house. This time a middle aged couple were buying their first house and seemed very happy and anxious to be on their way as if that would get them in the house sooner. As he was about to leave, Ms. Romaine grabbed his arm and pulled him gently away from the entry.

"Stay with me awhile and have a drink," she said. "I feel like celebrating." She had shrugged out of her suit jacket and kicked off her high heels. The long sleeved, high-necked blouse was shiny like satin, a deep blue, enhancing the simple pearl earrings and two-strand necklace. Her knee length skirt was lighter blue linen matching the jacket she tossed casually over the back of a stuffed chair. She still looked business-like in a casual way. "What's your pleasure," she called from behind the split counter in the kitchen. The breakfast bar served as her serving counter.

"I'll have whatever you're having," he said, looking around at the comfortable furnishings. The living room furniture was pretty much standard, similar to others he'd seen in the park—not the top of the line but more than adequate, certainly not cheap either in looks or quality.

"Gin and tonic OK?"

"Fine with me."

"I don't have any lime, just tonic water."

"OK"

She sat down in the sofa opposite him and turned the three-way bulb in the lamp down to a softer light. "Here's to success!" she said in a subdued tone, holding her glass up before taking a sip. "You have been a real help, Jake. I appreciate you coming over on such short notice. I never know when I'm going to need you but it really speeds up the deal for me. I can spend more time showing houses to other clients," she smiled briefly, her face weary. "Thank you."

"Doesn't it make for a long day? I notice your car is gone most of the day every day, even on weekends."

"Week ends are the busiest. A couple more deals like this one and I'll be able relax a bit."

Their conversation continued like this for awhile, Jake told of his writing goals and Mamie stuck to her realtor business. In half-hour Jake was on his way home. He wasn't expecting anything but somehow he felt disappointed, let down. Their discussion of real estate was like eating tofu, as far as Jake was concerned, the business had no flavor. He didn't know any more about her than before. She was proper and acknowledged his benefit to her and no more. A very disciplined woman, he decided.

A week went by and Jake was still struggling with his short story, now titled WHY THE FAT LADY NEVER SINGS TWICE. He was beginning to wonder if he'd ever finish the piece. Now he had her as a fading opera star stuck in the tub because she expended so much energy from singing an aria during her bath.

The phone rang. Her voice was soft yet business-like. "Jake, I have a client and need you to witness the contract. Can you meet me at my place in about half an hour? I would really appreciate it, if you're free."

He felt that warm feeling again. "No problem, Ms Romaine. I'll be there in a half hour."

Jake shut down the computer and with a quick glance at his wristwatch started pulling off his shirt. There was time for a shower. As he threw his clothes on the floor next to the bed he wondered about the background noise. There were a lot of conversations behind the sound of her voice. Certainly she hadn't called from the real estate office or a car.

Jake showered and put on clean clothes, one of his better sport shirts, dark slacks and black loafers. Maybe she would feel like celebrating again, offer him a drink after the deal was closed. Twenty-five minutes after Ms. Romaine's call, Jake checked his grooming in the bathroom mirror and headed for the door, taking a moment to turn one of the living room lamps on low, in case he was late…'much later', he smiled to himself. I like New York in June—How about you? he hummed to himself as he slammed the front door.

A midnight blue Mercedes was parked on the street in front of Ms Romaine's trailer, her tan Toyoda was parked on the stub drive next to her entry door. As he reached for the doorbell, Jake could hear laughter from inside.

"Ah, the man of the hour," Mamie Romaine greeted Jake with a big smile, "You're right on time. Thank you so much for coming." As usual she was dressed smartly in a business suit, this time a variation on the tan suit she was wearing when they met. The blouse was some sort of open lace pattern, which hugged her slim figure, the jacket unbuttoned. "Come right in, I have the papers laid out over here." She turned and led the way into the trailer.

The client was a beefy man, about Jake's age, perhaps in his early forties, close to six feet tall. He was wearing a silly smirk on his florid face that made his blue eyes look too small for his face. His blonde crew cut was receding fast at the temples and he was sweating profusely. His white, dress shirt was open at the collar and apparently that was his gray jacket lying across the arm of the sofa.

"Harvey, this is Jake, my lifesaver," she waved toward the big man.

"Hi ya, Julio," he waved a glass filled hand toward Jake, with only a quick glance away from Mamie as she walked past him.

"Jake this is Harvey," she threw over her shoulder.

Ms. Romaine seemed a bit giddy, yet nervous as she rearranged the papers for the signatures on the breakfast bar separating the kitchen from the living room. Her half-full glass was next to them. Apparently the celebrating had started a little early, that wasn't ice tea they were drinking.

Harvey sauntered after Jake and put an arm around Mamie, patting her shoulder, "Is this where we sign on the dotted line, honey?"

"You know it big boy. You get to lead off, sign right here and right there." She bent slightly pointing to the signature lines on the contract. Then she gave a little 'yip' and jumped sideways as he ran his hand down her back.

OK, little darlin', I'll do it." He set his drink down next to hers and took the pen she handed him and began to sign. Part way through he straighten, "Now, about the rest—" She slapped him playfully on the chest, "Silly, that's our unspoken protocol. That's not something we **ever** put on paper," she giggled.

"All right. But you promised an' I'm gonna hold ya to it." He pointed the blunt end of the pen at her and settled back to completing his signatures.

Jake was uncomfortable. Their easy familiarity was in stark contrast to the previous contracts he'd witnessed. "Now, you, Jake, if you please." She handed him the pen as their eyes met and quickly shifted away.

As soon a he signed, Mamie cupped his elbow and started to guide him toward the door. "Thanks Jake, I'll call you later." She seemed to wave toward the door.

"Yeah, Jamie, later," the florid Harvey clapped him on the shoulder as he turned for the door.

"JAKE," Ms Romaine, corrected, turning back in mid-stride to glare at Harvey.

"Whatever you say, baby," he added with a low chuckle, "See ya later, Jack." He gave Jake a broad wink when he turned back at the door. Mamie was patting him on the shoulder as she rolled her eyes with Harvey's clumsy humor. She didn't see his wink.

Jake walked into the darkness of Hyacinth, the porch light from Mamie Romaine's trailer fading into a single spot of light behind him. He hated Harvey and his easy, familiar manner with Ms. Romaine. Did she know him before? Was he her boyfriend? It didn't seem like it, since he was signing a contract. That call she made; that had to be from a bar; all that people noise. They must have spent the afternoon drinking. He stopped on the sidewalk and looked around. The porch light was still on, the front of the trailer now in darkness, no lights at any of the windows but the Mercedes was still there.

'What if she need's help? She seemed very nervous.' He looked down at the cement, the closer trailers with soft lights seeping through the Venetian blinds of most of them. A few with the lights of other rooms reflecting through darkencd, living room picture windows. Security wasn't his business yet he supposed Harrigan would expect him to be suspicious in case any of the tenants had trouble. He turned back toward her light halo, walking faster, his mind made up.

The trailer on the backside of Ms. Romaine's was in total darkness. Jake stopped, looked up and down the street, then darted between the two. There was a patch of light on the side at the end of Ms. Romaine's—the bedroom. 'This is wrong. If you get caught, Harrigan will kick you out...and that might be the least of your problems.' Standing under the window; the blind was all the way down. Still, he decided to check to be sure.

There were several concrete blocks scattered under the trailer, extras from the columns used to support the trailer. After stacking four them crisscross in pairs, he found two more to give him a platform high enough to look in the window.

At eye level, there was a half-inch under the blinds, which gave a limited view. Sighting through the inward slant of the blinds, he could see part of the bed. Until he got used to the limited view, Jake couldn't sort out what he was seeing. His footing on the concrete blocks was shaky. 'This was probably a bad idea.' As he was about to give up, he saw movement. In a moment his breathing seemed to stop; the scene suddenly made sense. There in perfect view he recognized a big, hard cock. Harvey was on his back, his pants down. Slim fingers with red nails were deftly unrolling a condom over the pale, pink obelisk rising from a tangle of reddish pubic hair. That was enough. Sickened, Jake jumped down off the shaky piling of concrete blocks. Quietly, in haste, he spread the heavy blocks around under the trailer as he had found them. Without hesitation, still breathing heavily, he visually checked in all directions. Satisfied, he set out for the street.

So she wasn't only the cool, professional realtor. Maybe his first irreverent thought when he met her was on the money, the realtor bit a disguise. Those contracts; he hadn't read them but they looked official and had the name of a real estate company on the letterhead. That was something he could check out. Hurrying through the darkness, his attempts at logic were only a disguise for the disappointment he felt. He had elevated Mamie Romaine to a status she didn't deserve. On the other hand, she hadn't hinted at anything between them, nor had she been provocative. What right did he have to assume anything? He felt sick, disillusioned and ashamed of himself, as well, for peeking in her window. Allowing himself to feel she might be threatened, was juvenile. She didn't need any protection. He wasn't security.

'She's giving it to him right now.' He could visualize the smug, beefy Harvey working her over. Why? Was he so attractive? Was it because of his big dong? Money and liquor—they'd been out drinking. If he was a boyfriend, why the contract? Was that the only way she could get him to sign?

He climbed into bed for a night full of lurid dreams, actually nightmares of Ms. Romaine and her possible connections with men. Was she a high-class whore? Did she screw him to seal the deal? Was it for pleasure? He woke early, grateful for the dawn, a clear cloudless day.

"Now listen," Harrigan was saying, "I want you to go over to Ms. Romaine's at ten thirty and install that disposal she's bought—you ever put one in before?" He frowned at Jake's blank look and negative nod.

"What's that song?" Jake interrupted, caught by the words of a song coming from the radio on a little table behind Harrigan's desk.

"What?" Harrigan's train of thought was derailed. "Ah…you never heard that before? The Mills brothers are famous. This is one of their big hits…aw, you're prob'ly too young. You never heard this before?

…Into each life some rain must fall and too much is falling in mine, the lyric ended on a low soft note as the background music took over before the second refrain. Jake remained in a trance, the scene in Ms Romaine's bedroom haunting him.

"You sure you never heard this before?" Harrigan was incredulous. "The Mills brothers have been around forever—they play this song all the time." His eyebrows were up, his eyes twinkling with more enthusiasm and interest than Jake had ever seen in Harrigan's face. His hands were laced behind his head now, relaxed, enjoying the song himself.

"I guess so…first time the words ever," he hesitated, not wanting to share his emotions with Harrigan, "ever…clicked," he finished, his voice almost a whisper, trying to disguise his disappointment. The song's tempo changed to a jazzy beat, the bass singer imitating the slapping of a bass…dumpt…dumpt…dumpt…pa…Into each life some rain must fall. "That's really cool," Jake smiled. A great weight seemed to lift from him, the music infectious. 'What the hell.'

Harrigan smiled, tapping the desk with his fingertips to the beat. "Ya know these guys have recorded more songs than anyone in history…true…heard it the other day on this station. They're the greatest. And you never heard this song before?" He shook his head sadly.

Almost reluctantly, Harrigan came back to the job for Ms. Romaine. "OK, this disposal thing—you ever put one in?"

"No." Jake was still listening to the song. The sad, almost prophetic lyrics mirrored his thoughts. Then the happy beat with the same theme—it was genius. He wanted to shout "So what? Take whatever comes."

"I know this isn't maintenance…extra in a way, but this Ms. Romaine, she's class—know what I mean? The kind o'tenant we like to have…to keep." He stared hard at Jake, making sure he had his attention. Jake nodded. He knew, all right, he knew.

Harrigan got up from his desk. "C'mon, I'll show you. It's easy." He threw an arm across Jake's shoulders guiding him toward the kitchen of the trailer.

"Into each life some rain must fall—but too much is falling in mine."

THE REALTOR

Mamie Romaine collapsed on the plush, crushed velvet sofa. At last she was set-tled—she had a place to live. She hadn't thought about living in a trailer park before her divorce but Shady Acres was certainly the best she'd seen. Her decree was now final and she was lucky her realtor license was still valid.

Next was to get to work. She settled back on the soft sofa, her long, auburn hair spilling over the scroll arm. Headliner Realty wasn't the top of the line but her references wouldn't support working at Century 21 or Better Homes. To make the best of it, meaning lower commissions, would have to be her lot, unless of course, Harvey came through. With $100 in the bank and about $50 in cash, now that she'd paid the deposit and first month's rent to Shady Acres, she had no time to waste.

The next two weeks were a blur. Mamie escorted potential buyers through the low-end house listings under Headliner Realty night and day it seemed and she was rewarded with a couple sales. Enough to keep the wolf from the door for a while and raise her bank account to a thousand dollars.

In a moment of reflection, as she was pouring water into Mr. Coffee one morning, she realized what a bonus it was to have Jake, the Shady Acres handy-man, around. Her first meeting with Jake had been at the main door of the Shady Acres clubhouse when they almost collided. He introduced himself and offered his assistance in getting settled. That was the beginning. Having him almost instantly available when she needed a witness to her sales allowed her to concen-trate on selling in the daytime and doing the paperwork in the evening. He was kind of cute too, dark good looks and always wearing his muscle shirt during the day. After a couple sales she had come to depend on him.

Then there was Harvey. That one instance when she brought Harvey to the trailer though was a mistake. In a moment of weakness, she had agreed to go to 'twofers' with him one afternoon and gotten a little tipsy. To compound the problem, she'd asked Jake to meet them at her trailer to witness the paperwork of a minor deal they had hatched while at a local bar. The details were slightly irregular. Harvey let her 'sell' some property listed by his company after he had lined up the client. And he gave her the whole commission instead of splitting it. The commission was small and Harvey extracted his share in a personal way. That was foolish, she admitted to herself.

The coffee tasted bitter, she'd forgotten the sugar.

Although she hadn't been intimate with Jake, she could see possibilities. With Harvey it was calculated—business. She screwed him because he'd broadly promised to get her hired by his realty company. That and the fact she'd had a little too much to drink that afternoon. A mistake—not good business, not good for personal relationships. Even then she could sense the discomfort, even embarrassment, in Jake that night when he witnessed the paperwork at her trailer. He had been kind and helpful to her and this was the way she repaid him. Relying on Harvey was unwise and she knew it.

A sip, the coffee tasted better now.

"Hello there. My, you're a strong swimmer," Mamie greeted Jake as he climbed out of the clubhouse pool. She'd watched him churn through several laps admiring the smoothness of his effort.

Jake smiled from behind his towel, drying his face and then his arms, the warm sun striking his broad shoulders from behind. "Hi, Ms. Romaine, good to see you're taking a break. I'm shocked." He laughed good-naturedly as he stepped a little closer to the chaise lounge where she was stretched out, almost totally in the shade of a beach umbrella.

She smiled up at him, "My first time at the pool, but I didn't escape the job entirely. I have to show a house at 2:30 and another at 4:30."

"Well, it is Sunday but that doesn't sound so bad—gives you chance to soak up some rays this morning anyway—although I notice you're staying in the shade." His eyes swept the full length of her figure, attractive in a one piece, black, bathing suit.

She put a hand to her broad brimmed, straw hat against the sun. "I've been listening to those health advisories—Say, listen," she spoke with the impulse of a sudden idea, "would you like to come over and have lunch with me in a little while?"

"Sure," he grinned. "Best offer I've had all day."

Mamie looked at her wristwatch, "How about 12:15?"

"Fine with me, I'll be there."

The lunch was very pleasant. They talked about their hopes and aspirations and Jake had been a charming gentleman. He was more polished than she expected. The maintenance man job was little more than a sustenance cover for his ambitions as a writer. He was well educated and had a gift for telling a story, a hint at his writing ability perhaps. In any case, the hour or so they spent together was very pleasant without any reference to the embarrassing incident with Harvey. She still felt bad about that, more because it threatened her plans than anything else.

Absently, she washed the luncheon plates and glasses thinking how to expand on this promising beginning. A plan began to form—perhaps there was a way she could 'reward' Jake. She had tomorrow afternoon off.

Reaching for the phone, she dialed up the Shady Acres office. Her discussion with Mr. Harrigan, the manager, was short but very satisfactory. Now she had to do a little shopping—buy a piece of hardware—and her plan would be complete; all but the installation. The installation was the thing, the centerpiece of her plan. She put a half-full mug of coffee in the sink and ran water into the cup for a few seconds; plenty of time to visit Home Depot or Lowe's before her first showing at 2:30. With a self-satisfied smile, Mamie gathered her things, briefcase and pocketbook, and headed for the door.

With Jake at work in the kitchen installing the disposal she'd bought, Mamie went into the bedroom to change out of her work clothes. A strong urge took possession of her, a feeling she hadn't enjoyed in some time. She took off the pale blue, silk suit she'd bought several years ago and carefully hung the skirt and jacket in the closet; the blouse went in the hamper. Down came the panty hose. She'd wash them out by hand later she thought as she tossed them on top of the hamper.

In the bottom drawer of her beautiful worm wood bureau she found what she was looking for—her black leather mini-skirt. From the drawer above she selected one of her long sleeved, high neck, open lace blouses—the fuchsia, after checking the lavender and the black. 'I'm in a red-hot mood today,' she smiled to herself. Then from the closet she selected matching red spiked heels and the wide, black belt with the leather covered, big 'O' buckle she always wore with this skirt. With her selected clothes laid out on the side of the neatly made bed, she stripped off her panties and bra and dropped them in the hamper.

Pausing, her hands on her naked flanks, she stood in front of the big bureau mirror. She made a critical inventory: Firm high breasts, not large but in proportion, a belly no longer flat but she knew many men liked a little belly with its enticing curve down to the pouting lips of her vulva. Turning slowly, she looked back over her shoulder satisfied with the firm, rounded curve of her hips and the long slender curve of her legs. Not bad for a forty-two year old. Then she undid the rich, deep auburn hair piled high on her head—a softer image. '—enough to arouse Mr. Jake. Him in his muscle shirt.' Her nipples got hard as erotic thoughts ran through her mind. With her finger tips she brushed them lightly, aroused by the sensation.

She pulled the snug-fitting blouse over her head, assuring herself in the mirror her engorged nipples were visible through the lace. With her hair brush she brushed out her hair then teased the dark hair of her crotch, making it stand out after being flattened the first half of the day under her panties. The black mini skirt was next, followed by the wide black belt, cinched as tight as possible without causing the skirt to crease. Last, she slipped on the red, spiked heels.

The mirror told her in a glance what she already knew. The last touch was to brighten her lipstick, the shade very close to her blouse and the spiked heels. Still she turned, carefully inspecting each detail to be sure she presented the wanton picture she desired, her creamy white skin contrasting sharply with her clothing. From the perfume bottle on her bureau a touch of Odalisque behind each ear and at the hollow of her throat.

Whenever she got this feeling, she wanted to be certain she was satisfied— fully and deliciously satisfied. After some slight adjustments, a tug here and tuck there, she was ready, confident—he didn't have a chance.

The preview ran through her mind like the coming attractions of a movie— delicious, teasing scenes. She had to hurt him, elevate his passion, then torment him, force him to get physical. Force him to the edge of violence, a passionate violence she would control while coercing him to take her. She was going to claw him and grab him so he'd have to do the same to defend himself. But that wasn't enough. It was also necessary to tease and entice him so that he wanted to rape her, even force him to do so because there was no other way to stop her. When she got him to that state, she knew her heat would be very high too. Bring him to a fever pitch, make him use force and gradually give in to him, let him overcome her, then work him hard and exhaust him. "Look at my black widow," she laughed lightly, hiking the short skirt up in front of the mirror.

When Mamie stepped out of the bedroom she was glowing with lust, excited by her thoughts, her anticipation. She left the door open. Her retreat would be into the bedroom when Jake reached the proper state of aggressiveness. Good timing, stretched and tormented to the limits, then cool judgment, in the white-hot heat of the sexual battle, were certainly required. She had been there before, high and excited, living at the edge, followed by that delicious pain of pure ecstasy. Could she manipulate Jake to reach that lustful extreme? Even the thought was exciting, the challenge, the anticipation. Her breathing had already quickened, her juices started, she was psyched.

She walked over to the kitchen sink where Jake's legs stretched out on the floor from under the open cabinet. "Can I turn on the water yet?" she asked. She almost gurgled with the tease knowing he would have to react.

"NO!" Then in a calmer tone, "Shouldn't take much longer, I…I…should be finished…. soon." His voice had gone mushy as if his mind and thoughts were distracted. Mamie inhaled deeply. With both doors to the under sink cabinet open, Mamie had a good idea what caused his voice to waver. She took a stride to her left reaching a glass on the counter, then a wide step back to other way to open the dishwasher and put the glass in the top rack, bending to reach as she pulled the dishwasher door open. From the corner of her eye, she got a glimpse of Jake's face. His mouth was open and he was motionless, staring.

Timing. Mamie squatted, her knees pointed toward his face. "Come out of there—I know what you're doing," she demanded, her voice harsh.

As Jake scrambled from under the sink, Mamie slipped off her belt, twice wrapping the buckle end around her right fist, clutching the 'O' buckle in her palm. Before he was fully on his feet, she began lashing him. "You were looking up my dress. You lecher!" She lashed out at him again. "Did you get an eyeful? Huh? Did you?" She continued to flail away.

Jake struggled for balance, the belt smacking across his shoulders and neck as he covered his face, backed up against the sink. "What's the matter with you? Are you crazy?"

"Admit it—you pervert—you were looking up my dress!" Her arm was getting tired swinging, still she continued.

He laughed from behind his arms crossed in front of his face. "I'd have to be a blind not to."

She closed in, feigning rage. Too weak to swing the belt any longer, she dropped it on the floor and attacked with her hands, slapping ineffectually against his shoulders and head as she shouted barely intelligible accusations then clawed at him.

He easily tied up her hands holding her very close to him, his eyes locked on hers.

"Now you're going to rape me, aren't you?" she said in a low throaty voice. She pressed against him, her hands digging into the front of his undershirt.

Surprise and shock registered in his eyes. "No!" He tried to step back and bumped against the sink again. "I would never do that." The blood had drained from his face, his stark look surprising to her.

This was not going well at all. "Yes, you are," she cried, pulling hard on the undershirt until the fabric gave way. "You're going to have to force me." In pulling his shirt and tearing it, she somehow managed to get both their hands on her chest. When Jake tried to pull away there was the sound of more tearing, a more delicate sound than that of his own shirt. A small hole above Mamie's left breast was immediately apparent. Mamie looked down and pulled her hands back covering the spot as she sucked in a noisy, deep, melodramatic breath, "You're ripping the clothes right off my back. You're a beast! A wild beast, ravishing me," she whispered, sounding shocked, her eyes mere slits like a cornered animal of the cat family.

"I...I didn't mean that!" His eyes searched the room frantically as if seeking escape.

At least his color had returned, she noted.

She renewed her flailing, forcing Jake to cover up again. When that flurry was over and before she threw herself on him again, the hole in her lacy blouse somehow had enlarged such that most of her left breast was exposed.

"You'll have to take me," she cried rubbing her whole body against him, pinning him against the sink.

His arms were around her and she sensed he was becoming aroused, about to kiss her.

She bit his neck, hard. "I'll fight. You have to take me." Her own arousal was peaking as she pressed hard against him

"Ouch! That hurt." He jerked his head back and put his hand to the spot. "What's the matter with you?"

"Can't take it? Momma's little boy hurtin'?" She brushed his hand away and bit him again taking care to hit a different spot.

"You vixen!" Roughly, he pushed her away from him then grabbed her by the shoulders, controlling her at arms' length. "Calm down—I am not going to rape you." His face showed the pain of the last bite less than the sadness that now seemed to overtake him. "Let me finish my job." His voice very quiet now.

Mamie looked at him, about to burst into tears.

He turned away from her and crouched down preparing to get under the sink again. "Anyway, I think you have me confused with someone else," he muttered, half to himself, lying down on the floor with a slight grunt and rolling to his back.

"What?" she sobbed, "Who?"

He stopped moving, glaring up at her, her slim legs visible all the way to her dark crotch, "That jerk you introduced me to last week who kept calling me by every name but my own—Julio, Jamie, Jack whatever." With an exasperated movement he ran the fingertips of both hands straight back through his jet-black hair.

In a voice that sounded strange, even to her, Mamie said, "I'm not a nice person—I take what I want," she paused, "when I want it. Can you understand that?"

"Yeah, I can understand that." His voice matched hers.

He slid under the sink.

Mamie turned and ran into her bedroom, slamming the door. That mistake with Harvey had come back to haunt her after all. She didn't cry although she hoped Jake might think she was. What she really needed was time to think—find a different approach. To be turned down was embarrassing yet the situation wasn't totally lost and she was almost certain Jake had been aroused. What went wrong? Her own heat had been so high she couldn't even remember the sequence of events—from the time she stood by the sink until he grabbed her by shoulders was a blur. And she wanted him now more than ever.

She stood in front of the mirror and pinned the torn part of her blouse, more or less covering her breast and prepared to face Jake again. Maybe it wasn't too late.

Tempting—inside she felt a familiar urge—but she knew exactly where such a rendezvous would lead. "No, Harvey, I can't—" she listened to his plea, "No, I'm sorry—I really can't handle that bar scene—I should be working." His voice became insistent and she recognized the subtle threat—only this morning he had mentioned her to one of the company bigwigs—a possible invitation to join the company. She skipped past that possibility. "Look, I have a client who seems ready to buy," she hesitated thinking of Jake and their close encounter with a shiver of anticipation, "with a little more encouragement," she lied. "Tell you what, call me next week, OK?"

As she hung up, she realized that was probably the end of it. Harvey wasn't likely to set her up to join his firm now. Somehow it no longer seemed important. Working for a big realty company had a lot of perks in addition to better commissions but she felt better knowing she didn't have to sleep with Harvey to gain that position. Trading her body for his support had been easy until now. Networking, it was called—her own version. She accepted that was the way things were in business, even enjoyed it on occasion, although she would never admit that to anyone else.

Yet in her heart she had to admit they were using each other. She was as guilty as Harvey.

What was it grandmother Bertha used to say? "To thine own self be true." Old fashioned philosophy that was so simple, even benign. It seemed unnecessary; an obvious statement for gray heads to nod over sagely, like 'he who laughs last laughs best' and 'the proof of the pudding is in the eating'. Who lied to themselves? Now, facing up to that simple axiom was painful, especially admitting her own guilt. Somehow Jake's words had triggered this quiet rebellion within her. Outwardly nothing had changed yet she felt completely different.

TRAILER TRASH

Beverly looked out of the open trailer door. It was a long way from a gated estate to a fenced Trailer Court. Reminded of her previous attitudes, the term "trailer trash" came to mind. Her anger rising, she decided she had been forced into this situation. Yes, she had made a conscious choice; even so, she was now in the midst of what she'd always regarded as beneath her. When his Eastern charm turned into thinly veiled dominance, she began to feel like his untouchable instead of his maharani. Sex lost its mystic quality and Hajii's mustache reminded her of an asshole instead of an intriguing accent to his swarthy face.

She sighed, leaning against the door languidly, one arm high on the doorjamb, the other holding the mug half full of her morning coffee. Beverly was dressed casually in a short sleeved, white, silken blouse and dark, velvet slacks. Simple pearl earrings and a triple strand pearl choker completed her dress. Unconsciously, she knew the combination emphasized her full breasts and accentuated the half-inch she'd lost in her waistline. She'd been so busy getting out of Hajii's manse, she'd had little time to eat or even think about food. After all, she now had to consider her ex-husband as well as Hajii. She didn't want either of them to find her. They might try—they shared a possessive nature.

Absently, her gaze fell on the well-proportioned man across the street, raking gravel in the vacant trailer's short drive. He was wearing one of those undershirts that reminded her of that old Clark Gable movie—what was the name of that picture? The undershirt over long pants didn't remind her of a workman, nor did it detract from the display of his fine muscular shoulders and long sloping neck muscles. Like a boxer she mused. Was he a new owner? As he turned she noticed with distaste he had one of those asshole mustaches like Hajii. A breath of contempt escaped her lips just as he looked up. Typical trailer trash.

The whiteness of his smile made her suddenly realize she was wrong. His appearance was actually a close, two-day growth of beard, black, like his straight back hair. She felt a flush creep over her neck as she realized he was staring at her. Earlier she had noted in the mirror with a certain satisfaction how youthful and full she looked at fifty. He was still looking and she smiled back.

Shortly, he began to walk across the narrow street between them, still smiling. A very good looking fellow, himself, she decided—her automatic appraisal, a ritual which ignored the fact her choices weren't always the best. Of course, he was just "trailer trash".

"Good morning," he said, "I saw you move in yesterday." He stopped as if sensitive to her personal space. "My name is Jake. Anything I can do to help you get settled?"

There was something about him that was reassuring. She dropped her arm to her side with a relaxed slap. "Why I don't know…I." She paused, her mind racing. There must be something…those boxes piled in the bedroom…She caught herself thinking of the bedroom first. Why was that?

"Would you like a cup of coffee?" she heard herself asking. Had it been that long? Those unconscious urges. Trailer trash—quite a difference from Hajii. Still. Stop it! This is only temporary until I can find a better place where Hajii can't find me—he's so demanding, thinks I'm part of his karma. The same as he thinks he's a rajah, she snickered.

"Yes, that would be nice," came the reply. He smiled again. "Give you a chance to…decide what you need," he hesitated, "…done." He seemed to understand her situation, his eyes direct.

She stood aside to let him pass. "Jake the rake," she murmured with a sudden laugh as he brushed by her. He was a head taller she noted with satisfaction.

"Oh, I'm sorry," he said, "forgot I was still carrying it." He quickly turned and leaning out the doorway placed the leaf rake against the side of the trailer. "Sorry," he shrugged. Those great shoulders again.

She found a mug and poured. He was seated at the oak table that came with the trailer, sturdy but definitely utilitarian. Another suggestive word she reminded herself—someone to be used for a purpose. "Do you work here?" she asked.

He laughed, a pleasant sound. "Well, I guess, I do—in a way." She sat down across from him, her arms and elbows in front of her, as she sipped her coffee. "I'm a writer…" he said. He made a little hopeless gesture. "I do odd jobs and help the tenants where possible in exchange for my place down the road away—maybe two or three hours a day." Still no reaction. "Keeps me fit and allows me to write. And I do enjoy getting to know people, so—" he stopped, taking a sip, both hands wrapped around the mug.

There was no dirt under his fingernails, she noticed. She brought her hands down, bathed in his gaze, then started to rise. "I guess there IS something you can do for me." She turned toward the back of the trailer and started to laugh, a low husky laugh, as she looked back, an invitation to follow.

She bent over on the far side of the queen-sized bed, her back to the doorway, and started stacking one box atop another. Straightening, she looked over her shoulder. Jake was pulling the tight undershirt over his head, his pecs and biceps alternately flexing and bulging as she watched.

"What are you doing?"

He stood there on the other side of the bed, the undershirt a bundle in his right hand, nonplused. "Getting ready for work," he said with only a hint of a smile.

Beverly paused, hesitant to speak.

"I figured this might be a sweat raisin' situation," he continued, tossing the shirt on the bed.

Finding her voice at last, "Yes. Well I'd like to start with all these boxes. I've put my clothes away, now you can't get near the bed for boxes. Can you do something with them?"

"Yes, ma'am," he said softly, "Ms. Romaine, down the street said she might need some."

Together they began to fit smaller boxes into larger ones, consolidating them. When they had done all they could, Beverly straightened up. Her eyes met his as she turned back and she felt that hot flush again.

He shifted to one foot, "I see you been working out," he stammered.

"What? Working out?" Puzzled, what's this about? "How can you tell?"

He ducked his head with a little motion looking up at her from under those heavy brows. "You're very firm."

In the dead silence following they stared at each other, each taking in the other boldly. He looked away, "I guess I better get these down to Ms Romaine…I'll put'em in the recycling bin if she doesn't need them."

He picked up two of the nested boxes and awkwardly stepped around the near the end of the queen sized bed. "I'll be back for those in a little while." He paused, calculating. "Might take three trips."

"You do that," she said smiling, "I'll be waiting—" She brushed the hair out of her face with a slow motion of her hand.

He wobbled his way through the doorway to the hollow sounds of cardboard striking each side of the jamb.

She fussed among the boxes for a few minutes anticipating his return, her back to the doorway. The thought of his arms encircling her from behind sent a delicious shiver through her. The feel of those strong arms catching her unaware and almost helpless pumped through her. Crawling up on the bed, she lay on her back, an arm across her forehead. Her other hand closed on the undershirt he'd tossed on the bed. She crumpled it, squeezing it, then held it up, the drooping shroud limp, sagging into folds. In a moment she released it, allowing the garment to fall back into a small shapeless heap. 'Who was he fooling? Working up a sweat.'

Time dragged—what was taking him so long? Where did that Ms Raymond live? Was it that far? She looked at the clock radio on the nightstand—11:20. Maybe he had to take the cardboard to the recycling bin. She heaved a big sigh— yes, it had been quite awhile. That terrible, demanding urge.

After all she'd just met the man. He may be another Blue Beard. What a thought! Actually, his dark two-day growth could be blue in a certain light, she decided. Still the growth was more enticing when she thought of it as black. Silly thoughts—wishful thinking.

He might be hungry she thought abruptly—after all it was nearing noon.

Beverly bounced off the queen-sized bed and went into the kitchen. She cleared the oak table putting the two coffee mugs in the sink, wiping it off with a damp cloth. Then she went to the refrigerator. There was a package of cream cheese, a bottle of milk, her special mixture of papaya juice with extra-added vitamin C, a jar of Skippy's crunchy, some cold cream and cosmetics.

She found a head of lettuce and decided cream cheese and crunchy peanut butter sandwiches would have to do—"Nuts to you," she giggled. Hoping the added lettuce with mayonnaise would keep them from being too dry, she made the sandwiches. He would probably eat two and have a big glass of milk, she decided as she cut the first one diagonally and placed it on a plate. Pulling the Glad wrap out of the utility drawer, she wrapped them and put them in the refrigerator. Then she looked around to see if there was anything else she might have for lunch and decided the bowl of fruit would have to suffice.

From the window over the sink, she could see no one on the road. He'd been gone an hour. She sat on the armchair in the living room opposite the open door and picked up Good Housekeeping. The gorgeous woman on the front cover, oh it was Sophia Loren—tips on Italian cooking to stay slim. "I live on pasta," was the caption under the picture inside with the movie star grinning broadly over a bowl of spaghetti. She was wearing a multicolored peasant blouse which was filled with a lot of Sophia, some cleavage spilling over the top. 'Must all go to her boobs,' Beverly thought. 'Maybe I ought to eat more pasta and become a double D—absurd.' She tossed the magazine aside. 'Where is he anyway? It doesn't take an hour and a half to take a few boxes down the road.'

In the midst of another thought about how else she might put Jake to work, she was startled by his double knock against the inside of the door jamb.

"Comin' in ma'am. OK?"

Startled, she looked up, started to ask about lunch then stopped, gaping. He was dripping with sweat. His face was expressionless. His eyes were down as he headed for the doorway toward the bedroom, turning slightly sideways to her. His glistening chest muscles aroused Beverly although his manner seemed odd— very subdued. An hour or so ago, he had a confident walk, even the hint of swagger. She got up from the armchair and followed him toward the bedroom.

"Sorry, I took so long," he threw over his shoulder as he seemed to almost dive toward the big bed. From her position, the marks on his back took a moment to register.

Was he working for Ms Roman or was it Romaine?

He reached for the balled up undershirt near the head of the bed, next to the window. The bright light as he bent from the waist now clearly revealed four parallel marks, red welts, on either side of his back. A couple of the thin red lines were interrupted by skin, which hadn't been penetrated. Beverly caught her breath with the sudden recognition. "Oh! That looks painful. Let me put a little peroxide on those—they might get infected." With her sudden realization of Ms Romaine's demands, Beverly felt her own breathing accelerate.

Jake turned quickly pulling the undershirt over his head. "No, ma'am." He stuffed the tail into his pants, "I'll catch it when I get home—better I get started on the rest of these boxes."

Beverly laughed and hurried toward the bathroom. "Wait! I'll be right back."

Trailer trash indeed…he was definitely utilitarian. She reached for the peroxide and drew out the box of Q-tips

"Oh really…ah, ma'am…I don't think," he reacted to the peroxide bottle and swabs.

"Nonsense," Beverly said, pushing him gently backward toward the bed, "those need to be tended to." He went over backward on the bed with surprising ease. "Now, roll over."

She pulled his undershirt out of his pants and ran her hands up his back slipping the bottom of the undershirt above the ugly red lines of scratches. His skin was warm to her touch, the sensation exciting. "This won't hurt—it might feel cold." She twisted off the cap to the plastic, brown colored peroxide bottle and tossed it on the bed next to him. Knee on the bed, she leaned over and applied the swab carefully to each of the long scratches. There was a slight foaming action over the bloody welts. "Lie still!" she commanded as he started to move. "Let that dry a bit." She blew across the wet scratches.

Pulling down the undershirt, "There that should be OK now."

He turned, propped on one elbow, a quizzical look on his face. "Thank you, ah…"

Beverly stepped back off the bed. "Did Ms Roman need the boxes?"

"Ah, no. Matter-of-fact, Ms Romaine had more than she could handle," he said straight-faced. He got up and resumed gathering and fitting the boxes together for removal.

Beverly didn't comment but that certainly didn't appear to be the case. A vision—she imagined herself in Ms Roman's place. Although the thought didn't repel her, she dismissed it—more "trailer trash".

"That's about it," Jake announced as he picked up two more armloads, awkwardly handling the boxes. "I shouldn't be as long this time."

With a grin, her arms folded across her bosom, "I certainly hope not—I may have other work…" The last was lost in the hollow sound of cardboard knocking against the doorjamb.

At that moment the image of Hajii flashed through Beverly's mind, a total abstraction. What would he do? Probably speed up she thought with a disgusted sigh. His solution to everything it seemed—he was a terrible driver—always too fast. But then Hajii's attraction seemed illusory to her now.

She looked around at the remaining boxes. Jake had estimated correctly, one more load would probably clear out the last of them. Unconsciously, she began to search for other tasks for Jake. What if…? She flopped on the bed on her back, her hands behind her head, her heated imagination at work. Had it really been that long?

Impulsively, she jumped up and pulled the long accordion folding door of the closet closed so she could check her profile in the full-length mirror attached to the first section of the door. With a slight effort she pulled in her tummy and noticed her slacks visibly drop a couple inches, her breasts standing out even more. 'That's the way they think—all white creamy skin and pink nipples.' For a gal past forty there were some advantages gleaned from life's experiences over younger women with their taut bodies.

The mirror image of her body pleased her, a plan taking shape. "Shame on you, Beverly," she half-whispered. "Would that be too obvious?" When was being obvious such a bad idea? After all how much can you expect from "trailer trash? She laughed at herself. The repeated ring of that thought brought her to the sense of the dramatic change in her fortunes these past two days—from gated estate to 'a secure mobile home park'—her own choice. She heaved a big sigh. Now she was among them—not to be found by Hajii or that SOB of an ex-husband Ernie—the restraining order on him had expired by now.

Speaking of "trailer trash", he couldn't even measure up to that level—what a fool she'd been to be charmed by his Ted Turner looks, the graying mustache and the Texas bravado. He didn't have a dime in addition to being stubborn and a lousy lover.

Did she dare move back into her home after her tenant's lease expired at Shady Acres? Would it be safe? She let Hajii think she had sold the place, a sop to his luxurious six thousand square foot mansion and his exaggerated sense of being of the Brahman caste. In three months the tenant's lease would be up and she could get her furniture out of storage and reestablish her genteel, cultured lifestyle once more—mix with the beautiful people again. She hadn't lost contact with all of them.

Meanwhile, there was Jake the rake—a project for a trailer dweller. Her project. He was 'utilitarian' and she knew she could use him—temporarily, at least.

The sudden, disruptive sounds, close at hand, confounded Beverly. She jumped up only to be abruptly and rudely shaken from her dreamy visions—literally.

"You bitch! You scheming bitch!" The red head muttered as she went for Beverly's throat, long, bright red nails flashing in the subdued light.

Gasping, Beverly instinctively avoided the hands threatening her throat and they clawed at her shoulders tearing off the top two buttons of her blouse. "You stay away from my man, you slut!" The angry, contorted face, painted with bright red lipstick was inches from Beverly's. The woman's breath offensive.

Without thinking, Beverly quickly brought her arms up knocking the red head's hands away from her face and neck to the sharp sound of her silk blouse ripping. She then delivered a closed fist to the red head's left eye. "Who the devil are you?" she cried out, amazed and inspired by her own quick reaction.

"Mamie Romaine, slut. You stay away from Jake or I'll scratch your eyes out," came the answer as the taller woman stumbled backward, off-balanced by the blow. Almost in slow motion, she continued backward off-balance, falling over the remaining empty boxes. Her legs flailed wide in a futile effort to keep her balance. The black, pencil slim skirt split up the seam revealing her slim, white thighs. She wasn't wearing any panties. Her left spiked heel, the color of her lipstick, kicked off over her head, the right somehow stayed on her foot during the last scissor-kick.

Beverly surveyed the awkward flail of arms and legs, the lavender, see-through lace blouse, the wide, black, patent leather belt, cinched around a thin waist and the dark uncovered thatch of auburn crotch hair. "You better get back to your trailer and finish dressing—you're a mess." She almost laughed, surprised by her own boldness. This despite her own disarray—her blouse, missing the two top buttons and slightly torn, hung open. Her slacks had slipped down low on her hips. She hitched them up. "Go on, get out o'here," she made a threatening move with her fists balled up. "…Trailer trash."

Mamie flailed amongst the empty boxes finally managing to get to her feet. She started limping through the doorway as Beverly reached the other red, high heel and threw it at her, hitting her in the backside "…and don't come back."

Standing in the doorway to her bedroom, Beverly watched the retreating Mamie through the kitchen, then the living room to the open trailer door. She allowed a slight smile to play across her face, her hands on her hips, triumphant. 'If only Hajii and Ernie could see me now—they'd really appreciate what a good 'bitch' they had.' She reveled in her new found aggressiveness, imagining their reactions—Hajji bemused perhaps and Ernie flabbergasted she was sure, his Texas braggadocio stilled for once. 'Who needs either of them?'

Her daydream broke with the realization Jake was standing in the doorway to the trailer. She had no idea how long he'd been standing there.

Looking directly at him, less than thirty feet away, she slowly unbuttoned the last two buttons of her blouse, then very deliberately, she pulled the two open sides across in front of her breasts and tucked the ends into her slacks. Jake didn't move and he didn't look away. The blouse gapped; the waistband of her slacks was too loose.

She smiled, brushing a hand though her hair, a luxurious gesture. "Where ya been, Jake? You missed all the action." She took a deep breath as if to puff up with pride.

He moved toward her, his face relaxed, his eyes locked on hers. "I don't think so." When he reached the doorway he murmured, "I don't think so," again as his arm encircled her waist and he bent to kiss her.

With that same enticing, low-throated laugh, Beverly spun out of his grasp, her blouse coming open again with the movement. "Not yet—be patient—remember the boxes." She turned facing him, out of reach, her silken blouse falling loose over her breasts.

In one motion, Jake pulled off his undershirt and lunged, his face intent.

"Easy—easy," she caught his bare shoulders, gently restraining him. "—the boxes." There was a calmness in her tone that surprised Beverly and concealed the surging excitement pumping through her. Two more steps and they would have fallen together on the bed—her resistance gone. Then, just as calmly, she pointed with one extended finger to the biggest box, the one with one side caved in where Ms Romaine sat down so abruptly. The action created an enticing movement which riveted Jake's eyes. She laughed again and with her other hand gently pushed his face toward her pointing finger and the box. "Concentrate—think HARD," she teased, glancing at his bulging fly.

With a sullen look Jake tossed the undershirt on the bed and started gathering the boxes. He was able to nest three of them under one arm and carried the big crumpled box under the other. As he headed for the doorway, he gave her a glance from under those hooded brows, the trace of a smile easing his features. Beverly had moved to the far side of the bed.

Now she slithered up on the bed on all fours the blouse gapping. "Hurry back."

Glancing back at her, Jake said something incoherent, his eyes wide, to the muffled sound of the boxes striking the walls as he wedged through the doorway.

'Trailer trash", be damned, it's going to be an exciting 3 months.' Beverly took off her blouse and tossed it next to the little heap of Jake's undershirt and lay back.

Then a laugh, unbidden, erupted from her as a perversion of Forrest Gump's homey philosophy ran through her mind. She had seen the movie at one of those cut rate theaters a week before.

"Life is like a box of chocolates—you never know what's in the next piece," she pronounced half-aloud through the dying eddies and swirls of laughter, only to be consumed again.

THE SUPER

Harrigan turned from the window of his office and ran a hand over his sweating bald pate. Jake was moving—no longer standing in front of the manager's office—on his way, reluctantly. He understood Jake's moodiness. He collapsed into the squeaking, old wooden swivel chair. 'Better him than me.'

The handyman was, at last, on his way over to 629 Floral Avenue—Sylvia's. Jake was helpful. He conceded to himself the part-time handyman made running Shady Acres easier. With a squeak, Harrigan leaned back in the swivel chair and turned up the volume on the cheap plastic radio set on the table behind his desk. The Mills Brothers swung into the rhythmic song Cab Driver. Harrigan liked the Mills Brothers, their music didn't intrude—no clashing guitars, no monotonous drumbeat or sound penetrating your pores.

Cab Driver, drive by Mary's place
I just want a chance to see her face

However his mood didn't match the happy beat, the Mills Brothers seemed to put into even the most melancholy songs.

The problem was Sylvia. Jake would take care of her plumbing for sure. That wasn't the problem.—not the real problem. Luckily, Harrigan realized that months ago. Leaning back in the old swivel chair, he laced his fingers behind his neck, ignoring the open account ledger.

Don't stop the meter let it race
Cab Driver, drive by Mary's place

A few weeks ago, Sylvia's big breasts were flopping in his face as she rode him. The thought of those big soft things swaying gently into his mouth caused him to start getting hard. By now she was probably riding Jake just as hard. 'Let him take care of that horny bitch.' was his conflicting thought. It was smart to let Jake live in that empty trailer on lot 14 in exchange for doing the handyman chores at Shady Acres. A write off besides! Harrigan congratulated himself.

Cab Driver, once more round the block
Never mind the ticket or the clock

Then his conscience: 'Face it, you were lucky! And you loved screwing that heavyweight—one hundred eighty pounds if she's an ounce. How many times does 55 go into 40?' He chuckled aloud, aroused. 'She was good—too good— Maddie should try so hard.' Maddie was a good woman, a good wife, honest, straight forward—maybe a little too reserved—'If only she were a little wanton in bed,' he mused. Still, no doubt, he had done the right thing. He had to give up being seduced by that horny jumbo. If Maddie ever found out about Sylvia—or May—or what's her name a couple years ago—

Only wish we could have had a talk
Cab Driver, once more round the block

"Oooh ooh Eddie—ready for lunch?" The call drifted from the kitchen.
With a start, Harrigan caught himself about to fall over backward, both feet desperately hooking the desk keyhole under the center drawer. Maddie was calling. If she found out—he struggled to right himself, his gut muscles straining, the old wooden chair trying to roll under the desk—that was one thing. If her father found out—he got back to the normal sitting position, breathless, his knees aching—that was quite something else again!

Cab Driver, once more down the street
There's a little place we used to eat

The Shady Acres account was $2000. short. He looked at the account ledger unseeing. The $2000. shortage happened to coincide with Jake moving in and taking on the handyman chores. Using that, Harrigan could cover part of the money as a loss—no an expense—an expense for handyman services. Plausible, but he knew it wouldn't stand close inspection, like an independent audit. Maybe a thousand would, not the whole $2000. And somehow he had to come up with $3000 more!

> *That's where I laid my future at her feet*
> *Cab Driver, once more down the street*

"Hurry, Eddie. come and get it while it's hot."

So far he'd managed to keep the 'collectors' away from Shady Acres. Any tenant's question about a couple of hard looking men couldn't be answered by calling them some of Tony's construction men. Even Maddie would pick up on that—her father's construction crewmen would never be seen in an upscale place like Shady Acres without construction in progress. A possibility—an idea he might pursue although unappealing—more juggling the books.

> *Cab Driver wait here by the door*
> *Perhaps I'll hold her in my arms once more*

When he made the last payment, they were very clear about the balance and he knew they were serious—very serious. Ten days to raise the remaining $3000. Fast women and slow horses, the old gambler's saw went. How true. Could he squeeze another $3000. out of the books? Next month's rental fees were due on the first, less than a week away. Madeline's father seldom had the books checked, however Tony was sly—made all his money in construction and was very protective of his daughter. Even a random check of the books spelled disaster.

> *Then things'll be like they were before*
> *Cab Driver, wait here by the door*

Every Sunday they were expected for a big family supper over at the Maggedali's. He wiped his head, sweating again. The numbers in the ledger in front of him blurred with his foreboding. Tony was generous but you didn't miss a Sunday without good reason. The tradition was suffocating for Harrigan—being Irish didn't help—he was sick of trying to explain both sides of the IRA mess whenever there was an outburst in Northern Ireland which so far covered most of his married life.

> *Cab Driver, better take me home*
> *I guess that I was meant to be alone*

And God help you if they suspected a lack of sincerity or enthusiasm for the Sunday meal—embezzlement! The word shocked him. He could imagine Tony's reaction. How did he get into this mess? He tried to focus on the ledger as if the neat columns of figures held the answer. Where in hell was he going to get $3000?

I hope god sends me a loved one of my own
Cab Driver, better take me home
Cab Driver, better take me home

"Eddie!" Maddie was at the doorway frowning. "The Mills Brothers, I might have known—"

"You wouldn't understand." Harrigan reached back and turned off the radio. "—besides I was workin' on the books." He rose from his desk, slamming the green clothbound ledger closed. Carefully he put it in the lower right hand desk drawer, then locked and tested his desk.

"Honestly—" exasperation in her voice, "you'd think you were in charge of the mint—come on your minestrone is getting cold." She turned shuffling over the wall-to-wall carpet in her fleece slippers.

Harrigan followed her to the dining nook of the big, double—wide, his thoughts still jammed with the details of his financial woes.

As he sat at the place she had set for him, she wrapped her arms around his shoulders from behind and kissed his ear. He could feel her breasts against his shoulders through the thin wraparound housecoat she was wearing.

The place setting was complete from the colorful Mexican place mat, full silver setting to the basket of poppy seeded hard rolls she knew he liked. "You have a hard morning, dear?"

He looked up from the brimming bowl of minestrone, his face blank. "Huh? Oh, it's that damned ledger—," he blurted before hesitating—he didn't really want to go there, "I...well you know how I am with figures." He looked away from her dark eyes. "Got any butter?"

"Right there," she pushed the plate closer to him, her own soup untouched.

"Oh, yeah." He reached a roll.

"How's this new guy, Jake, working out?" She watched him dip the hard roll in his soup ignoring the butter.

"Fine—" A thought came to him. "I probably ought to check on him—"

Maddie rolled her eyes, a knowing look as if she understood, almost as if she could read his mind but didn't want to intrude. "Eat, eat—want me to heat it up?"

"No—I'm not very hungry."

They ate in silence. Harrigan finished his soup and a couple rolls. He pushed back from the table. "Maybe I'll take a walk, my stomach's been unsettled lately—need some air, a little exercise."

"Wait!" She jumped up and came around the table. "Wait," she said softly, "let me relax you." Maddie gently pushed him back down in the chair and began to gently massage his shoulders. "You're all tense—don't let the books get you uptight—take off your shoes, come into the bedroom. Let me give you a massage, get you relaxed. Daddy can get someone to take care of the books for you." She bent closer. He could feel the softness of her against his neck as she ran her hands down his arms and he began to sweat.

Now, right now, he had to get out of there. The thought of Tony having someone take over the books scared the hell out of him. "Please! I gotta get some air." Abruptly he bolted from the table, brushing by Maddie, heading for the door.

In the bright sunshine, he put up a hand shielding his eyes, turning blindly up the street around the corner past the windowless end of the manger's trailer. Walking blindly, he was on Floral Avenue before he realized where he was or which direction he'd been walking. His random, scrambled and incoherent thoughts found a focus. 'God Tony checking the books! Just what I need.' He turned left walking up the slight incline. Maddie's off-hand remark was the direct result of his unthinking comment about the books—how stupid. He was going to hang himself if he wasn't careful.

He stopped. Now, he was in front of 629 Floral—'Well, might as well get it over with.' He sighed and walked up the three wooden steps to the storm door and tapped on the glass, the inner door open.

Sylvia was visible as she approached the door. 'What the hell is that she's wearing? One of those whatcha-m'call-it's—a…a…leo-leotard.'

"C'mon in Harrigan," she called from inside, gesturing. She twirled toward the breakfast nook her cheeks jiggling as she pranced, barefoot, toward the coffee maker.

He stuck his head in the door. "Hey you lost a little weight, haven't you?"

She did another funny turn, her breasts waving wildly. "Oh, you noticed." She struck a pose that would do credit to a nineteen fifties movie star, stretching to her maximum five-foot-six height. "C'mon in, take the load off—have a cup. I got some good news."

Harrigan stopped, two steps inside the door. With her tummy sucked in like that, one hand low on her hip standing in profile, Sylvia was voluptuous. The wispy green sash didn't disguise the fact she was wearing nothing under the leotard. He started to get aroused. "Oh I can't stay…I…just wanted to see if Jake took care o'you." She relaxed her pose slightly, "I mean handled your problem," he fumbled.

"What's t'matter Maddie got you on the clock?" She lowered her chin looking at him from under her brows, smiling slightly. "What makes you think Jake could handle my problem?" She breathed in her best sexy voice.

Harrigan, hesitant, was still cataloging the leotard. She turned again and bent over, checking the cupboard under the coffee maker. Now he wanted to wipe his head, he was beginning to sweat. "Oh, here it is right here," she smiled broadly picking up the mug beside the coffee maker. "Let's see, it's been a long time—straight black, right Harrigan?"

He sat down. "I mean did Jake fix your pluming?" he said, at last wrenching his eyes away from decoding every subtle curve under the leotard.

"Yes, he did his best, I suppose." She set the mug in front of him and settled opposite, her breasts and those big nipples seemed to rest on the blonde oak table top like two huge eggplants on display in a jeweler's case. The incongruity of this image was lost on Harrigan as he struggled with his impulses. He was fully aroused. "Ah…you said somethin' about good fortune—you inherit a million?" He laughed to show he was kidding, as he tried to control his erotic thoughts.

She raised her eyebrows as if surprised and reached across the table grabbing his arm. "Can you believe it—I'm a wealthy woman." She squeezed his forearm.

"I'm glad someone's luck has changed," he mumbled, his thoughts roughly driven back to his overwhelming money problem.

"You got problems? I'm sorry to hear that, Harrigan. Is that why you haven't been around lately? You know I wouldn't say anything to anyone," she patted his arm, her expression sympathetic. Clearly, she wasn't talking about money.

The bulge in Harrigan's pants was gone, still he wanted to wipe his bald head. He looked down at the coffee mug, then took a sip. "Naw, I been busy—gotta keep track o'this new guy. Know what I mean?" He looked into her eyes knowing she knew he was lying.

"Can't Tony help?" Her gaze was steady, as if she knew the arrangement for running Shady Acres with his father-in law.

The thought sent a shudder through him "Matter o'fact I need to do some more checking right now." He started to rise.

As he rounded the table, Sylvia came very close to him, one big breast easing up against his elbow. "You know me Eddie. All you have to do is whistle."

"Yeah," he turned toward the door.

"You know how to whistle, don't you, Eddie?"

Harrigan looked at her, his hand on the storm door, "Sure, doesn't everybody?"

"You just put your lips together and blow." she said in a breathy voice.

He shook his head pushing open the door. "That something you heard on TV? That soap opera you watch?" He laughed as he caught the curve of her lips through the leotard as she moved into the bright sunlight through the doorway and immediately the flash picture of those same lips under him several weeks ago.

Outside he hurried down the steps, feeling that aroused tingle again.

*   *   *   *

Typically, they were in the library at the small, fold-out bar, away from the rest of the family. Tony liked to talk politics—man talk—and insisted on having a drink with Ed, alone. Tony never called him Harrigan like everyone else. To his surprise Tony started out on religion. They never talked religion. Even when he was pinning Harrigan down about violence in Northern Ireland, like it was Harrigan's responsibility to control the fighting, religion was virtually ignored.

"So Ed, what d'ya think about this thing with all the Priests and the choir boys? The scandal?" Tony sipped his bourbon over ice and raised his eyebrows expectantly, his dark brown eyes nailing Harrigan in that familiar way.

Harrigan, caught by surprise with the religious question, hesitated trying to get his thoughts off his money problems.

No matter, Tony went on with barely a pause. "Here I was pushin' young Ant'ny, you know my oldest son, for the Priesthood—to take the vows an' all 'at. There's always been a Priest in the family since I can remember. Would you believe it! Wow!" He slapped his forehead with an audible smack. "I coulda made a crucial mistake—you know what I'm sayin'?"

Harrigan nodded his head, wondering where Tony's talk was leading—sometimes he came in the backdoor with things that could trap you.

"I mean, Ed, those faggots oughta be shot, smooth collar or not, hell, Catholic or not." He stabbed a pudgy finger into Harrigan's chest, his eyes still locked onto Harrigan's.

Harrigan nodded again hoping his uncertainty wasn't apparent. He wanted to wipe his head.

"If I ever caught any o'my relatives playin' footsy and coverin' it up, I'd hang'em by their balls or stick'em in a barrel o'cement," he grinned maliciously at the thought, "—ya know somethin' drastic?" The ice cubes in his glass clinked.

"Such a violation of trust." He shook his head sadly, his eyes at last turning away from Harrigan's.

Tony turned toward the dining room. "C'mon, Ed let's eat." Tony reached up and put a heavy arm around Harrigan's shoulders. "Ya know, I didn't mean to get so riled up—after all it's Sunday f'crissakes."

Harrigan, call me Ed, was visualizing Tony's reaction to his $2000 'violation of trust'. 'Something drastic'—one of those cement trucks could deliver nine cubic yards of cement. That was a lot of concrete.

"Hey you hav'nt finished your drink—how come?" Tony suddenly focused on Harrigan's glass. "Last time I heard of an Irishman not drinkin' he was plottin' an uprisin' in the old country—right, Ed?" He laughed and slapped Harrigan on the back Harrigan felt a trickle of sweat run down behind his left ear. He took out his handkerchief and mopped his bald head, smiling weakly. He stopped as they were about to enter the dining room. "You got it Tony." Raising his glass in a semi-salute, he downed the gin and tonic.

"Whoa," Tony roared. "People! Watch out for this guy. Time t'eat, right now, baby!"

Harrigan picked at his food. But for the sudden rush of warmth from the gin, he felt sick. Maddie, across the table from him, was laughing with her brothers and sisters recalling an incident from the past when they were all at home. They were all talking at once, each trying to get his version in before someone else could bias the story. Usually Harrigan felt left out when these uproarious exchanges got started, today he was grateful. The spaghetti and meatballs was delicious. Anna, Tony's wife, was an excellent cook, but his acid reflux was acting up again. At least that's what they called it on television. He had never had any stomach problems, now it seemed he had indigestion—acid reflux—constantly.

"Hey, Ed!" Tony shouted over the din of his offspring from the end of the table. "How come you're not eatin'. You don't like Anna's sauce? Fresh made today. Right honey?" She nodded silently, her face sober.

Harrigan looked up, surprised, the wine glass of Chianti half way to his mouth. Suddenly everyone was quiet. "I don't know. Don't have my usual appetite, it seems." He paused uncomfortable with the attention. "The sauce is good, like always," he added—an after thought. Anna was staring at him.

Tony was frowning over the huge linen napkin as he wiped his mouth. "You seen a doctor?"

"Oh, it's nothing," Harrigan waved a feeble hand, "maybe a little touch of indigestion—something I ate this morning," he added hastily with a glance toward Anna, her straight pulled back, mixed gray hair seemingly sinister.

Harrigan stood in front of the open closet in his shorts, shirt and tie, carefully folding his good sharkskin trousers over a wooden hanger. Maddie was behind him in front of her bureau in nothing but her black pantyhose unscrewing one of her gold pendant earrings. In the light from the bathroom, the mirror reflected her firm, pointed breasts. She was well proportioned for her 48 years. Harrigan avoided looking at her as he unknotted his tie and smoothed it before hanging over the tie rack inside the closet.

She turned and walked over to him still wearing her high heels, her arms open to embrace him.

In front of him, her arms around him, she kissed his cheek. "How are you feeling, Eddie?"

"Oh, OK I guess," he answered, fumbling with his cuff links through her embrace. "Let me get this off." He pushed her arms down to unbutton his dress shirt avoiding her pert nipples as he did so. She turned away, stepping out of her high heels as he pulled off the shirt and shoved it in the laundry basket.

Standing in his boxers and tee shirt he watched her slip the long loose night grown over her head and in one fluid motion pull her panty hose down as the gown fell with her hands to her ankles.

Shaking out her panty hose and folding them, she caught his glance and smiled, her lips still red with lipstick accenting her dark flowing hair and dark brows. "What?" she smiled, seemingly excited and a little embarrassed at the same time.

In the soft light his face was serious, reflecting something deeply affecting him, "You're a beautiful woman," he said quietly, "I'm lucky to be married to you." Then he walked past her into the bathroom.

He set the alarm and climbed into bed, settling on his side, his back to Maddie. After a deep breath he felt better. Apparently that commercial gas stuff was doing its job—maybe he could sleep.

Maddie turned toward him, hiking up the long nightgown to put a leg on top of Ed's hips. "You OK Eddie?"

"Yeah, I'm fine."

"You know Daddy really likes you."

"Yeah? That's good."

"I think he was worried about you tonight."

"I'll be OK.

She kissed the back of his head and snuggled closer, running her fingers through the hair on his chest. He was drowsy, comfortable, his stomach quiet. 'I wonder if there's any dope in that stuff.'

The big concrete truck backed up to the hole in the ground—a basement for a new house. 'There must be enough concrete in that truck to fill this whole base-ment,' Harrigan thought. He struggled but couldn't move, he was rooted there in the center of the basement. The heavy flow from the truck encroached on him slowly, a thick gray taffy full of small stones, menacing like lava from a cold vol-cano.

As the concrete reached above his ankles, he noticed the two 'collectors'. He called out to them—One nodded and they turned away—fading into an unseen mist. Another man appeared as they vanished. Harrigan couldn't see his face, then the figure walked toward the concrete truck—Tony!

He hit the thick rug floor with a thump still struggling in the cold lumpy con-crete, his senses confused in the darkened room, his arm tangled in the sheet he'd clutched and dragged off the bed.

"Eddie?" He heard Maddie's voice as though in a tunnel.

The rest of the night wasn't very good either.

Harrigan put the phone down—a signature loan wouldn't work. Two to three days they said plus he'd have to have a cosigner. The VISA card was maxed-out. Besides, the chance of Maddie finding out was high, she used the credit card to shop. He leaned over the open accounts book, his head in his hands—two days, that's all that was left to raise the $3000. His head throbbed despite all the coffee he'd had.

"All you have to do is whistle, Eddie," he remembered—hell, he'd never for-gotten—he got a hard on every time he thought of her in that black leotard. 'Did she really have any money?'

For the next five minutes Harrigan debated with himself, twice picking up the phone, then thinking better of the idea, putting the phone down again. He had to be careful. Just having the door to the rest of the trailer closed wasn't enough. Outwardly he needed an excuse in case Maddie found out, that was why he sent Jake up there before. But he couldn't delay any longer, the 'collectors' specified cash—no personal checks, no IOUs, no VISA cards, no Postal Money Orders, no Western Union, no traveler's checks. Harrigan almost laughed, who in hell was going to give those guys traveler's checks? He had to come up with something now—suppose Sylvia needed a couple days to get the cash?

At last, an idea; something that would allow him to go to Sylvia's at least a couple times, if necessary. It might work he told himself—'now if only she has the money'. He looked up at the ceiling, a little prayer.

With the positive action of an executive, Harrigan picked up the phone. On the fourth ring she answered. "This is the Shady Acres Superintendent," he announced formally, "will someone be there in the next half hour?"

"Oh, hi Harrigan, I'm always here for you. Just now, I had to slip out of the shower to— " Brusquely, he interrupted, "We'll be sending someone around this afternoon or sooner to inspect the gas stoves on your street. A potential explosion—er that is—ah, nothing to worry about," he added hastily trying to think what to say next. "The connector nipple, ah, that is a part replacement—the inspector will provide all the details when I get there." He hung up flustered. Trying to sound official he had raised he voice, so he reached back to turn up the radio. Now he'd have to call all the other tenants on Floral Avenue.

"Good grief, there's fifteen others," he groaned, as he looked though the master tenant's list, "that might take all morning." Then brilliantly he decided to fake the calls. With that he decided to turn the radio down again.

Holding the disconnect down he officially told everyone on Floral Avenue about the gas leak, that is the potential gas leak—he got it right on the last five phony calls. Rubbing his hands together he felt better. He had an excuse.

Sylvia greeted him at the storm door wearing a long white Turkish towel bathrobe. The ends of the belt hung loosely on either side as she held the middle together with her folded arms. Harrigan gaped at her lumpy figure looking around furtively.

"Don't stand there! Come in, "she ordered. "What's this gas leak all about?"

"You said I should whistle if I needed help." He tried to keep it light.

"This way, Harrigan."

He followed her toward the far end of the mobile home. "Well?"

His mouth fell open as she turned, no longer holding the robe together.

"Eddie," she purred, "sit down beside me. Let's talk," she patted the bed. "You know I'd do anything for you." She smiled allowing the robe to fall open further. "See anything you want?"

For the next forty minutes Harrigan alternated between expressing his needs and fulfilling Sylvia's. When he staggered out of 629 Floral, exhausted but relaxed, he was sure she said she would have the $3000 cash tomorrow afternoon. He sauntered home, his stomach growling, ready for lunch, his big problem solved.

Almost as soon as he finished clearing off his office desk, Maddie called him to lunch. He greeted her warmly and sat down to the baloney sandwich she had prepared, a glass of milk on the place mat and a golden delicious apple to the side.

"I had to fix you a cold lunch," Maddie said, her voice apologetic. "One of the tenants called about the gas stove leak. You weren't here so I called Daddy. He said it could be serious and not to use the stove, he'd send his best man over as soon as he could."

Harrigan froze, half a baloney sandwich suspended in one hand, his appetite curdled by sour stomach.

Maddie looked at him, concerned, "Eddie are you all right? I did the right thing didn't I?"

He looked at her, then at the sandwich, then around the room, desperate. "Yeah." After he swallowed, clearing his throat, "I think I got a handle on the gas thing—ah, there's a part I need to check. Possible recall by Whirlpool. Doesn't effect everybody. Excuse me, I need to check something."

Harrigan scrapped back his chair and hurried back to his office and closed the door. Automatically he turned on the radio and sat down—in a trance—

Cab driver, once more round the block.

SYLVIA'S CURSE

Sylvia pressed the TV mute button silencing another one of those diet commercials—now they had invaded her favorite soap HOPE FOR TOMORROW. This one was plugging pills.

She picked up her empty coffee cup and walked to the compact kitchen of her double wide.

From the kitchen cabinet she pulled down the prepackaged popcorn, opened the microwave and set the timer. She reached a bowl under the cupboard and got the squeeze butter out of the Fridge—not enough butter in the package to suit her.

The diet commercial reminded her of the exercise machines in the closet: Suzanne Somers Thigh Master, Butt Master, the Nordic Ski track and others she couldn't remember. Maybe she'd get back to the Thigh Master one of these days. Harrigan even said he noticed a difference the last time.

She smiled thinking of the Super—Superintendent of Shady Acres his full title. Harrigan was a little caught up in himself these days. He owed her $3,000. She didn't know why he borrowed the money but he must be in a jam. Otherwise why didn't he get the money from his father-in-law, owner of Shady Acres. And this thing about the stove problem in her part of the park. What was that all about? There wasn't anything wrong with the stoves—she'd checked with old Mrs. Shanty over the back fence. The woman knew everything—The microwave dinged. Yet somehow the situation was favorable for her—Sylvia knew whenever she pulled the string Harrigan had to come.

She squirted butter over the popcorn and added her own special seasoning, ginseng, taro root and other stuff to 'enhance life' the fine print on the bottle, above the asterisk with the FDA warning, said.

Hurrying back to the sofa she clicked the TV mute button. Della was just opening the hospital room door—Sylvia only missed the opening line. She identified with Della, a big woman like the ones those old painters liked to paint in the nude. She had been on the show at least twenty years. Della filled her nurse's uniform as if the show's costume people ran out of money ten years ago. Big hearted, she never lacked for a man despite the risk—she'd been kidnapped twice since Sylvia found the show. Both abductions were due to trusting the wrong man—usually the rough, tough guys you could see at first glance were no good but were oh so good when a woman needed them to be. Harrigan?

She liked the show despite a critic's three line review in the local newspaper:

"TV soaps: 'WA'S HAPPENIN' TOMORRA?' (HOPE FOR TOMORROW) Cast: From yesterday's has beens and today's wanna bes including veteran voluptuary, nurse Della, played by Agnes Moorestud. A story of hope and promise for the castaways and losers of today—"

The door bell buzzed causing Sylvia to start, interrupting the closing moments of HOPE FOR TOMORROW. Della was about to be entrapped in a dubious money deal by her latest paramour.

Sylvia had intended to replace the buzzer with chimes almost since she'd moved in. Maybe she could get Jake—Frowning, she got up to answer the door, silently cursing that damned buzzer, unconscious of her attire or lack of it. She had pulled on a pair of panties and slipped into her American styled, genuine Japanese, silk kimono when she got up. Around the house she never tied the belt to the robe, the feeling of being half-nude pleased her. Now, almost at the entry she made a vague attempt to pull it closed ignoring the fact that her body was almost as well defined through the silky sheen with it tightly closed as when she breezed though the trailer.

There, through the glass storm door, was a trim young man professionally dressed complete with black imitation leather briefcase, staring off in the distance, uncomfortable in the warm morning sun. As his gaze snapped back, his mouth fell open and his blue eyes widened behind the rimless glasses.

"Yeees?" She cracked the storm door a few inches allowing the robe to fall open slightly.

"Ms. Holbein? Ms. Sylvia Holbein?"

She frowned, again, "Yes, what do you want?" Salesman? No, not allowed in Shady Acres. Who could this guy be?

He colored slightly. "Ma'am I'm from the IRS. I wonder if I could talk to you a few minutes," he said averting his eyes while he fumbled for something from his hip pocket.

Sylvia, wrapped her arms around her body, catching the door with her bare foot. "What about?" Her first thought was her discrete manicure business; cash only, she reassured herself.

He peeked back at her holding up his wallet, showing his credentials. Then with a determined look, he faced her fully. "I'm not at liberty to discuss the case here on your doorstep," he said, his voice very official, "but if it will ease your mind, this is not about your income tax return. May I come in? If you'd like to get dressed first I'll wait here."

Sylvia relaxed her grip on the robe, grinning, "You don't like my Japanese robe?"

With an effort, it seemed, he smiled. "Ah—yes—it's very nice, I'm sure."

She pulled the royal blue robe tight with one hand looking down at a huge yellow chrysanthemum bulging over her breast, her nipple swelling off center on the flower, "Giant mums are my favorite—aren't they're beautiful?" She smiled at him.

Blinking, he cleared his throat, then continued, "Ah…yes…Ms. Holbein, I'm Agent Charles Libertine, my card." He held out the little white business card.

Sylvia took the card, "Come in, I'll fix some coffee." She led him to the round butcher block table across from the kitchen sink in an alcove surrounded by indoor plants.

With a mug of coffee in front of him, Agent Charles Libertine began to question Sylvia. He wanted to know about her Shady Acres finances—how much was her lot rent? What fees did she have to pay for maintenance services, garbage pick up and the club/pool? Did she own her double wide or was it rented from Shady Acres? What was her mortgage payment since she was the owner? Did she have contact with the manager often and was he conscientious about answering complaints? Were there any special charges, particularly cash only charges? All the while the agent seemed to be inspecting the interior of her double wide, avoiding her eyes.

Sylvia became more anxious as he continued despite his assurance this interview wasn't about her tax return. The background he was collecting was aimed at her more than anything or anyone else. She tried to distract him in her trips back and forth serving the coffee, but he doggedly continued. Finally she blurted, "I thought this wasn't about my income taxes?"

"It's not," he answered as if surprised by her reaction. "This is background." He waved a hand, "Ah…I'm…ah…establishing a pattern, that is…a mosaic. Yes, a mosaic—" Then responding to her continued stare, he added, "You're one of a larger sample within Shady Acres. Ah…I can't be more precise. I hope you understand," he trailed off, seemingly caught between his inability to explain the situation and the restrictions of confidentiality.

After a short pause, his eyes focused on the wall behind her, then his face brightened with an apparent breakthrough, an idea, "You could consider yourself as sort of an agent—Yes, that's it. We need to find out things about the Shady Acres management/ownership team." He looked at her boldly, his blue eyes bright behind the rimless glasses.

Sylvia gave a shiver-like shake of her shoulders, causing a seductive sway below, an almost automatic reaction for her under the gaze of a man. Her mind, however, immediately focused on Harrigan. Maybe that $3,000 was for back taxes or a lawyer. Could she use that? Maybe she could get Harrigan to send Jake over to put in her chimes—She remembered the time Jake was under the sink fixing her clogged drain and got a warm feeling. This agent thing might work out—generate possibilities.

Agent Libertine watched her face, expectant—the first time he'd looked at her for more than five seconds. "Is Harrig—I mean the Superintendent of Shady Acres in trouble?" She asked.

As she returned his gaze, the IRS agent looked away coloring again. "Of course, I can't disclose information about a pending or potential case—you understand." Then that quick, meaningful look, straight out of the IRS Agent's Handbook she was sure.

"Yes," Sylvia said absently. "I suppose—"

"Then I can count on your support?"

Her thoughts still alternating between Harrigan and Jake, Sylvia said, "What?"

With a very sober look, emphasizing each word, "This, of course, must remain secret—you are now an unofficial agent of the US Government." He soft pedaled 'unofficial'. "I will be in touch." He started to rise.

"Wait! Wait!" Sylvia jiggled raising a hand from her wrap-around position, his statement pulling her from her reveries of sex and maneuvering Harrigan. "What do I do? And what about my protection as a government agent? A secret agent—I should at least have a code name."

"Secret Agent? Code name?" Agent Libertine gave her a blank look. "Code name?" He repeated softly. Rising slowly, he considered her request, his face expressionless, then with a look as if he were having an epiphany, a sharp nod of his head, "Yes. I suppose so. Any suggestions?"

Sylvia couldn't resist, sensing full control again. "How about Lolita?" She tried to hide a grin, standing opposite him at the butcher block table, her kimono pulled tightly around her.

The agent blushed and turned toward the door as if to deny her suggestion. Then after a long hesitation, turned back. "Yes…ah…that's fine…Lolita." He made a sick smile as new Secret Agent Lolita pranced ahead of him toward the door

"Don't forget your briefcase there." She pointed back to the table as he started to follow her, mesmerized.

'Secret agent Lolita!' Sylvia turned off the TV as she sat back on her plush sofa, pulling her legs under her like a bird sitting on a nest waiting for something to hatch. So Harrigan owed the IRS money—well maybe—Agent Libertine said the 'management/ownership team'. She had only seen Mr.Maggadole, the owner and Harrigan's father-in-law, a couple times. Mrs. Shanty said she didn't trust him, whatever that meant—he had nothing to do with the Shady Acres tenants directly nor for that matter did his daughter Madeline—Maddie as Harrigan referred to her. She knew there was more but her thoughts kept drifting with hot anticipation to the men available and how she might use her new status.

And Agent Libertine—he was a strange one. His shyness was intriguing.—a little boy looking though the window at all the candy. Had he ever seen a 'real' woman up close and in person before? She doubted it. The man blushed whenever she caught him starring—a good sign—innocence. Interested but uneducated.

She chuckled aloud visualizing what it would like teaching him what she liked and how she liked it, agent-to-agent, of course. Agent Lolita, could mold him exactly as she chose. He wouldn't be like Harrigan or even Jake—not that that was bad, oh no, deliciously different. Libertine was a new and exciting challenge. What if he was a virgin? Wouldn't that be fun?

She looked at the closet door concealing the Suzanne Somer's thighmaster and Butt master and the other exercise hardware. Maybe she'd give Harrigan a call this afternoon. She didn't have any manicure appointments and after a couple days she got edgy—

The loud buzzer reverberated though the double wide shocking her with its insistent rasp for the second time in the morning. Harrigan? She guessed who was at the door. After the first visitor anything was possible. Unfolding from her couch she headed for the door. Passing the window over the kitchen sink she glimpsed two men on the stoop and hastily drew the silk kimono around her.

The men were in work clothes, wearing silver painted hardhats with Maggedali Construction in Chinese red letters over the short brim. One was clean shaven, the other with a two day growth. She wrapped her arms around her middle. "Yes, what do you want?" she called through the storm door.

The clean shaven one spoke, as his partner nudged him in a not very subtle manner. "Sorry to bother you ma'am, we're from Maggedali Construction. The boss asked us to check out your gas stove—you been havin' any trouble with your's?"

Sylvia thought of Harrigan's call a couple days ago—something about a recalled part—his message garbled and confusing. She looked from one to the other and decided she'd rather deal with Harrigan than these two. "No, I've had no problems. I don't need you to look at my stove."

The clean shaven one looked pained. "Are you sure, Ma'am? It won't take long I promise. And the boss'll be mad if we don't check your stove—think we're not doin' our job—maybe come over here himself." The rough looking one mumbled something and looked at his feet.

Sylvia looked at both men again, carefully, then after a long hesitation, "OK, but make sure you wipe your work boots on the mat before you come in…and…Oh! Let me see some ID first." The last came with remembering a recent HOPE FOR TOMORROW episode.

The two men looked at each other blankly. Again the clean shaven one spoke, "Ma'am Maggedali Construction doesn't have passes—we checked in with the Shady Acres Super. Actually his wife—he wasn't available." The other man nodded dumbly.

"Sorry. Come back tomorrow. I got to check this out." She closed the front door in their bewildered faces. 'Check with the Super—You better believe it, Buster. I'll check with him all right.'

"Damn, woman! Do you always come to the door undressed?" Harrigan looked in both directions and hurried inside the double-wide, his heavy brows furrowed in disapproval.

Sylvia grinned at him, flipping the kimono in a suggestive motion. "You seem to like it."

"The door's open, people can see—" She grabbed him by the waist band and pulled.

"What are you doing?" He protested reaching into his hip pocket, his bald head sweating.

"Did you come to make a payment on the $3,000 you owe me?" She continued tugging at his waistband, drawing him past the kitchen.

"What? Listen a minute, will you?" He stopped moving. "I heard you had a visit this morning—"

"Oh, that guy," she thought of the bespectacled IRS agent. "that was nothing, I had the—" Secret Agent Lolita took over, "I had those guys pegged from the start. I didn't tell them anything," She started unbuckling his belt.

Harrigan was trying to mop his head with a handkerchief and grab Sylvia's busy hands at the same time. He apparently didn't notice Sylvia's slip, "What did they want?"

"They wanted to check out my..." she giggled allowing her hands to wander—noticing a growing response to her fumbling.

Harrigan shoved her against the wall, "STOP! Who were they?"

Surprised, Sylvia's eyes opened wide. He had never been rough before—this was exciting. "Didn't your wife tell you? Two guys from her father's construction outfit, Magg-something."

"Goddamit, what'd they say?" He held her against the wall pinching her shoulders, the kimono gapping open. Then one hand releasing for another quick swipe over his sweating head.

Sylvia smiled, she'd never seen Harrigan so forceful. 'Kinda nice, manly,' she thought. "Relax, Eddie boy, I told them to come back tomorrow after I checked with you." His grip eased and she took one of his hands and placed it on her bare breast. "Forget your troubles and just get happy—Now, you don't have any troubles do you?" He began to respond. She went to work on his belt again. "You can tell me Eddie—I know what you need. That's it. I can relieve all that tension...matter-of-fact I got a little tension build-up myself."

Although Harrigan rose to the occasion as usual, she didn't learn any more about his financial problems—the borrowed $3,000 still a mystery. Nor did he reveal why he started the gas stove inspection routine. Clearly, he was upset about both. Perhaps 'upset' wasn't strong enough. Could he be in trouble with the IRS or was it Mr. Magge-what's-his-face? The gas stove thing had to be some kind of cover-up. One thing, at least, she could have him relieve her edginess whenever she wanted now, a distinct change from his recent refusal to come near her double-wide for several weeks.

Next was to get her chimes. She bubbled at the thought. Harrigan had absently agreed to look into the problem and see about sending Jake over. He didn't promise—you had to pin Harrigan down—but the thought had been inserted. Della from HOPE FOR TOMMORROW would have been proud of her.

She felt so good she decided to have four peanut butter crackers with her milk and cottage cheese fruit salad for a late lunch. Maybe she'd get out the Thigh Master this afternoon.

It came to Sylvia as she was watching HOPE FOR TOMORROW. Della, at last, was wising-up. The guy she was sleeping with was cheating on her (like all the others) while stealing money from her for his wild schemes.

When he asked Della specifically for $3,000 to bet on the Perfecta, Sylvia heard chimes and not from her front door. As soon as her boyfriend left her apartment after breakfast, Della got on the phone and hired a Private Investigator. The over-night romp hadn't fogged her brain. Sylvia clapped, "Go girl! Way to go! That's showin' some smarts." As the program concluded with its theme music, she settled back in her big sofa to think. The stove problem was phony and Harrigan still owed her $3,000 and somebody in the management/ownership team was in trouble with the IRS.

Harrigan hadn't called or visited for almost a week—not at all what she'd envisioned. She called him once about fixing her chimes and got a curt answer. He was too busy. Agent Libertine hadn't been around either. All her leverage seemed to have evaporated and she was getting tired of the Thigh Master day after day without anyone to admire her progress. She needed a PI just like Della.

After a phone call or two Sylvia decided a real PI cost too much money—she may have a good bank account because of her recent inheritance from her favorite aunt and her manicure business was good—but neither could support $60 an hour and expenses with $300 minimum deposit up front—the cheapest offer she'd had. What was needed was a substitute and a little self-help, she decided. After all she was a secret IRS agent, sort of. And old Mrs. Shanty knew more about Shady Acres than anyone. Why couldn't she get what she wanted on her own? With the right information and little more Thigh Master they'd crawl, willing to do what she wanted.

Her start was miserable. Talking to Mrs. Shanty over the back fence after wading through the honeysuckle proved to be a disappointment. The woman ran on about the owner, Magg-what's-his name. All about the 'old days' before he had a construction company and Shady Acres was half as big as now. "Tony Maggedali is Sicilian, you know," she raised her eyebrows, "and connected...back in the 80's before the FBI crackdown." And she'd heard Maggedali Construction was in financial trouble with outstanding loans and slow housing sales.

Sylvia wasn't interested in the old lady's gossip, she wanted something she could use to get the IRS agent's attention or at least more on Harrigan. Then came the insult. Sylvia mentioned Harrigan and the old shrew gave her that insinuating look then something about the gas stove problem, adding, "—but I guess you already know all there is to know about that." After that and the lingering smile on the old widow's face, Sylvia decided maybe Mrs. Shanty knew too much.

Scratching her ankle, Sylvia realized she shouldn't have worn shorts on her foray to the back fence. Poison ivy. And she'd missed HOPE FOR TOMORROW. She tossed the Suzanne Somers Thigh Master to the other end of the sofa as she considered her next move.

She waited another day. Despite her desperation she had resisted calling Harrigan. Now, even with her legs coated in Calamine lotion to halt the Poison ivy's upward advance, she decided to confront him—get his attention. If nothing else she could demand some payment on his $3,000 loan—besides she wanted her chimes. She slipped into a pair of tan pedal-pushers and a sleeveless mauve, tank top to draw attention away from the chalky pink daubs around her ankles and open toed, leather sandals. After applying lipstick matching her shirt and a brush of her short, golden-brown hair, Sylvia checked the mirror—not too sexy but enough to remind Harrigan he'd been away too long.

At the Shady Acres office door, Sylvia turned the knob and plunged in with two sharp knocks. Standing directly in front of her, across the room, was a short, dark haired man with intense brown eyes focused sharply on her. Vaguely familiar, he was well dressed in an off white, linen suit and pastel blue tie. His face showed no surprise and was fixed as if chiseled from granite. To her left, Harrigan flipped a big green ledger book closed with a slap and started to rise from his old wooden desk, face pale, bald head beaded in sweat.

He was surprised. "Sylvia, er, Ms. Holbein...what are you doing here?" Then, recovering, Harrigan looked toward the shorter man, "Ah...excuse me, this is Mr. Maggedali, the owner of Shady Acres—" He made a weak gesture toward the man still staring at her.

Mr. Maggedali nodded. "We meet at last—You're the one who wouldn't let my men check your stove, right?" His face relaxed a little.

Disguising her shock as best she could, Sylvia met his penetrating gaze fully. "A girl can't be too careful these days—y'know?" How in hell was she going to confront Harrigan in front of this guy?

He looked her up and down. "Yes. I can see why you mighta been concerned with them pink-albino leopard spots." There was a parting of his lips that might have been a smile.

"Your men didn't have any identification," she flared, "Anybody could steal a couple construction hats or paint Maggadole on them—if they could spell it," she added as an aside.

"Maggedali…it's M-a-g-g-e-d-a-l-i," he almost whispered, instructional in his manner. "Perhaps you need to check your lot contract, it clearly—"

"Ah, tell me Sylvia, what can I do for you this fine morning?" Harrigan interrupted, rubbing his hands together. His color had returned and he was showing some teeth in a forced smile.

Before Sylvia could answer: "No matter. It's no matter. We've fixed the stove problem, haven't we Ed?" His voice was soft but his eyes were on Harrigan like hot pokers.

Harrigan: "Oh yeah—it's fixed all right." He coughed. "Go ahead Sylvia. You were about to say?"

Sylvia turned toward him, realizing at last, they'd been arguing before her abrupt entrance. "My chimes, remember? You said you'd send Jake over." She smiled sweetly, enjoying Harrigan's discomfort.

"Oh, thank you," Harrigan exaggerated, rubbing a hand across his bald head, "thank you for reminding me. I'll get him over there first thing tomorrow morning."

"Not till then? Couldn't you get him to come over today?" With a glance at Mr. Maggedali, "I've been waiting a week."

Harrigan grimaced, "Sorry, Jake's only available mornings. That's the work agreement we have." He looked at his wrist watch, "Too late this morning." A sick smile toward the owner.

Sylvia started to ask Harrigan about the money he owed her, hoping to embarrass him fully, but didn't—the phrase 'manager/owner team' used by Agent Libertine made her hesitate. That and Mrs. Shanty's long harangue. She wished now she had listened more closely. Instead she faced Mr. Maggedali's unwavering gaze, "Nice to meet you, I hope I didn't interrupt anything important," and turned to leave.

There was a dry chuckle, "Not at all, ma'am, I was just givin' Ed a little fatherly advice."

HOPE FOR TOMORROW opened with nurse Della in the isolation ward—as a bed patient! They were running tests for the SARS virus. Soon it was revealed she'd come down with flu-like symptoms over the weekend. Sylvia was absorbed in the drama as she absently scratched.

The buzzer, raucous, jolted her from the scene as Della moved languorously in a filmy nightgown, the covers well down, about to speak her first line. On the second buzz Sylvia punched the mute button on the remote, struggling out of the deep sofa. Because of the poison ivy she was wearing her old, faded purple, chenille bathrobe over a long cotton nightgown, her hair unbrushed. In fact she hadn't yet brushed her teeth. Wrapping the robe around her she hurried to the door, the buzzer blasting again as she passed the doorbell box in the hall. She covered her ears, cursing the device.

Jake stood at the glass storm door, broodingly handsome in his sleeveless muscle shirt, his lips pressed in a thin line.

Sylvia was overjoyed the instant before realizing how unkempt she looked. "Oh, Jake—you're my hero—come in…ah, Do you have my chimes?" She saw his bag of tools but no box or device that could or might be chimes.

He opened the door. "No, I have to look at the doorbell box first, maybe—"

"God, I look a fright—it's right down the hall here," she pointed ahead as she fled toward her bedroom. "I'll be with you in a minute or two—check it out," she tossed over her shoulder.

In the bedroom she pulled open her bureau drawer reaching for the black leotard—the one she wore when Jake was here last. She remembered how he looked at her then. As she threw the old faded chenille robe on the bed and the cotton nightgown after it, she glanced up, the full length mirror across the room reflected all her nakedness. The Calamine pink spots half way up her heavy thighs were like huge beacons against her white skin. "Oh, that'll never do," she murmured. She turned back to the bureau stuffing the black leotard in the half open drawer. Frantically, she ripped through the clothing; shorts, halters, one piece playsuits, nothing appropriate. In desperation she hurried to the closet and grabbed the dark blue Japanese kimono, flung it on and rushed into the adjoining bathroom, a big slug of mouthwash, and furiously began brushing her hair. The kimono half open, she turned from the bathroom after one last swish of the mouthwash. A wipe of the towel across her mouth and a glance in the full length mirror before bolting into the hallway for the living room. 'At least the Calamine spots won't be the first thing he sees,' she thought.

She crossed the living room eyes shining, ready for Jake.

The hallway was empty, the box for the doorbell in place. 'Where is he?' She looked back in the living room, even went back to her bedroom in hopes he might have gotten anxious and taken the lead, although she realized it was impossible not to have passed him enroute. There was no sign of him. She ran to the hallway, then for the kitchen, the entire front of her voluptuous body, spots and all, exposed, but no Jake. The storm door was hissing closed as she breathlessly reached the kitchen.

She flung open the storm door a few seconds later, heedless of her exposure. Jake was just turning off the bottom step of the stoop. "Jake!" She gulped air," Where are you going?" Another intake, "My chimes," she swallowed, "my chimes, what about my chimes?"

He turned, a lazy smile across his face. "You're in luck, they're fixed. I flipped the switch—that's all it took. Now everyone can ring your chimes—See ya." He half-waved and turned away, whistling.

"NBC!" Sylvia musically greeted Agent Libertine, "You're the first man to ring my chimes."

The Agent blinked a few times behind his rimless glasses, lost for a response. At least he didn't look away although Sylvia was wearing a tank top and shorts. Without moving to enter, as she held open the storm door, he spoke, "Is there some reason for your call Ms. Holbein?"

"Ssssh! Not on the stoop." Sylvia leaned out and looked carefully in both directions. "Agent Lolita, remember?"

The IRS agent rolled his eyes and entered the trailer. Turning toward her, his briefcase hugged to his chest, he asked, "What have you got?"

"Sit over there at the table," she indicted the butcher block table in the alcove across from the kitchen, "I'll fix some coffee. I thought you'd be back long before this to get better acquainted."

Agent Libertine took a couple hesitant steps toward the table, "The IRS frowns on us getting too close to our informants—"

"You mean like this?" She shimmied her breasts against him, nudging him toward the table.

He took two quick steps and went to the far side of the round table, a bushy fern to his back. "Agents can't have relationships with their co-workers either," he blurted, coloring slightly.

"But you said I was 'unofficial'—doesn't that mean the rules don't apply?"

"Ms. Holbein, why did you call me?"

Sylvia fixed two mugs of instant coffee. "Because I think you're cute when you blush like that," she giggled. "By the way—have you ever seen a strip tease?" A wicked smile.

"Please, I don't want to be rude but unless you have something related to our previous discussion about the management/ownership team here at Shady Acres, I'll have to leave."

The automatics again, right out of the Agent's Handbook. "OK." She set a hot mug in front of him and sat opposite with her own coffee, "Ya got me, Charlie—I've got plenty." She shivered seductively and laughed when he looked away. "You never have—have you?"

Agent Libertine looked back at her with a steely glance, "The IRS is about to charge Maggedali Construction with income tax evasion and fraudulent claims," he said heatedly. "What do you have to add to that?"

Sylvia hid her surprise with, "What about the Superintendent of Shady Acres, Mr. Harrigan?"

He squinted, suddenly more cautious, "We're still investigating."

"I know he had to borrow $3,000 recently—"

The Agent cut her off, nodding, "Gambling debt. He plays the horses. He's a real loser."

"Huh! He's more of a man than you are," she retorted with sudden vehemence. At once she bit her lip, surprised at her own lapse—this wasn't the way to get Agent Charles Libertine into bed.

"Really? You defend him? He's your idea of a real man?"

"What do you mean?" Sylvia expected to hear him say he knew where the $3,000 came from.

"He's also a thief," Libertine spat out. "He stole $2,000 from Shady Acres— more gambling debts." The agent threw up his hands, the only gesture she'd seen him make. "I must be going. Thank you for your help. I'll see myself out."

As he turned toward the door, Sylvia jumped up and grabbed him from behind by the seat of his pants and lifted—hard.

A peculiar sound wheezed from the surprised agent's lips as he experienced his first 'wedgy' and was propelled toward the door, barely maintaining his balance.

"I'd say I'm sorry if I thought you had any balls," Sylvia snarled, "But you haven't and I won't…" she finished as she shoved the agent through the storm door adding a push from her free hand.

TONY'S TORMENT— THE SHADY ACRES SHIMMY

"What do you mean you don't understand? What could be plainer, Ed?" Tony Maggedali screamed at Harrigan, his eyes boring into his son-in-law's. "In simple terms: do you want to lose your job managing Shady Acres for me?" His voice ended in a near whisper as Harrigan ran a hand over his thinning hair, his face blanched white.

There in Harrigan's office, the door closed shutting off the rest of the swank trailer and any chance of Maddie overhearing, Tony began to execute the first part of his plan: to get out of trouble with the IRS. "You think I want to see my daughter married to a failure?" His voice rose again and he pounded a fist on his son-in-law's desk. "Because he *doesn't understand*?" He mocked the now sweating superintendent of Shady Acres, the most up scale trailer park in the city. "I don't have a job for you at Maggedali Construction. You have to get this done here— *capisca*?"

Harrigan nodded, the movement barely perceptible as if he was holding his breath.

"First, you need to form an organization—get one of the tenants to act as the president and become the Shady Acres Limited Partners. Then we sell Shady Acres shares to them—a percentage of the total property value and we raise enough money to get Shady Acres out of this lousy IRS trap.

"Unfair, as it is, I'd fight them in court but there isn't time—we need action, **now**. You need to get on this right away. Now, who have you got for President?" He leaned over Harrigan's desk challenging him.

Harrigan sat there behind the desk in his squeaky, wooden, swivel chair, his mouth gaping like a gaffed fish, "Ah…ah, I'll have to go over the tenant roster." He mopped his balding scalp.

Tony could see Harrigan was totally lost, intimidated by the task and frightened—just the way he wanted him to be. "What about that bimbo who interrupted us last week when we were discussing the gas stove problem—the **non-existing** gas stove problem **you** created. That. incidentally, could have panicked the whole park if word had gotten out." He knew Harrigan had over reacted to something. Luckily Maddie had called him while Harrigan was out stirring up trouble and he'd been able to get the situation under control before half of Shady Acres was alarmed and thinking the trailer park was unsafe or worse. With tenants like Charlene Shanty you never knew—the woman was a gossip of the first order as well as a shrew.

"You mean, Syl—" Harrigan cleared his throat, getting back to the question, "ah…Ms. Holbein, as president?"

"Yeah, that's the one—" Tony chuckled, "bounced in here like she owned the place…couldn't pronounce Maggedali—spunky kinda girl—big—big tits," he held his hands in front of his chest for emphasis.

Harrigan half-smiled and looked down at his desk, hiding his expression, "Oh, I don't know…she wouldn't suit…no business head. Maybe Ms. Romaine, the realtor—"

"Ed!" he cut him off, "You're missing the point…she's exactly who we want," he looked hard into his son-in-law's face, "You read me?"

Caught in the surgical beam of his father-in-law's eyes, Harrigan closed his mouth and tried to swallow, nodding his head.

"Of course, there's a stipend that goes with the job," Tony grinned, relaxing his piercing gaze.

"Ah…ah, a what?—oh yeah that…" he caught Tony's inflection. "How much?"

Tony looked around as if someone might be eavesdropping on the other side of the closed door or the room might be 'bugged'. "Couple a thou', maybe more, whatever she needs to…" he raised his eyebrows for emphasis, "to be cooperative," he hissed. Then, straightening abruptly, "Within reason, of course."

Harrigan took on a crafty look, he was in synch, at last. Tony heaved a sigh. This was such tedious business with his son-in-law—not like dealing with his construction crew who were much more savvy. Maybe he was holding out—more money? "You got something goin' with this broad?" His look hardened.

Harrigan made a face, that 'aw'shucks me?' look Tony had seen before, "You don't want her askin' a lot o' questions do you?"

"What d'ya mean? This deal is legit," Tony winked, "—right?"

The conflict within Harrigan flashed across his face like the lights on a movie marquee. Tony was pleased. Ed was on board but tentative, sure but uncertain, confident but scared, firm as Jell-O—perfect. "Now go talk to Madam President and feel her out, give her a little hint, a warm feeling—not too much—and get her on board the team, understand? We'll give her some details soon."

Harrigan's eyes narrowed, he became tough detective Sam Spade in spirit as he met his father-in-law's purposeful look. "Yes, sir. She's all mine."

"Good. I'm glad you understand how important this is," he reached across the desk and slapped Ed on his shirt-sleeved shoulder with a loud smack. "See you Sunday for supper."

Tony walked to his Mercedes in front of the superintendent's trailer, his brow furrowed. At best he'd made a shaky beginning to solving the IRS problem. He felt the sun penetrating his white linen suit, accelerated by the high humidity—'heat and pressure, just like the IRS,' he thought.

He needed over one hundred thousand to satisfy the judgment or go to court and fight the claim—a fight he knew he couldn't win.

Although he didn't think they would add jail time, that had been a threat from Agent Charles Libertine.

If he could sell shares to a limited partnership and raise a few thousand, that would provide cover. Then he could funnel in cash from Maggedali Construction and pay the whole thing off, side stepping any real penalties from the IRS. At least that was his plan. Of course, there was a bind—cash flow—he could only raise about fifty thousand comfortably from his construction company within the time limit.

'Better make that a hard sell to the tenants,' he thought realizing Harrigan was central to his efforts dealing with the tenants whether he liked the idea or not.

Starting the car, he turned the AC on high as he checked in the mirror to make a U turn back toward the fancy field stone entrance to Shady Acres.

He needed to look into the state thing about some new highway construction near Shady Acres. There might be some potential work there for Maggedali Construction. A lucrative contract to supply concrete would be ideal. Perhaps Shady Acres was near the right of way, and he could sell the property, certainly he couldn't use it as a write-off for Maggedali Construction any longer, the IRS had seen to that.

Another possibility, the city-county recently declared the landfill, three miles down the road. would close in two years. Since a new site would have to be found and land near Shady Acres had been considered once before the park might come up again in the search to locate a new landfill.

As he drove clear of the decorative stone entrance to the trailer park, Tony began to think back over almost twenty years. Charlene Shanty—recently widowed at the time—she was hot, as they liked to say now. Their affair had been torrid for a brief period—long enough for him to come to his senses and stop thinking with his dick. The sense of her and the lust he felt were easily revived. Fortunately, he remembered he had a family to consider and needed to make a living. Maggedali Construction was a budding dream at the time. There was no sense in risking it all for some woman with hot pants even if she did talk of marriage. He wondered what risk she might pose now. This organization, which he planned to turn into a legal Limited Partnership, he was trying to get Harrigan to start with the tenants would surely involve her. Charlene was an activist and talked a lot, although she hadn't said anything to harm him over the past years. He realized he needed to be cautious. That and knowing Harrigan probably couldn't pull this scheme off by himself. Most likely, Tony would have to expose himself to the tenants at some point. 'I gotta stay out o'this as much as possible—let Harrigan be the buffer.' he decided.

Sunday was a miserable day. Under low, threatening clouds, the showers began at daybreak and continued on though the day. Maddie and Harrigan arrived at his-father-in-law's house right after a heavy downpour. Tony greeted them at the door, "Hi, nice weather we're having." He hugged his daughter laughing at his weak joke, and took her umbrella and put it in the stand in the corner next to the front door. "Ed, how's it going?" He grinned up at a dead pan Harrigan.

As was their custom the two men went off to the parlor for a before supper drink while Maddie went to greet her mother, brother and sisters in the dinning room—kitchen area.

Drinks in hand, Tony wasted no time. "So, Ed, were you able to get that Holstein dame on the team?"

"Excuse me?" After a few seconds, Harrigan's blank look dissolved, "Oh, right,…you mean Ms. Holbein? I did mention the idea but she had a lot of questions…you said—"

"Come on, Ed!" Tony's exasperated look registered.

Harrigan looked away as if searching for the right words. "She's hung up on a TV soap and Della, the main character, recently found out her boyfriend embezzled a lot of money from the bank he works for and—"

"Ed, what the fuck has that got to do with anything? For crissakes." Tony slammed his glass down on the little built-in bar slopping bourbon and water all over the fine walnut finish. "What did I tell you?"

Harrigan rubbed a hand over his scalp. "Money. She wants money," he rolled his eyes. "She thinks this soap opera is real. Right now anything with 'legal' involved anywhere, she…" he dropped off unable to explain how Sylvia's favorite soap influenced her thinking.

"Where does money come into it?" Tony controlled his voice. "How much money?" Now he began wiping the bar with a terrycloth towel. Reluctantly, he realized he had to give Harrigan more of the details, now that the plan was more resolved in his own mind—he'd been thinking of little else since their last meeting. "Ed, come over here and sit down." This was a first—something they never did. As long as the Sunday suppers had been a ritual, not once had Harrigan been invited to sit down. Always it was a 'men's get together' with Harrigan and Tony standing near the small built in bar, under the perfect rows of books in the formal bookcase, and discussed world affairs or whatever Tony wanted to discuss.

For the next ten minutes Tony explained the Limited Partnership plan to Harrigan, cautioning him to tell Sylvia Holbein only as much as necessary to get her ready to sign the papers. "Ed, you got to sell this. She's got to want to sign up as President and be a salesman—salesperson—to sign others up to buy shares in Shady Acres—one thousand bucks a share. Now, most important, how much will it take to get her on board?"

"You mean a…a bribe?"

Tony looked at him, his patience running thin. "What did **you** just say?"

"Oh, yeah. Ah…ah, three thousand."

"Now, see, that wasn't hard, was it?" Tony forced a smile. "You're sure, you can get her for that?" There was still some 'sweetener' left for persuasion but Ed didn't need to know about that yet.

"Yes, sir. I can get her for that." He sipped his gin and tonic for the first time.

"All right. Keep in mind, your goal, you and Madame President, is fifty thousand or more. That's fifty shares in Shady Acres, one share sold for at least half of all Shady Acres tenants. There might be another small bonus if you two can reach that goal in the next week—ten days at the outside—right?" he pointed his little finger off his highball glass at the now sweating Harrigan. Then raising his glass, "To Shady Acres Limited Partners."

Harrigan raised his glass, the look on his silent face almost peaceful, no apparent conflict within.

Tony wasn't sure he liked Harrigan so calm, "Once more Ed, deliver the goods. No stumbling, no hesitation we gotta beat the IRS—right?"

"Right." Harrigan replied, unruffled.

"Let's go eat." Tony put his glass down on the bar, unsure what had come over Harrigan—was it the three thousand? Was Ed, sandbagging him? He started calculating how he could check on Harrigan.

Harrigan's acid reflux was quiet. For the first time in recent memory he had actually enjoyed supper at his father-in-law's—well maybe not enjoyed—he wasn't as depressed or as uneasy as usual. He even loved his wife, Maddie, after they had undressed for bed—a Sunday night, all time first.

The very first thing he did though when they got home was lock the three thousand and the legal paperwork Tony had given him in the bottom drawer of his office desk.

Maddie had accepted his brief explanation about the Limited Partnership except when he mentioned Ms. Holbein as the President. Very carefully he told of how her father had insisted on Sylvia Holbein to be the President of the Limited Partners against his advice. When she asked why, he shrugged, "I don't know" and shifted the conversation to the overall plan, "Tony probably needed some capital for the construction company what with those houses in the new subdivision unsold."

Harrigan tried to follow his father-in-law's example not to involve the family females in business.

Conveniently, Tony had solved a worrisome problem for Harrigan. Now he could go over to Sylvia's without inventing some excuse or sneaking over when Maddie was out shopping. Best of all, and a great relief, Tony had provided the money to repay the three thousand dollars he owed Sylvia—borrowed to cover his gambling debts. Tony's bribe to sell Limited Partner shares could work for him as well as bind Sylvia to the deal, he was certain. Besides he knew what Sylvia really wanted—and he'd give it to her. Then she would be the President if Harrigan asked her.

The next morning after what he thought was an appropriate delay for Maddie's sake, shuffling papers and acting busy, Harrigan left the Superintendent's trailer via the office door and headed for 629 Floral Avenue, Sylvia's. The three thousand bulged in his pants pocket and he had the rolled legal papers establishing the Limited Partnership stuffed in his hip pocket. He had rehearsed what he was going to say and, more importantly, the timing and sequence of his actions which he knew would be most important.

There was no doubt in his mind that Tony would somehow slither out of this IRS problem and if anyone got hurt it would be him not Tony. Somehow he had to avoid that even if he had no idea how. First, he had to get Sylvia.

"Oh, Harrigan, what a pleasant surprise," Sylvia held the storm door open for him. "You're early—what's up?"

Typically, Sylvia was wrapped in her fancy, Japanese kimono loosely tied at the waist. To Harrigan, she represented a Christmas present from overseas, ready to be unwrapped. All he had to do was pull the string. "I couldn't wait to see you," he said with a wide smile, pushing her away from the door. "I even have a surprise for you."

"What?" She faced him, radiating pleasure, standing close enough to encourage his hands.

He pulled her to him and kissed her lightly. "I have some money for you," kissing her again, a little more emphasis. He knew it wouldn't take much to arouse her yet he had to control himself and not rush. "A lot of money," he kissed her cheek and slid down her neck—'not too fast' flashed through his head, his erection growing. Then down inside the kimono, a couple flicks with his tongue then remembering his caution, back up, his own excitement rising with Sylvia's. She was breathing hard now.

"Oh, Eddie…What are you talking about?" She pulled back and he realized he was caught like a circus rider with one foot on each of two horses galloping around the center ring, disaster lurking if the horses split. One horse was all he could ride at a time to carry out his intention.

"Can't talk now, I'm too hot for you." He pulled the kimono apart and went for those huge, milky orbs, postponing his real purpose while cautioning himself to go slow until she was ready and led him to the bedroom. His ambivalence also reflected the reversal of their usual pattern as his own passion began to overwhelm him.

Lying naked together on her bed, Harrigan ran his hand over her wet belly, "I've got your three thousand. How about that?"

"Harrigan. You're full of surprises. That last one was terrific," she humped playfully into his hand, "what's the catch?" She laughed at her nonsequitur.

He hesitated, the sequence he planned had begun. She was now supposed to be 'ready' for the follow-on, but her off-hand reaction was too close to the mark, unsettling. He ran his hand up over a generous nipple, "I do need a favor—sort of the reason why I was able to pay off what I owe you." Now he had to keep his hand on her sex, keep her warm and fuzzy, anticipating more, knowing she was easily aroused more than once. A more positive approach, his intention.

Sylvia rolled up on one elbow toward Harrigan forcing him back on his back, her ponderous breasts slapping his chest as they followed gravity. "You mean all of this," she grabbed him between the legs, "was a setup?" Her voice was no longer soft or warm with anticipation.

Out of desperation, he cupped one breast in his hand, he couldn't fail now. "Sylvia this is a terrific deal—Maggedali's in a jam—he has to sell part of Shady Acres and—"

"What? You mean the IRS finally got him?" She surprised him, giving his testicles a firm squeeze.

She knew as much as he did, it seemed. Unable to stick to his rehearsed line, he blurted, "Would you rather have the IRS as your landlord? And sell Shady Acres to the highest—"

"What difference would that make?"

"I wouldn't be superintendent, for sure," he uttered in an unconscious moment of truth. "Rates might change, ah,…" He wasn't prepared—this wasn't going at all as he rehearsed, "Tony wants you to be President of the Shady Acres Limited Partners." Quickly, he went on to explain that 25% of Shady Acres was available at $1000. per share with one hundred shares for sale. "We need to sell at least fifty shares this week." he concluded, realizing how lame his explanation sounded.

"This week!" She rolled back down on her back, "Why me? Oh, why me?" She sighed.

Harrigan quickly followed her body with active hands, "He was impressed with you," he whispered after sensing her arousal. "that time down at the office—remember?"

She sighed, "Damn you, Harrigan, why do you have to be so good in bed?" She squeezed him again.

He grazed both nipples with his palm, knowing he'd won, no matter how much she might argue and grumble over the details.

'**Yes!**' Somewhere inside he crowed, 'It worked'. He really did know what she wanted and that would save his job. Now all he had to do was satisfy her and seal the deal.

Tony rang the bell. To his surprise, the door opened instantly. She stood there, staring at him, impassive, "Well, if it isn't the phantom owner of Shady Acres." Her face was fixed, her eyes penetrating. "What do you want?" she snapped.

Tony looked at her, searching for the right approach. "Hello, Charlene, how are you?"

"Twenty years older and a lot smarter than the last time you saw me—as if that makes any difference to you."

"I did what I had to do—what I thought was right," he reached to straighten his tie. "Can I come in?"

"Aren't you afraid someone will see you and start rumors?"

"No, I—"

"Well, I am. So state your business." she folded her arms across her chest.

Embarrassed and angered, he turned away then back again—.

"Tony! Tony! Wake up! What's'a matter with you? You eat too much lasagna?"

Her poke brought him upright. In the predawn light he looked in her face, answering Charlene Shanty…"You witch, you're," mumbling, "—oh. Anna, I…I musta…A dream…some witch chasin' me."

"Witch? What witch? Who? You want something'—maybe a glass o'warm milk?" She started to throw off the covers.

"No. no…it's nobody. Go back to sleep. What time is it?"

"You sure?" She was sitting up, looking at him, then turned to the luminous dial alarm clock on the beside table, "Almost five." She yawned, settling back.

"Last time I read Shakespeare before bed," he mumbled as he got up and pulled his robe around him. Shuffling into his slippers, his thoughts were fleeting and multiple but Shakespeare wasn't among them—'Harrigan. Gotta check on that fool somehow'.

✶   ✶   ✶   ✶

Without a conscious plan, Tony found himself driving slowly around Shady Acres, ignoring the lush greens of the trees and the well-kept lawns. 'There has to be a way.' He turned passed the cub house/swimming pool area down Hyacinth Lane. Ahead he could see a man in jeans and undershirt raking the stone drive to one of the trailers. 'Is that what's-his-name, the handyman? The one Harrigan mentioned when that woman, Holstein no Holbein, came over asking about her chimes.' He slowed, lowering the passenger side window. "Excuse me, aren't you the handyman who works for Superintendent Harrigan?"

"Can I help you?" He came to the car window.

"Get in, I want to talk to you for a few minutes. Put your rake down, have a seat I'm Tony Maggedali, the owner." He held out his hand as the handyman got in.

"I'm Jake." They shook hands.

"Tell you what, Jake—You might be able to help me. See, I'm tryin' to get a feel for some of Shady Acres' tenants—gotta couple projects where I may need some support from responsible, informed and intelligent folks. Know what I mean?" He locked into the younger man's eyes. "You probably know some of them. Maybe you could give me your impressions"

Jake returned his stare, his face blank.

"Nothing I'd hold you to, understand—I don't know any of these people…" Jake's expression didn't change. "I don't want to go over Ed's head or anything, but I'd like to get a different slant, OK?"

Jake rubbed the sweat off his forehead. "Well, sir. I'll give you my impression, but I…."

Tony held up a hand, "Fair enough,. I have to start somewhere. How about this woman, the realtor ah…ah—"

"Ms. Romaine?"

"Yeah, that's her."

For the next fifteen minutes or so they talked or rather Tony asked questions and Jake replied—briefly. All too briefly to suit Tony. He went through all the names he could remember and got nothing of significance, much less any tidbit that reflected on Harrigan and the Holbein woman. He even asked about Mrs. Shanty to no avail.

Driving away, he concluded Ms. Romaine threw herself into her work. She was the only one Jake seemed to know much about. Tony was a little surprised that she used Jake to witness some of her legal paperwork in selling homes. Perhaps he might be able to use her to dig into the future plans the state had for road construction in the area. She might know somebody on the planning board. He could even throw a bone her way and sign up with that rinky-dink real-estate outfit she worked for, enhance her commission a bit if she could learn anything. Hell, she might even sell one of those $250k houses he had been trying to unload for six months.

Frustrated and feeling morose, he parked in front of the Super's trailer—time to shake Ed out of his lethargy.

He opened the office door without bothering to knock. "Morning Ed, how's it goin'?" He turned to see Ed stretched out behind his wooden desk, his feet crossed over a desk corner, the radio playing a sixties song by the Mills Brothers. Harrigan came from his relaxed position upright with a loud squeak of his swivel chair in a flurry of arms and legs. "Jesus! Mary and Joseph!" he gasped, clutching his chest.

Noting the roll of bills on the desk, "Haven't you given that broad the dough, yet?"

"What?" Harrigan looked around wide eyed, then recovering slightly, "Oh, that?"

"Yeah, **that**." Tony moved toward the desk, pushing the door to the rest of the trailer closed.

A cheesy smile, "That's our first limited partner, three shares."

"Looks like the three thou I give you for what's-her-name—the one to be president of the investment group."

"It is. She invested her fee." A forced laugh.

Digesting that information, Tony realized he'd just given away a piece of Shady Acres, in fact bought it for someone else. "Where's the money from the other shares? How many have you two sold? Have you issued the stock certificates?" He tried to cover his chagrin.

"Well, ah…ah," a swipe over his baldness, "as a matter-of-fact, ah…ah—"

"You haven't sold any, have you?" Tony felt his face flaming.

"We're planning to set up a tenant's meeting to announce the stock sale, ah…ah, sort of our own IPO." Ed gave him that cheesy smile again.

"When? When are you going to do it—next week, for crissakes?" All of the frustrations of the morning were right there before him in his hapless son-in-law. Nothing accomplished, yet he sat there daydreaming in his damned, squeaking, swivel chair. "If you'd get up off your ass, you'd have sold ten or twenty shares by now." Without waiting for a reply he stormed out of the office, angry with himself for losing his temper. If pushed too hard, Ed would simply lock-up and choke like a machine flooded with fuel.

And then there was Maddie. He didn't want her to suffer as a result of breaking Ed down. At best he wasn't much but Tony lived with his daughter's choice of the man—marriage was a sacred institution…' we all have to live with our mistakes,' he thought, a vision of young Charlene Shanty flashing through his mind.

✳   ✳   ✳   ✳

Tony sat in the back of the well appointed meeting room of the Shady Acres club house. Beside him Maddie sat quietly, hands folded in her lap, watching her husband and Sylvia seated near the podium at the front of the room. "You OK baby?"

She smiled at him, her dark eyes shinning. "Yeah, Daddy, I'm fine. I hope the meeting goes well. Ed and that woman, Sylvia Holbein, have worked hard to get the word out and prepare for this meeting." She turned more toward him to look at him directly "Daddy, did you really recommend her?"

He chuckled, "Yeah, baby." he shrugged, "She was the only one I'd met in Shady Acres," he grinned, a bit sheepish, "We needed to make this limited partner offering tenant involved—give them a warm feeling—not corporate—*capisca?*"

Maddie laughed softly, "Yeah, I *capisca*,"

The room was filling and few paid any attention to Tony and his daughter sitting in the back. Tony noted Mrs. Shanty, Charlene, slide into the second row of the padded folding chairs, ignoring him completely. With perhaps thirty people scattered over the front part of the meeting room, Harrigan rose to begin the meeting.

In five minutes he covered the basics of the stock offering and the potential benefits to the new stockholders. His words were a repeat of the information on the fliers many had brought with them. There were a few questions which he answered rewording most of what he'd already said. Then Mrs. Shanty stood and asked: "What influence will the limited partners have on the management of Shady Acres? And will the books be open to their inspection?"

Tony sucked in a breath through tight lips.

Harrigan smiled and looked at Sylvia Holbein, the answer so obvious. "Well, of course," he began, "we **are** talking about **a limited partnership** here so management will continue as it is at present. As for the books, ah…ah they will probably be open to inspection at the end of the **next** fiscal year."

Without hesitation she came back, "What, then, is the advantage to owning shares in this limited partnership?"

"Dividends—those dividends based on the number of shares and the operating profits of Shady Acres at the end of the next fiscal year. Then too if Shady Acres is ever sold they would be worth 25% of the sale price after expenses, taxes etc, so there might be some profit over and above the $1000 cost."

Tony let his breath out. Harrigan was holding his own but after two further questions by Mrs. Shanty there was a long, awkward pause—no one said anything—the details totally covered. Tony looked around considering. What could he do to generate some activity? At this rate the meeting would be over in five minutes or less and it didn't appear anyone was ready to buy.

Before he could think of anything, Sylvia Holbein was on her feet next to Ed, her face filled with a look of anticipation, apparently some secret she couldn't hold back any longer. "I have it from a very good source," she announced, "as a special incentive, that those who purchase shares within the next week will get $50 off their lot rent for the next three months for each share they buy." She beamed at Harrigan's look of total surprise as if revealing a very generous streak he was too modest to openly acknowledge.

"Personally," she continued, turning back to the seated tenants with another secret, "I've already bought three shares and plan on buying two more—How 'bout you?" She threw her arms toward the audience as if to embrace them.

Alarmed, Tony grunted, then started to rise, about to shout something when he realized the audience was engaged. There was a buzz of discussion as couples and individuals began to turn to each other, considering this more immediate benefit that the Limited Partners President had thrown out to the group. He sat down with a sigh and began to mentally calculate the cost of madam president's generosity.

Harrigan recovered after a long, dumfounded look into Sylvia's smiling face. He turned back to the now active audience, "Folks, there you have it. There's no time to waste. This is a bargain, a pay off as soon as you sign up." He spoke in his best carnival style, "Your money is earning interest in advance. How 'bout **that**! Step up here and buy or reserve your shares, now."

Tony recognized Harrigan's cheesy smile; 'damn, that broad I chose to be president made this up on her own—this could cost up to $5000 a month for three months'.

Maddie looked at him, her face alight. "Oh, Daddy that's a wonderful idea—you're so generous. That ought to convince the tenants you're sincere on this offering."

"Yeah," Tony said, "—wonderful."

People were beginning to approach Harrigan and Sylvia at the card table set up in front to record the sales of shares in Shady Acres.

With his thoughts in turmoil, Tony rose and leaned over to kiss his daughter. "Tell Ed I'll check with him tomorrow morning on how the sales went. Goodnight, honey."

Driving home, Tony went over the events since he'd initiated his idea to sell stock in Shady Acres to get out of trouble with the IRS. He needed at least $50,000 from that stock sale to be able to meet the assessed IRS penalty. The rest of the money he intended to raise from Maggedali Construction. He hadn't counted on losing $15,000 from the Shady Acres lot rental money. That would drag down his cash flow at the most critical time—right after paying off the IRS penalty fine. He needed a little more cushion. Selling one or two of those new houses, he'd been trying to sell for six months, would make a big difference, adding almost $100,000 down stream. With that money, to bridge the gap, he would have no worries—the IRS fine would be paid with no cash flow problems.

For the future, he needed to get that realtor woman, the one the maintenance guy told him about, on board. He'd probably have to offer her an 'incentive' to get her attention but that was the only way to get things done in a hurry. He had a lot of practice offering 'incentives', it all depended on the person—most of the time money was the key but you never knew, some people were peculiar.

Following a recent pattern, Tony spent a restless night, filled with lurid dreams of empty, unfulfilled promise. He rose early, insisting Anna stay in bed and not bother with getting his breakfast—he wasn't hungry, he'd stop at Krispy Kreme for doughnuts and coffee on his way over to Shady Acres.

He read the paper; he lingered over his coffee; he even talked with the store manager about business and how Krispy Kreme was doing in the stock market and still he arrived at the Shady Acres office at ten minutes to eight. The door was locked. Tony pounded on the hollow metal door until Harrigan, sleepy eyed, coffee mug in hand, opened it. "What? Are ya already restin' on your laurels?"

Harrigan blinked a few times, moving slowly to his totally clean wooden desk. "The news is good, Tony." He sat in his squeaky wooden, swivel chair carefully setting his coffee mug down on the desk. He looked at his father-in-law as he sipped the coffee with a big slurp, "We sold 43 shares last night, including the pledges—that's 46 total."

Tony remained standing in front of the old desk. "How many pledges?"

"Oh, ten to fifteen, I'm not sure of the exact count," he half smiled, "And there's at least ten more we need to follow up—the 'maybes'."

Tony was both surprised and angered—the anger won out. "Well, why aren't you and Madam President on the phones following them up?"

"We're going to do better than that," he answered after another noisy sip, "We're going to visit each prospect over the next two days and give'em the full treatment. Sylvia says she saw something on her morning soap that'll fit right in with—"

"For crissakes, Ed, this is business, not make believe—we need to get the money in five days." Tony felt his face flushing. Ed was so damned calm.

"Look," Harrigan squirmed in his chair with a big squeak digging a ring of keys out of his pants pocket. "Wait till you see this." He bent over inserting one of the keys in a wooden drawer. Shortly, he sat upright, his face red with the effort, and tossed a bundle of checks bound with a green rubber band on the empty desk top. "Thirty thousand dollars."

Impulsively, Tony reached for the small bundle.

"I'll need a receipt."

Tony looked at his son-in-law for a long moment, Sicilian eyes penetrating, then began to count the checks without disturbing the green rubber band. "There's thirty one—"

Harrigan shrugged. "I rounded it off." He took a big gulp of coffee, settling back in the swivel chair with another loud squeak.

Gritting his teeth, "Write it up, I'll sign a receipt," Tony said as he began to recount the check amounts.

As Ed pulled a blank piece of paper from his desk, Tony satisfied himself on the count—it was thirty one thousand—and thought of the 'other' business he needed to set up with the realtor. "Ed, this dame that sells real estate, was she at the Limited Partners meeting last night?"

Distracted, Harrigan looked up, then returned to the receipt he was writing, "No."

Tony waited for more, then after a long pause, "You surprised by that?"

"No."

"What's she like anyway?"

Harrigan finished the receipt and turned the paper toward his father-in-law pushing the pen across the desk. Absently, "I dunno…she's the kind of tenant you like to have—first class. She and the other one, who **was** there last night. Maybe you saw her—dressed to the nines, very striking—reserved five shares."

"What's her name?"

"Who?"

"The realtor—who do you think?"

"Oh. That's Ms. Romaine, nice lady, she's—"

"That's the one." Tony grabbed the paper and signed it in a rush, shoving it back toward Harrigan brusquely, almost throwing the ball point at him. "Yeah! Spare me the build up. Set up an appointment with her today—as soon as possible."

Harrigan blinked, frowning, "I don't know what her schedule—"

"Now, Ed! Pick up the phone and get to it."

"I could ask her to come up to the office," Harrigan said as he reached for the card index of tenants.

"No. I want to meet her over at the club house—privately."

Harrigan's expression didn't change but Tony knew he was dying to know what business he had with the lady realtor. As far as Tony was concerned, Harrigan would remain that way. He intended to keep his dealings with Ms. Romaine secret along with his future plans.

✳   ✳   ✳   ✳

Sitting in front of him was a slender woman in tan slacks with an open, matching jacket, an old fashioned, frilly, high necked, white blouse with a large brown and white cameo at the throat and a copper road runner pin on the left breast of the jacket that matched the highlights of her upswept hair. From her snake skin pumps to her dark brown eyes, Ms. Romaine was striking, her demeanor implied awareness and self confidence.

With a certain caution, he began. "Ms. Romaine as a businessman I have to look to the future in order to set a course for Shady Acres that will allow for all possibilities, yet continue to move in a positive direction. I understand you didn't attend the tenant's meeting on the limited partner's stock offering last evening." She nodded, "May I ask, why?"

There was a brief smile, nice even teeth, "I wasn't interested." Her body seemed to straighten in the club chair, perhaps poised to make a quick departure.

"Please. This isn't a sales pitch," he held up a hand, "I was giving an example of what I meant about preparing for the future." She crossed her legs, slender ankles exposed. "You work for Headliner Realty I understand."

"Yes, and I'm late for—"

"Hear me out, Ms. Romaine, it may be worth your while in the long run. I can't make promises before I get to know you better, but I may be able to throw some business your way if…" he paused, a new thought crossing his mind "I figured since you live in Shady Acres and I own the park we might be able to work together for the future benefit of the park. As you know I'm selling 25% interest in the park to the tenants under this limited partnership deal—you interested?" He locked onto her eyes hoping he hadn't been in too much of a hurry—he had to be careful; dealing with a business woman was not an everyday thing with him.

"Are we talking real estate or limited partnership?" Her expression was open, business-like.

He skirted the question. "Do you know anyone on the state highway commission?"

She considered that without looking away, "Not off-hand. That's a pretty big office—if I had a roster of people, maybe—what are you looking for?"

"As I said, I'm looking ahead for Shady Acres." Tony decided to gamble. "Any construction plans the Department has that might effect the park would, of course, be important to our future—" pausing, "yours and mine," he added, hoping to appeal to her own needs.

"Why don't you just ask them?"

"I've tried that without success," he lied. "Their usual answer is 'when future plans are firmed up the communities affected will be notified in due time.' Of course their 'due time' is always too late to make adjustments and realize the maximum benefit from the information—the deals are already set."

"What deals?"

Tony looked away. "The most obvious is the right of way—where do they intend to route future construction. Then, of course, there's the construction contracts and material suppliers." He engaged her eyes again. "I'm in the construction business—I guess you know."

"Yes—how does this involve me?"

"If I know where and when, I might be able to confirm or put to rest any rumor going around."

"And you want me to find out—"

Tony, nodding, "I have some new homes that need an aggressive real estate agent to get them sold.—they're in the range of $250k and up. With the right information I might be willing to add 1% to the commission you're getting at Headliner Realty—in fact they don't need to be involved at all, if you prefer."

"That's an interesting proposition," she smiled, "let me think about it awhile."

Tony was sure he saw something in those lovely eyes when he mentioned the homes he had for sale. "Don't wait too long Ms. Romaine…a little research on the state highway commission might help too," he said gruffly, then reached inside his suit jacket and withdrew a business card. "You can reach me at the bottom number. Oh, and let's keep our little conversation here confidential—no need to fuel any rumors that might be floating around. Agreed?"

"Agreed." She offered her hand as they both stood up.

✳   ✳   ✳   ✳

Tony was in high spirits, he even smiled at IRS Agent Libertine who was a witness to his payment of the fees and penalty due the US government as a result of his investigation of Maggedali Construction. "Now, let's see, how much is the total?" He asked with a big grin.

"One hundred three thousand, four hundred fifty three dollars and sixty seven cents, sir," the clerk read from the court document in front of him.

Rattling the change in his pants pocket, Tony withdrew a handful of coins and carefully counted out.67 cents, "There you are young man. That's a down payment," he started to turn away as if the transaction was completed, then turning back, "Oh yes, that's right, you'll need a check for the rest, won't you?." He glanced at Agent Libertine who's mouth was pressed in a straight, thin line. Tony reached into his suit jacket and pulled out a check made out to the US Treasury for $103,453.00. "There you are. Have a nice day," he beamed at the IRS Agent as he turned to leave.

With great relief Tony tripped down the steps of the Federal building, his spirits singing. The sour look on Agent Libertine's face was in his mind, a pleasurable reminder he had escaped any jail time which he knew the agent was planning as the next step if he couldn't come up with the back taxes and penalty by the expiration of the time limit.

All this and Ms. Romaine had telephoned him that she had a lead, a contact in the state highway commission who worked in contracts. They were to meet that afternoon at the Shady Acres club to discuss the details. His scheme was simplicity itself. Something she wanted for something he wanted. What did she want most? Money. That gleam in her eye when he hinted at what he would give for the right information, that was the key.

Clear of the IRS, he now could turn to business, selling houses and turning Shady Acres into an even bigger cash cow. With the right information there were some very interesting possibilities, like selling the right-of-way and grabbing the contract to supply concrete for highway paving—mouth watering.

He even considered throwing a bouquet to Harrigan and that woman so generous with his lot rent money—her impulse worked to the tune of $50,000. in stock sales. Acknowledging Sylvia Holbein's success came with a certain amount of grudging respect—all he wanted was a figurehead to front the Shady Acres Limited Parternership, not someone to be a vocal representative of the shareholders. This, in turn, he reminded himself, was a caution in dealing with Ms. Romaine. She was much more astute than the Holbein woman, he was sure. Might she come up with a hidden agenda as well?

He drove out of the Federal Building parking lot sobered by the realization he had more problems to solve. Getting out of the IRS trap was only the beginning. The relief he felt must not be allowed to become euphoric carelessness, he reminded himself.

"Ah, Ms. Romaine, you are as punctual as you are efficient," he gushed. "Sorry I'm a bit late. I had to clear up some business with Mr. Harrigan," he smiled, emphasizing the word business for effect. Actually, all he'd done was stop by to compliment his son-in-law and invite him to Sunday supper, per usual. The club house was deserted as she met his gaze with a steady, unblinking look.

"You seem to have made contact quickly," he continued, seating himself opposite her in a matching club chair.

"Yes, I was a little surprised, myself."

"You said this person works in contracts for the State Highway Department?"

"Would you believe it—he is a high school classmate."

"What are the prospects? What's he working on?"

"I don't know." She smiled as if to tease him before continuing, "I'm having lunch with him tomorrow. I should be able to get some general information but..." she hesitated, frowning slightly, "I gather you don't want a direct approach...Correct me if I'm wrong." Her look said it all.

Tony's admiration for her perception was tempered by his concern for caution. "Ms. Romaine, I appreciate this is a delicate and sensitive situation for you and I certainly don't want to push you. My goal is to learn what highway construction plans affect Shady Acres and possibly what opportunities exist or will exist for Maggedali Construction. If you can get an advanced idea of the Highway Department's intentions, it would facilitate my planning for the future of Shady acres." He felt like he was rambling—a long speech, a round about method to hide the stark truth—he wanted information before the normal public release, an insider's edge.

Ms. Romaine controlled her features but obviously, she wasn't fooled by his circumlocution trying to camouflage his intent.

"Mr. Maggedali," she looked at him in a very direct manner, "I **know** this man." She hesitated as if considering further explanation before finishing, "I'll keep you informed, as necessary," she smiled, almost a grin, "We can negotiate then, OK?" She rose from the club chair, even as she spoke.

Tony nodded as he sank back in the comfortable chair. Relaxed, yet with a sense he wasn't totally in control of this effort. 'Maybe it's just as well,' he thought, reminding himself that after all Ms. Romaine was the one making direct contact and nothing she did led to him if the effort didn't go as desired.

For fully five minutes he sat there, strangely at ease, mulling over the desired information and how she would get it, what she would say and how the State Highway contracts officer would react. Would he be alarmed? Would he squeal to his superiors? That was the risk.

Then another thought at random. The famous female spy in World War I he'd read about; the one who was executed by a French firing squad as a spy. She subverted and seduced some very senior officers on the French General Staff to gain important military information. In his lurid thoughts Ms. Romaine was surely attractive enough to be the seductive Mata Hari. He laughed, wondering if she'd do the same seductive oriental dances? How far would she go? And, as he thought logically, coldly, back in the present, what was it going to cost him? How much would she demand for her services? Had he offered enough incentive?

Two weeks passed without contact with Ms. Romaine, then one gorgeous day in September she suggested they meet.

She had everything. Listening closely, Tony realized there was a good possibility she could control her friend on the Highway Planning Commission, 'steer him' as she put it, into the right choices for both the route of the highway construction as well as the contract for the concrete necessary to build a full clover leaf access near the Shady Acres area—part of the projected Highway plan.

As the full impact of his potential gain hit him, Tony, for the first time in his life, became introspective, unconsciously evaluating himself. Until now he considered himself pragmatic, although he would never admit to even that, being uncertain of the meaning of the word. His style was to adjust to the problem and solve it in the most direct and efficient manner—some might say ruthless manner.

At this moment he felt positively brilliant. Getting Ms. Romaine to work for him on this problem was inspired, he admitted to himself. In fact if someone knowledgeable had used the word genius in connection with how he had foreseen and guided this business, he would not have uttered a protest. He had asked all the right questions and she had provided the answers; then made sure the choices were the ones he wanted. Her perception was uncanny. For once he wasn't terribly concerned with the cost beyond what he'd hinted in his offer to her.

How she accomplished all this didn't concern him either. Like Mati Hari or otherwise, she had supplied the answers to his questions and manipulated her source as he suggested—the rumors Harrigan brought up to the contrary. What did he care who visited her trailer and what they did? That was her business as long as it didn't disturb anyone else in Shady Acres. Harrigan's information sounded like something Mrs. Shanty planted with the Super anyway.

This brilliant triumph vindicated his clever moves, leaving him giddy. Simply put, he was soon going to be a millionaire, without doubt. "Are you sure?" He managed as he forced his thoughts to the present and the need to seal the deal.

Ms. Romaine smiled that smile, that knowing smile he almost feared, "I know **my** guy. And may I say also, I expect to have a buyer for the house on Mulberry street tomorrow—just remember your promise." She leaned forward a bit in her club chair for emphasis.

Tony reached across and patted her hand, "You can count on it, my dear. And as soon as the state signs the contract for the concrete supply there will be a substantial bonus for you, as well.

"By the way, is there anything else we need to do to persuade your contact to follow through?" Distasteful as it was, a bribe was sometimes necessary.

"Not yet, but there's a possibility he may need a little more encouragement. I'll let you know."

Tony couldn't suppress a grin, "You've managed him so well, I would almost be disappointed if you needed any help," he winked.

Her only response was that knowing smile again.

That same gorgeous September morning a seemingly unrelated tete-a-tete was about to take place in Shady Acres. IRS agent Charles Libertine rang the doorbell at 629 Floral Avenue.

The door opened fully in five seconds. Sylvia stood behind the storm door, her arms folded across her abundant chest, the faded chenille bathrobe almost colorless in the bright sunlight. "What do **you** want?"

Agent Libertine forced a smile, showing some teeth. "Once a secret agent always a secret agent," he replied lightly, "remember?"

Sylvia frowned, "So?" Her favorite soap opera was in its first commercial break and she had come to the kitchen to pour another cup of coffee.

"The IRS likes to reward it's inform…er, secret agents and keep in touch. I thought you might like to know…" he hesitated, "May I come in for a few minutes? I have something for you." He actually shrugged nonchalantly to disarm her suspicion, remembering their last encounter and the hostility of his departure.

She held the storm door open with a bare foot. "All right," she answered with a sigh of resignation. "I suppose you want a cup of coffee too," she turned back toward the kitchen as he caught the door with a hand.

"Yes, that would be nice of you." He forced himself to be sociable.

When they were seated at the round butcher-block table, Agent Libertine, with his back to the small forest of ferns and plants, Sylvia studied him over the rim of her coffee mug," What's this about? You out to get someone else in Shady Acres?"

With a forced chuckle, "No. I'm here to present you with a small token of the IRS appreciation for your assistance in the Maggedali case. We were able to settle the case in a very satisfactory manner and you were very helpful." He pulled a small scroll tied with a blue ribbon from his inner suit pocket and handed it to her, cracking his face in another functional smile.

Sylvia put her coffee down, surprised, then with a sudden inspiration. "Thank you…Hold on a second, I got something to show **you**." She didn't know why, maybe it was suspicion, maybe it was the need to show this patronizing SOB that she was not some kind of hard up, female, lap dog needing his crumbs to find self respect or self worth.

In less than two minutes she returned, the chenille robe flapping open with her haste. The extra large vellum had her name inscribed as the President of the Shady Acres Limited Partnership. Her official recognition for the sale of over fifty shares at $1000. apiece. "What do you think of that Mr. IRS agent?" She pushed the document in front of him "Secret Agent, huh, I've gone beyond that. I own five shares of Shady Acres now." She declared, enjoying the surprised look on Agent Libertine's face. Him and his little thank you scroll.

She wanted to tell him she'd even been paid to become the President of the Limited Partnership but something inside told her to hold back.

Reading the scroll carefully the Agent noted there was no incorporation or mention of licensing mentioned anywhere on the scroll much less any registration information with Securities and Exchange Commission. "What's this?" he asked. "You appear to be an officer in charge of a public company."

Now was the time, she thought, "Yes, and I got a bonus for being the President too." Sylvia proceeded to tell him all she knew. She was enjoying herself with this pipsqueak. Basically she repeated the same information she told perspective Limited Partners who purchased shares during the recent campaign with Harrigan.

"So, Mr. Maggedali has sold Shady Acres to the tenants?"

"No, just 25% of Shady Acres. He still controls the park. Oh, you know, some of us made a very shrewd deal too," she gushed, her coffee untouched, growing cold, "We get fifty dollars a month off our rent for each share we bought. Good for three months." She giggled thinking of the $250. a month she would save over the next three months. "That was my idea."

"Just for buying the shares?

"Well, yes, for buying them right away."

"Right away?" The agent's eyebrows shot up with the question. "Please explain."

Sylvia looked at the agent, he obviously lacked business sense. "Yes, of course, **that** was the incentive to buy within ten days of the offer." How could he miss that, it was so obvious.

"There's no date on this vellum, when was the 'offer' made?"

"Oh, last month, maybe three weeks ago."

"I see," The Agent's natural suspicions were fully aroused. "My congratulations." He spoke slowly, "I hope this deal is profitable for you."

"Now I must take my leave—thank you for the coffee, it was delicious." The Agent rose, concealing his look, afraid his suspicions might be reflected in his glance.

At the door he turned, presenting his best façade, "Now don't forget: once a secret agent, always a secret agent," he smiled, raising a finger to add a lighter touch.

Sylvia grinned, "Huh! You can call me Madam President now."

"Yes," he grimaced, "Well, goodbye…ah, Madam President."

Sylvia clapped her hands with delight and skipped back to the living room, scooping her vellum off the butcher-block table as she passed—humbling Agent Libertine, the old sourpuss, was fun.

✳   ✳   ✳   ✳

Sylvia was comfortably settled on the plush divan in her Japanese kimono as HOPE FOR TOMORROW's theme music came on. As the scene opened Della was getting dressed, preparing to go to her boyfriend's hearing for embezzlement, the charges being brought by Citizen's Trust, the bank he worked for—until recently. She paused before the mirror to look down at the huge square cut diamond he had recently given her after proposing—

Sylvia jumped, startled at the second ring of the phone almost at her elbow on the end table. Frowning, she reached for the instrument, annoyed with the interruption. People had no consideration for others. It seemed she was always being called by someone during her favorite soap. "Hello," she barely concealed her irritation.

"Sylvia this is Charlene Shanty. Have you read this flyer from the Management?"

Sylvia let out a sigh, "What flyer?"

"The one I just pulled out of my storm door about Shady Acres Limited Partners turning in their shares—"

"What?"

"I thought you'd be interested, Madam President," she cackled, "You're going to be getting a lot of phone calls, I'll bet." Ms, Shanty hung up still laughing to herself.

Sylvia starred at the TV screen, unseeing, the receiver still in hand. Slaming it down an instant later she fought her way out of the deep cushions and scrambled to the door, the kimono flapping open as she went, all sorts of questions running through her mind, beginning with what she was going to ask Harrigan.

Drawing back the dead bolt, unsnapping the latch and finally twisting the snap lock, she ripped open the big door, immediately clawing at the pink flyer stuck into the jamb of the storm door. Belatedly, she fumbled with the lever lock, pushing the storm door open, Then she grabbed at the pink paper as it floated away from her like a falling leaf, coming to rest on the wooden deck. Without hesitation she scampered after the piece of paper, frontally exposed to the whole neighborhood as she crouched to retrieve it.

After a hasty reading the only thing that registered was the phrase "…recalling all Limited Partner shares for redemption…" She walked to her bedroom as she read. Now she sat on the unmade, queen-sized bed and reread the flyer. Ms Shanty was right, the telephone would be ringing all day long. Without pause she shrugged out of the kimono, pulled open her bureau draw and reached a pair of panties. Wiggling into the panties she stepped toward the closet and grabbed a pair of gray sweat pants and matching shirt. In less than thirty seconds she was dressed and pulling on a pair of dirty, white tennis shoes. Harrigan was going to hear about this all right—that snake in the grass. Recalling all Limited Partner shares—they had only been issued two months ago. Why?

Harrigan gave her his best smile, the one she had seen so often when he was thinking up some story to cover his butt. "Now, come on Ms. Holbein, you're upset." He craned toward the door leading to the rest of the trailer, his dark eyebrows moving up and down like old railroad semaphore signals "Let's look at this calmly."

"Why is he doing this to us?" She spoke out, ignoring his attempt at sign language or whatever he was trying to signal with his eyebrows.

"Doing what? The original offer clearly states that management can recall all Limited Partner shares at 125% of face value within six months of issue—that's a 25% profit."

"There's something shady about this—I just know it!"

His smile became broader as he leaned back in his swivel chair with an irritating squeak, hands behind his head. "Remember, Ms. Holbein, this was one of the selling points we made to prospective buyers. You, yourself convinced at least two of the holdouts using that clause in paragraph 3c to show they couldn't lose money—what are you complaining about?"

Now Sylvia was convinced something was up, Harrigan was too sure of himself, too smooth. "C'mon, Harrigan. What's the deal here?" The image of Agent Libertine flashed through her thoughts.

He shrugged, "Nothing'. You know how it is—business. Mr. Maggedali sold a couple houses and got the IRS off our backs—things are swingin' again. Business, that's all, business.

"Just tell the shareholders we'll have a meeting at the club house to redeem the LP shares in the next day or two." Then squeaking forward in his chair, his voice fell to a whisper, "I'll be over tommora…wear that Japanese kimono."

Pacified but not satisfied, Sylvia half smiled, knowing she'd pump the rest out of him tomorrow. She turned to leave. With the office door knob in one hand she pulled up the sweat shirt with the other, flashing him. "See, ya."

Walking home, she wondered if Agent Libertine's recent visit had any connection,

For Harrigan, Sylvia's little visit brought an anxiety which quickly replaced the lurid anticipation he felt after seeing one of those big tits. Sylvia was right, Something was going on. He felt it too.

Last Sunday, Tony played the most gracious host. Never had Harrigan seen him so relaxed and hospitable. He thought back to their pre-dinner chat over drinks. Not only were they drinking Crown Royal over ice but Tony hinted there was an even more dramatic deal to follow the repurchase of LP shares. Apparently the new deal was related to the repurchase in some way.

Harrigan was surprised the buy back clause was ever in the contract from the beginning. He didn't believe Tony would offer a 25% gain within six months simply as an inducement to buy the shares—that was not like him—there was something more involved right from the beginning. Tony was clever, no doubt about it.

*   *   *   *

The pencil quivered in his fingertips as if some tremor from within had erupted, maybe a heart attack. With a dry mouth, he reviewed the simple, basic figures he had just worked out on the back of an old envelope pulled from the trash basket. No question, they were accurate. Tony sighed. Six million dollars, maybe more. Those limited partner shares were worth 10K each but he bought them all back at $1250! He congratulated himself on his foresight to include the buy-back clause—good business.

He had convinced the Highway Department contract negotiators with actual receipts that Shady Acres was worth six million dollars over the next five years as a business—his livelihood, he pointed out—not including the actual land value they used to compute their offer of one million for the highway right-of-way. When they mentioned taking the land under rights of eminent domain, he acknowledged they could do that but promised a fight in court if they tried. That option would be very time consuming, he reminded them. Then he offered to sell them Shady Acres for four million provided they gave Maggedali Construction the contract to supply concrete for the clover leaf entry/exit they planned for that location. Taking such a bold move would have been unthinkable without Ms. Romaine's spying. Having a friend in contracts didn't hurt either, again thanks to Ms. Romaine. The commission agreed that settling for his figure was preferable to a law suit and the attendant delay in construction especially when he reminded them how fickle the courts could be. They might award an even higher sum for Shady Acres with the presentation of hard evidence like that he presented the Highway Commission.

Turning to the figures for the concrete; by his calculation the clover leaf, two lanes wide, would easily require two million dollars worth of concrete, maybe as much as two million five.

With the contracts signed and the construction scheduled to begin in the spring, all that was necessary was to notify the Shady Acres tenants—the eviction notice—before the local paper ran a story about the highway project. There had been enough grumbling about the LP shares buy-back. Some people weren't satisfied with a 25% profit in only four months. Not to mention the rent reduction bonus, Madam President handed them (and herself) as an incentive to buy the shares in the first place, He shook his head at the sad reality—such greed.

That Holbein woman was to blame. She was the worst—an agitator like Charlene Shanty who didn't buy any shares—thank god. He was glad he didn't give Harrigan any advanced information about the highway project. That woman was far too active and Harrigan was far too weak. Whatever he told Harrigan was sure to become an open secret in a short time.

*   *   *   *

Tony walked up the Federal Building steps his jaws clenched tight. With a barely perceptible nod he acknowledged an acquaintance's 'Good Morning.' The fall chill suited his mood perfectly, brisk and to the point, all business, 'Agent Libertine ought to be castrated, The bastard is trying to build his career hounding me. That letter, that damned letter—I'm going to stuff it down his throat—'Summons to an Informal investigation'. What kind of business is that?'

Inside the old, ornate building, he descended the stairs to the basement finding his way through the labyrinth of dully lit corridors towards the back, past half-paneled, lettered, frosted glass office entrances, until he found the one with guilt lettering 'Special Agents'.

Walking in, his way was bared by a waist high counter. The desk behind the counter was flanked on three sides with floor to near ceiling files, cutting off any view of the room behind except for an aisle through 'the Andes' opposite the hinged counter break.

A middle aged woman looked up from the computer centered on the desk suddenly distinct from all the clutter. "Yes. sir. May I help you?"

"Agent Libertine? Is he here?"

She pressed a button on the desk and he heard a distant buzz from somewhere behind all the files, "George is Charlie in yet?" She asked into what appeared to be an old call box.

"Yeah. He's back in his cubby-hole—might be on the phone, can't tell," came a disembodied voice.

She looked up at Tony, "Can you hold a minute? I'll go check." As he nodded she was on her way. He checked inside his jacket pocket feeling the 'Summons' letter he'd received the day before.

She returned shortly and lifted the hinged counter, "Through here, sir. Agent Libertine will see you now."

He passed through the gap in the tall cabinets into a big room to find it broken into warrens by green partitions topped by corrugated, translucent, panels, the combination about shoulder high. The short walk could have been a passage through the metal security check at the airport and was awash in government green.

Federal style office equipment from at least twenty years past, except for the computer terminals, populated each cubical. The whole thing was accented by wiring and cables strung in random patterns across the deck gray cement floor and snaking under the green panel sides of every cubical. He followed the narrow corridor flanked by the green partitions and turned right at the first intersection, noting a man's legs stretched across an opening about fifteen feet ahead. The legs retracted under the chair and straightened upright propelling Agent Libertine into the entry.

"Mr. Maggedali," his tone in mild surprise, "the meeting's not until tomorrow."

Tony reached into his jacket pocket and drew the letter as if he were pulling out a concealed weapon. "What's the meaning of this!" He stopped almost nose to nose with the agent slapping the envelop across the palm of his other hand with a snap.

Libertine's expression didn't change, after all this was almost a daily occurrence here in the Hive, as the agents called their crowded office. He turned his head slightly, "George, have you got the visitor's chair over there?"

From behind a green panel close by, "Yeah, I'll bring it right over."

"I don't need a damned chair—why ya holdin' this meetin'?" Tony's face was flushed.

George appeared behind Tony as Libertine backed into his cubical space. "Have a seat, Mr. Maggedali." He indicating the entry way as George pushed the chair up from behind. Tony more or less fell into the chair cushion as a result of George's push.

The chair was high backed and very much like a full sized, cloth covered, dining room chair someone had discarded when he bought a new dining room suite. Rocking forward in the big chair, Tony repeated, "What's this meetin' about?"

Very patiently Agent Libertine began, "As the letter states, sir, this is an informal meeting to determine if a Grand Jury should be called to look into your failure to report income, bribery, violation of Securities and Exchange regulations and possible fraud. You aren't required to attend, we're merely extending that courtesy to you, but you should be aware that as a result of this meeting a Grand Jury may be empanelled and formal charges may be brought against you upon recommendation by the Grand Jury."

"Why me? You think you're gonna make a big reputation puttin' me in jail?" He jabbed his thumb into his chest as he spoke.

For the briefest moment there was a predatory gleam in Agent Libertine's blue eyes. "I don't put people in jail—they do it themselves," he said quietly.

The man had more backbone than Tony gave him credit. He realized he couldn't threaten him, at least not here. Gaining control over his temper at last, Tony had run out of things to say. The agent's statement was broad and to Tony's surprise included areas he hadn't expected. "Most o'that doesn't sound like IRS business."

Agent Libertine cocked his head slightly, "Call it inter-agency, federal-state cooperation—your tax dollars being used efficiently."

Tony was stunned—how much did they know? He stood up, awkwardly pushing the bulky chair back as he struggled for something to say, something with an impact, something to recover his aplomb. All he could muster was, "We'll see about this." Flustered, he squeezed around the chair and retreated the way he came, chastised—this was real trouble.

"Have a nice day Mr. Maggedali—the meeting's at 10AM upstairs," Libertine called after him.

✳   ✳   ✳   ✳

"What are ya doin' home at this hour? Ya want somethin' t'eat?"

Tony looked up at his wife from the comfortable arm chair in the library. "S'all right. Anna, I don't want nothin'. I gotta a lota thinking' t'do, that's all. Go on back to the kitchen."

She remained standing in the doorway, a worried frown fixed on her plain features, watching him go to the bar and pour some brandy into a snifter glass. "I guess so—hittin' the bottle at ten in the mornin'. What's wrong? You been out t'the job?"

"Nothin'," he snarled, "yet." He waved a hand in dismissal as he lifted the brandy snifter.

With a clucking noise Anna turned away from the library doorway." Keeps everything to himself," she breathed, feeling rejected.

Tony sat down again in his comfortable chair and took a small sip of the brandy. He began the process. 'First, do I need a lawyer?' He made a face. The idea conflicted with his natural instinct to stay away from lawyers. 'They cost money and you can't count on the results, besides they want to know too much.' If Agent Libertine got this to a Grand Juery and charges were brought, then he could still get a lawyer. The thought of being forced to get a lawyer made him scowl, he really didn't want a lawyer.

'What have they got? I need t' think this through.' Mention of the SEC really surprised him. Another government agency, bureaucracy—he wasn't sure he knew what they did.

'And how did they get the state into this? Who squealed? Ms. Romaine?' She's been paid in cash, nothin's on paper. What could she tell them? That I was interested in where the highway right-of-way went; that I wanted the concrete contract for the interchange the state was going to build right over Shady Acres? What's wrong with that? I'm a business man—always looking' for a deal. So what? I'm no different than any other business man—gotta look after business, get an edge if I can, like everybody else.'

His thoughts turned to the Limited Partnership—Harrigan? 'He's got those receipts for a total of 56K. Has he been talkin' to anyone? I can control him. Still…couldn't watch him as close as I wanted when he and what's-her-name—Holstein, the cow'—he almost laughed out loud, 'it was Holbein, that's right.' He remembered her aggressiveness at the sales meeting—the little incentive she tossed out that cost him an extra five thou to get those LP shares sold. 'Was she involved somehow?' He took a big sip of the brandy. As the warmth suffused through him—'did Agent Libertine make contact with her? That possibility bothered him. The fancy scroll they had presented her, he and Harrigan, to recognize the success of the Limited Partner sale, the money he used to pay-off the IRS the last time. Was there any way that scroll could be used against him? The brandy couldn't erase the bad taste in his mouth contemplating what Ms. Holbein, Madam President, might tell the IRS and what impact her words might carry.

'Charlene Shanty? What could she do?' She didn't know anything—just a gossip with a big mouth—might whip up bad feelings but there was nothing she could prove about any of his dealings.

It all boiled down to Harrigan, Ms. Holbein and Ms. Romaine. Which one had talked to Agent Libertine?

And where had the bribery charge come from? He didn't bribe anyone. He paid for services rendered. That's the way he'd always done business. 'You want somethin' you got to pay for it—always been that way. The guy Ms. Romaine contacted, whoever he is, that's the man—maybe he squealed. Did they twist his arm? Did Ms. Romaine screw him for the information? What if she did? 'What difference did that make? She wasn't Mata Hari spying for some foreigners,' he reminisced, thinking of his library and the book on WWI he enjoyed so much.

After all, the State Highway Commission made the decision on the right-of-way and on the concrete too. 'I gave 'em my side and backed it up with proof; they accepted my offer 'cause they knew I had a good case if some judge had to arbitrate the deal. Good sense on their part, anyone could see that. So what's this bribery thing Libertine's throwin' around?

'Maybe I do need a lawyer to sue them for false charges,' he chuckled to himself, feeling better. The last full swallow of brandy went down with a satisfying warmth.

*   *   *   *

The meeting was brief—less than an hour. Tony was disturbed by the brevity, knowing some of the principals had traveled for several hours to attend—as if they already had decided to call for a Grand Jury, their minds made up. With rising anger, he questioned the lack of specifics and was told that he would have ample opportunity to testify to the Grand Jury when specific questions would be asked under oath. They said this was an informal meeting with no charges actually filed, no witnesses called; they simply dealt with the overall limits of the charges they intended to bring and whether or not they had enough information to call for a Grand Jury. The vagueness of the proceeding left him feeling helpless. He wanted to yell at them. 'Who told you that? Who said I bribed them? What's wrong with trying to get a contract?' The circle around him was closing from all directions, squeezing him. What was he supposed to do? What did they want—money? That always seemed the end result—the final threat.

*   *   *   *

Tony was almost happy to learn that lawyers were not allowed in the Grand Jury hearing. He didn't want one anyway. To Anna he said he was invited to give testimony just like Ms. Holbein and Ms. Romaine, even Harrigan, no big deal. So he was off to a good start, anyway.

As it turned out, if any witness wanted a lawyer, he (the lawyer) had to remain outside the Grand Jury room and could not advise his client while actually giving testimony. On the other hand, witnesses were put under oath. That was the part that made him suspicious, maybe a little uneasy about not having a lawyer. The reasoning that the Grand Jury hearing was only an attempt to formally decide whether 'an indictment should be handed down', sounded like so much legal 'mumbo—jumbo' to him—an obvious attempt to nail you before you went to court for the 'real' trial where they officially 'stick it to you'.

When it came his turn, he denied everything from bribing Ms. Holbein to run the Limited Partners 'scam' (they actually used that term, to his surprise), to bribing Ms. Romaine to 'suborn' (whatever that meant) the contracts guy working for the State Highway Commission. Did they actually expect him to admit he paid her to get information from this guy? Apparently the contracts guy was really in hot water with the State Highway Comission. The man passed on 'privileged information' on highway right-of-way and construction matters involving costs and bidding—imagine that? Shocking. Tony denied any contact with the man, in fact he declared, voluntarily, that he didn't know the man until the highway people at the Grand Jury introduced his name, a Mr. Timothy Coskerelli—sounded Polish or Irish to Tony.

The whole thing was a setup, just as he suspected. Agent Libertine accused him of cheating on his income tax—seems you're supposed to estimate and pay federal tax quarterly on you're income. Thanks to Ms. Holbein's testimony backed up by Harrigan's receipts Libertine asked him where that 56K was in his quarterly estimates? 'Hell they were lucky to get it reported at all,' he thought, inwardly chuckling. He'd report that money in April when he knew all of the income he'd made for the year, after all Maggedali Construction had several sources of income, new houses, the state contract for concrete for a complete clover leaf to be built on the land now called Shady Acres (he particularly liked the expression on Agent Libertine's face when he started expanding on this one)—what the hell he paid his taxes every year, this quarterly business was the government's way of puttin' the squeeze on people. He'd estimated and paid quarterly the way he had for the last couple years, what more do they want? Greed, nothing but greed, that's what this so called fact finding was about.

And then there was the guy from the Securities and Exchange Commission asking about filing with them for the IPO for the Limited Partnership of Shady Acres. Initial Public Offering? What public offering? They weren't going on the Stock Exchange. The people living in Shady Acres were given a chance to buy up to 25% of Shady Acres at $1000 a share that's all—what 'public offering? The residents bought 56 shares…and,…and…they actually made 25% on their money within, what, about four months—not bad, hey? What's this registration and offering public shares about?

So then the SEC guy comes back, "…and what if one of your tenants decides to sell his shares to someone who isn't a tenant? What then? This isn't a 'Public Offering'? Show me on the contract where this is prohibited."

'I'm not telling them nothing.' he said to himself.

*   *   *   *

The Grand Jury handed down several findings for formal prosecution:

1).Income tax evasion, one count: Failure to estimate and pay quarterly Federal Income tax.

2) Felony Bribery, two counts: Offering a bribe to sell stock not registered with SEC, Offering a bribe to obtain confidential information on highway construction routing and materials contract.

3) Perjury, two counts: Lying under oath to Grand Jury regarding the offer of money to sell fraudulent stock; lying under oath to the Grand Jury regarding offer of a bribe to suborn an official of State Highway commission.

4) Fraud, one count: Offer of public stock based on improper pricing versus evaluation. Failure to register Initial Public Offering of stock with government regulatory agency (SEC).

*   *   *   *

The trial went pretty much as expected. Reluctantly Tony hired a lawyer and as he suspected the guy wanted to know too much. "That's all there is—all you need to know," Tony told him at one point. Later, at another point in the proceedings he thought, 'Maybe I should tell him more,' but quickly decided against the idea.

Ms. Romaine, bless her heart, tried to tie the money she received to the sale of Maggedali homes but was forced to admit she made a big bank deposit very soon after Maggedali Construction got the juicy contract for all the concrete to be used in building the clover leaf where Shady Acres had been.

Although there had been many surprises, Tony was shocked to see Jake, the Shady Acres handyman called to the stand as a witness. Under oath, Jake identified Mr. Timothy Caskerelli as the man he had seen many times entering Ms. Romaine's trailer and implied Mr. Coskerelli remained over night on more than one occasion.

Challenged by Tony's lawyer as irrelevant and immaterial to the case, the judge ordered the jury to disregard Jake's testimony about Mr. Coskerelli's visits to Ms. Romaine. And of course the jury immediately forgot and totally disregarded Jake's testimony of some twenty minutes in their deliberations. That is, if you believe in the tooth fairy.

The biggest single thing was the Prosecution was able to find a chink—they called it 'perjury'. They couldn't nail him for anything he did but instead for what he **told** them he did in the Grand Jury. Unable to prove any of the charges, they crossed him up with the questioning and got him to say something false. He was amazed. Tony knew he hadn't said anything false but there it was right in the 'transcripts'—a slip-up, a misstatement.

Despite the fact that both Ms. Holbein and Ms. Romaine received money from Tony for their 'services', as he put it, he denied that either was for an illegal purpose, much less anything so crass as a bribe.

It was at this point in the trial, just after Tony returned from the witness chair to his attorney's table, that the legal eagle leaned over and hissed, "Why didn't you tell me about this?" What with Ms. Holbein going on about how she didn't know anything but took the three thou and turned it into shares which were priced on an estimate not fair market value. Had someone offered Tony an equivalent sum for Shady Acres his pricing per share would have been OK—they said.

The whole thing was a set-up. Agent Libertine was going to get him no matter what and that slut was helping him: Going on about some soap opera and how this case was just the same—fraud. And this was testimony? Somehow the fact that she and every other buyer made 25% on his money in about four months didn't cut any ice. Tony knew after that part of the trial, he was dead meat.

At least the lawyer had kept him out of jail—mostly. Tony got a year and a day with six months reduced to house arrest and the rest to be served in the county jail with the possibility of time off for good behavior. The lawyer said he was 'lucky', the sentence could have been three to five years—if you want to believe that.

Anna cried a lot but was somewhat consoled thinking of all the baking and cooking she could do to cheer him up on visiting days.

The judge also decreed he could not manage the concrete contract through Maggedali Construction, assuming his company won after the contract was bid again. Further, he would have to resign and someone else would have to be the CEO, at least until he served his time and the courts approved his reinstatement.

Just thinking of Ed Harrigan running Maggedali Construct gave Tony a headache and he had nightmares his first week in jail visualizing Harrigan behind that clean desk in his squeaking, swivel chair listening to the Mills brothers. The whole bad scene subsided a little when he thought, 'at least Maddie will be provided for…so long as that idiot doesn't completely ruin my business.'

The county Sheriff, a friend of almost fifteen years, assured him he had the best cell in the jail. Not that it was equipped any better, oh no, simply the view. Nice.

Alone with his thoughts, he found himself watching a beautiful scene from his cell window, as the sun set over the tree topped hill, white with snow. After a while he turned from the peaceful scene, dusk almost complete and country lights springing on in the farmhouse in the foreground.

"Greed, everybody's so greedy now," he said to himself. There was no contradiction in this, no irony did he sense. "They don't take the risks, they don't understand business but they want the profits."

In spite of this, one way or another, in cash or escrow, he still had almost four million dollars less taxes, of course. 'Blast that Agent Libertine anyway.'

SIDNEY, AN AMERICAN TOURIST

Carcassone—La Cite—a fortified Medieval city in France. There, in front of us, was a sand-table model of this most advanced fortification engineering before the advent of cannon. Our guide was beginning our indoctrination before the guided tour of this fully restored medieval town-fortresses—one of the few still inhabited in Europe.

"Who was there before the Franks?" Sid, our resident octogenarian wanted to know.

"The Romans," our guide answered, adding an interesting tidbit about their contribution to the town/fortification.

"And who was before them?" he came back quickly.

"The Visigoths," she responded and returned to her lecture.

"I won't ask her who was there before them," he muttered *sotto voce*.

I laughed out loud, drawing frowns from those nearest me who were having enough problems hearing with Sid's questions. Apparently, I was the only one who heard Sid's sly comment on his self restraint. This incident was the first time I appreciated Sid, the tour group's resident curmudgeon. He had been a gadfly since the beginning.

Enroute, I sat one seat behind and across the aisle from him on the Air France 747 flight to Paris. In the huge, crowded cabin he was an unremarkable, faceless man who resembled nothing so much as Woody Allen, 30 years older—wispy, grayish hair, sallow complexion and horned rimed glasses over watery, blue eyes.

The only reason I remember that now is he soon became a great deal less anonymous, at least to those in his immediate vicinity.

He stopped the French stewardess offering coffee and tea and asked for Perrier water. "Yes, sir, right away, she responded in clear English and hurried off to refill the empty coffee pot she was carrying.

Some time later, after she had passed by a couple times, Sid reached out and caught her arm as she was hurrying in the opposite direction. "Awhile ago I asked you for Perrier water," he rasped, fixing her with his watery blues.

"Oh. Yes, sir," she said, "would you like Guiness or Perrier?"

"I SAID, Perrier water!"

"Right away, sir." She blushed and took off to comply.

There was something in that exchange that didn't sit well—despite the stewardess failure—a touch of rudeness that left me uneasy. Nor did his querulous interrogation of the steward about the dinner menu, roughly an hour later, help. Sid wasn't satisfied with either of the entrees offered and wanted a simple bowl of soup. Was that too much to ask? Apparently it was. Soup, however simple, was not available, not even vegetable.

I didn't know then that Sidney was on our walking tour group of Southern France, but decided I would as soon not have to deal with this prickly pear.

He was and I didn't, at first. And I wasn't the only one to note his behavior. Within a couple days of our settling in for the tour, people were kidding T.G. (short for T.G.Nakazawa) for bringing Sid on the tour. After one jibe as we were settling on the tour bus one morning, T.G. felt compelled to explain.

"Hey, I didn't invite him—he called me from Miami to ask where we were vacationing this year. He used to live in our apartment building, in Chicago," he shrugged, not sure he'd convinced those around him who were still chuckling.

I usually sat at the back of the bus. For three or four days I didn't have to deal with Sid although it was impossible to ignore his interrogations of guides that seemed to go far beyond the interests of the group, to the point of distraction. At meals I avoided sitting in his proximity, but I often heard his pointed remarks and sometimes his gastric demands.

When we changed locations and moved to the hotel Donjon in Carcassone the situation changed. After an enormous country lunch one day we started to hike back to Carcassone, about six miles away, along the Midi canal. Everyone, as well as our accompanying guide, was concerned about some of the older, less active of our group. so the guides arranged that our bus would park ahead and those who only wanted to hike part way could board the bus after a short stint.

Sidney lasted three miles which impressed those of us who went the whole distance.

That evening at our three crisp, white linened tables it was apparent one person was missing. There were eight to a table and ours only had seven. The chair to my right was unoccupied.

As we were being served the salad course, simple deduction led us to conclude Sidney was the missing diner.

Because of my aversion to him, or perhaps in spite of it, I noted Sid's room was only two doors down the hall from mine. "I'll go check," I volunteered, "he's in 319 down the hall from me."

Who knows? Maybe I was trying to impress the beauty to my left, maybe I was subconsciously worried about Sid after his hiking with us for three miles—afraid of what I might find in 319. Morbid curiosity? Whatever the motivation for volunteering, I wiped my mouth and put the large napkin beside my plate and hurried down to the third floor.

He was there. After a couple sharp raps on his door he answered and was quickly ready for dinner. That's the good news. The bad news is I became his hero.

He was delighted to make dinner in time to be served the first course as the rest of us had barely started the second. Volunteering led to my becoming his official 'make sure I'm awake guy'. The next day we were scheduled to tour the famous Frontfroide Abbey some distance away. Zi, Zi, our guide, wanted everybody to be ready to board the bus at 0730 sharp.

Since I was still doing a little hand laundry each day, I had to get up early to see what was dry. I beat on Sid's door promptly at 0635, got a satisfactory response and went on to breakfast. We all boarded the bus on time and everything went smoothly for the next few days until the end of our stay in Carcassone when we proceeded to Toulouse, a large city, and Le Grand Hotel Capoul, a very modern hotel compared to our previous lodgings.

Here, the first day after our arrival, I was late for lunch, another first. Our group was split. There was no room at the three or four small tables inside the cafe bar so I went to the tables pushed together along the wall immediately before the exit to the sidewalk cafe. As the only route into and out of the cafe from the street, it was bustling with traffic. The waiters danced a ballet with artfully balanced trays floating magically above heads, coming and going, as they scurried in and out with their orders.

The only seat available was next to Sid on the inside. "Come on, sit by me," he grinned yellow teeth.

Zi Zi and I pulled the table out so I could get in, disrupting all flow momentarily. I sat down and was quickly served the opening course. Zi Zi and Bruno, the bus driver, sat opposite us.

I commented on how poor the restaurant fare was compared to the country meals we had been used to during the earlier part of our stay out in the country-side. Even Zi Zi agreed.

"Got any baked beans?" Sid interrupted my ruminations, halting a long-necked, goosey waiter. The man stopped so abruptly that the elevated tray tipped forward dangerously.

Zi Zi's bushy eyebrows went up in surprise. "Baked beans?"

"Baked beans? Do you have any baked beans?" Sid focused on the waiter who obviously didn't speak English. I am at a loss as to why he stopped in the first place.

Zi Zi tried to interpret. An attempt from ignorance, even though he'd been to Boston. Clearly he didn't know baked beans. So Sid's reference to Boston baked beans only complicated the problem. Even Bruno was trying to help the waiter understand and I don't think he'd ever been to America, much less Boston.

In spite-of-myself, I snickered. That was bad. Without intending to, I was beginning to enjoy Sid's malicious outbursts. What was the waiter supposed to say (.assuming he finally understood), "Yes, we have no baked beans today?"

"Sid, you ought to be ashamed of yourself," T.G. admonished from halfway down our makeshift table. "They don't know what baked beans are here."

"You mean like French fries?" Sid shot back.

Zi Zi *was* in earnest discussion with the waiter, the french flowing in a torrent between them. Now, Sid began to back off in a pseudo stab at graciousness. "Aaah, that's all right, don't worry about it…if they don't have any, they don't have any It's not important," he offered, his voice reaching a melancholy level, as the waiter nodded and turned back toward the kitchen, his intended service in the other direction aborted. "I don't want to get'em all shook up in the kitchen," Sid generalized, half turning toward T.G.

"You should cancel the order when the waiter comes by again to make sure he understands," T. G. scolded.

Sid half smiled back, "Well, let's see what happens," Sid answered while nudging me, his new pal.

We were nearly finished the meal, Sid's order and the translation problems put aside for the more immediate interest in the next place we were to visit and the details of how to get there on foot, when the tall, gangly waiter appeared and with a huge smile, reached across the table and placed a dinner plate heaped with string beans in front of Sidney, then stepped back still smiling. He was obviously pleased with himself for completing a difficult task—Boston baked beans—delivered.

Sid looked up at the waiter then back at the plate as if he was totally mystified. You would have thought Sidney was a character from silent movies. This nonplused state lasted maybe two or three beats, enough time for everyone at the table to spy the big pile of string beans, then Sid said, "Not what I ordered…but it's OK…I don't want to send them back and get you in trouble in **the k**itchen. Like the long hesitation, it was a perfect. The Woody Allen, straight-faced—'you totally screwed up a perfectly simple order' to the waiter, who beamed in blissful ignorance. Fortunately, Sid didn't raise his voice to help the waiter understand.

Then grinning raffishly, he passed the plate down the table, each **of** us taking, three or four string beans to share Sid's 'baked beans' and dilute the blame for one ugly American.

This incident was vaguely reminiscent of a lunch at one of those country places before I became Sid's buddy. I was reminded of the previous incident because Sid was served fresh strawberries in addition to the regular desert the rest of us received at the end of the cafe meal. At the country place Sid asked if they had any fresh strawberries when they attempted to serve him chocolate pudding. Was this Zi Zi's apology for the baked beans or a reminder of the previous strawberry incident? Or was it language again? In spite of the shame I felt, I laughed, totally subverted by Sid's perverse humor and bad manners. In all, the most memorable part of a walking tour of southern France.

IS ARCHOLOGY
REALLY A SCIENCE?

Culture is a funny thing, there are so many odd parts of life no one ever considers. My dormant curiosity was prodded to life by a trip I took to Mexico and the famous, ancient Mayan ruins—many partially or fully restored. These magnificent structures, chiseled from stone, offered evidence of Mayan lives and culture back then. Vaguely I sensed something was missing. Surely even archaeologists must tacitly admit to some shortcomings. Viewing and photographing the magnificently restored Chichen Itza, I was reminded of the sharp contrast with 'Garbology' which I read about in National Geographic, I believe. Something about sorting through 30 year old garbage in a landfill—soft culture for want of a better term. There are similarities here also. Probably both fall loosely under the heading of archaeology—the history of life and culture of the past.

After returning to Cancun from Chichen Itza, I examined my own opulent, 'three star', surroundings more closely: marble floors, stone facings, steel structure—certainly they could still be here ten centuries from now for some archaeologist to ponder. Intrigued, my own senses sharpened, I spied the fresh roll of toilet paper in my gilded bath, the beginning sheets precisely folded into the form of a blossoming flower, not unlike a carefully folded linen, napkin at a fancy dinner banquet.

Archaeologists would miss such clues to our civilization. They would no longer exist. At that moment I realized their deductions are either severely handicapped or full of magnificent insight, drawn from a paucity of evidence. That was my intellectual stimulus.

Do they teach toilet paper folding in maid school I wondered? Is there even a maid school? I mean it must take time to learn to make all those tucks and folds at the beginning of the toilet roll; a sunrise, a flower blossom unfolding. In my US travels I had never seen this before with one possible exception. I do vaguely remember stopping at a motel one night and finding the end of a fresh roll of toilet paper folded into a point, something like an arrowhead. I remember because at the time I wondered if I was in Indian territory. Culturally speaking it was meaningless to me.

Some days later, my awareness piqued by the Chichen Itza visit, I had an occasion to notice that the toilet paper at the fancier place up the street (the 'five star', Cancun Palace) was folded in an even more elaborate pattern than at my hotel. Assuming my maid was not a trainee, I concluded that the fancier the hotel the more elaborately the toilet paper is folded—hence the 'five star' rating.

The experience also left me wondering. Is Decorative Toilet Paper Folding (DTPF) handed down from generation to generation like the crafts of the Middle Ages? Think of it: a family profession. Or is there some training course maids have to attend?

My education obviously has been limited. When I commented on this phenomenon, friends told me toilet paper is artistically folded in US motels too. How did I fail to notice fancy folded toilet paper before or is that why Motel 6 can offer a room cheaper than Hampton Inns, even when they leave the light on?

As a child, I always thought it was funny when mom and dad argued over whether the toilet paper should be hung 'over' or 'under' on the roller. This was a running argument which mom always won because she always hung the toilet paper. Aggressive people, I'm told, always hang it over. The subtler way is under. A friend made a point that the makers of toilet paper favor the 'overs' since the design is on the other side if it is hung 'under'. I didn't know that. Design? In mom and dad's day there were two choices, yellow or white. 'Designs'?

Here I must divert momentarily to speak to a related area and this gets back to 'garbology' so it does apply. I have to confess that a question has bothered me ever since Sears, Roebuck and Co. closed down its catalog business. To wit: Did the passing of the Sear's catalog indicate the end of a significant era? Even indirectly?

Let me explain. For years the catalog was the main prop under that company and one of the major reasons for their success, I believe. People in rural areas particularly, without easy access to a Sear's store, could order things through the catalog and that helped propel Sear's into a nationwide company. Surely, everyone is familiar with the entertainment value of the catalog. Many young boys got their first sexual knowledge (anatomical at least) from the ladies underwear section. In addition, everyone is probably aware that rural areas were the last to convert to indoor plumbing. I've heard stories that the Sear's catalog was sometimes used for more than its entertainment value in those old outhouses. Archaeologists, 'Garbologists', are you taking notes?

Is it possible, barely possible, that the decline of privies in rural America had some indirect, hidden effect on Sear's decision to abandon their catalog sales division? Consider the effect. Could that conversion from outdoor to indoor plumbing have had even a remote impact on Sear's catalog sales? I suppose it's far-fetched, but is it not also possible that the availability of toilet paper in colors and even in patterns changed, forever, the real value of the Sear's and Roebuck catalog?

On the other hand, ten centuries from now, will some archaeologist find a 'one holer' perfectly preserved in amber and puzzle over the purpose or meaning of the Sear's catalog inside? Is there a remote possibility he might draw the wrong conclusions? Might he mistake this for a place of worship and the catalog a version of the Bible—a cult Scripture? Or perhaps a silly earthling's attempt to become immortal using his own, self-constructed space ship in a vain attempt to latch onto the Hale-Bopp comet? Might he come closer to the truth and assume this was the way we entertained ourselves, isolated in our own pleasure house, reading? It's a puzzlement, I agree.

As for toilet paper, when I laughingly describe my amazing discoveries in Mexico to friends (discreetly, of course, I always wait until they have finished their first cocktail) they often look at me with that 'where have you been?' look, especially the ladies. Apparently giving toilet paper a fancy coiffure is not only prevalent in American hotels, it is *de rigor*, something Motel 6 doesn't offer. I guess Tom what's-his-name figures 'leaving the light on' is enough of a perk (Probably makes the cheaper rates possible too since he doesn't have to put his maids through the DTPF school.)

All of these ruminations leave me in something of a quandary. Will the archaeologists of the future miss all these signs of our culture? Will they find no trace of the fancy folded toilet paper and/or the Sear's and Roebuck catalog? Or will they misinterpret their findings if they do run across them?

I'm also beginning to worry that the Mayan ruins I spent so much money to go and see with their temples and significant religious connotations may be misrepresented. Did archaeologists find all the evidence before proclaiming them religious temples? Is it possible communal bathrooming was right up there with communal bathing? Were these huge pyramidal structures merely splendid, large, group...naaa couldn't be. Everyone knows Mr. Sears and Mr. Roebuck weren't around then. Besides their catalog would have to have been carved in stone, right? Stone? The catalog was heavy enough in paper. (All right so some archaeologists claim they had some form of paper back then—you get the idea. It would still be a heavy catalog.)

So I ask you: Is archaeology really a science?

IN REMEMBERANCE
OF A TRIPLE HEADED
MONSTER

Ed Dew was a radar-navigator on a B-47 crew like me. We were called triple headed monsters because we navigated, bombed and operated the radar. The B-47, built by Boeing, was the world's first operational, all jet, atomic bomber. It had a crew of three, two pilots and a radar-navigator.

I remember, one scorching day at a base in North Africa. Ed was padding barefoot on the duck boards from the shower building to his hootch, his stocky body almost wrapped in a sheet. I was headed in the opposite direction wearing a towel, soap in hand. The huge flies were droning around us like WWII bombers looking for a place to strike.

"Hey, Sam, why don't you pay me now so we don't have to stay up till dawn?" he jabbed.

We had a $5 bet on the Rocky Marciano—Jersey Joe Walcott heavyweight, championship fight.

"What d'ya mean," I countered, "Walcott will cold-cock him in seven."

The bout was to be broadcast on the Armed Forces Radio network beginning at 2AM local.

Ed hooked my arm swinging me sideways onto the burning sand. "Is that a prediction? You wanna double the bet?"

"Ha, ha, ha," I feinted a punch and jumped back on the duckboard, bobbing and weaving away, my feet burning: Five dollars was all I could afford to bet.

I don't remember how many days we three crews remained at our temporary assignment at Sidi Slameine, that hot, dusty base in Morocco, but the lost bet sticks in my memory because Ed Dew was killed in a plane crash a couple years later when we were on another temporary duty assignment to Japan.

Half a dozen B-47s flew from our home base at Mt. Home,Idaho, via great circle route to Misawa, a base on Hokkaido, northern most of the Japanese home islands. We were tweaking the big bear's tail. Our route shaved past the Kamchatka Peninsula by a mere 60 nautical miles so precise navigation was critical.

After crew rest, overnight and refueling we flew past Mt. Fuji, southward to Okinawa, southern most of the Japanese islands, and landed at Kadena base, near Naha.

Ed and I enjoyed a few beers at the Officer's Club bar where he hit me again with the heavyweight fight we bet on and what a poor loser I was. I countered that low blow with a shot reminding him Walcott almost had Marciano in the seventh as I had predicted. (Marciano was a 'catcher' who counted on hitting his opponent more often with heavier blows than he caught—mostly with his face.)

"Aw bullshit!" he said with a roundhouse grin, "I don't remember anything but the 13th when Rocky clobbered him—he was counted out flat on his back."

We returned to Misawa to stage for the long flight home over the North Pacific and Alaska; back to Mt. Home, MUO by abbreviation.

Ed was in the flight of three aircraft taking off ahead of my flight. Low rain clouds and a wet runway were part of the take off calculations that day and we were briefed to simulate the Emergency War Order by taking off at one minute intervals, fully loaded at 190,000# gross take off weight.

Some say that two of the six jets on Ed's bird had compressor stalls just before they lined up on the active runway after the lead aircraft started its take-off roll. The word was the Aircraft Commander didn't get those two engines stabilized before Ed counted off the seconds to go to full power and the start their take-off run. Did all six engines deliver full power when the AC rammed the throttles forward? We'll never know for sure. The heavy aircraft staggered off the wet runway briefly and settled back down again on its belly, skidding along the over run and up a slight grade in the rough ground off the runway, shedding pieces as it shot straight ahead at 120—130 knots, the fuselage splitting open just forward of the wing root as it slowed. About half a mile later the broken fuselage came to rest and began to burn.

The two pilots climbed out as the fire was starting, neither injured seriously, just shaken and bruised with superficial cuts.

Ed had no chance, He was literally ripped out of his position in the nose, still strapped in his ejection seat the whole, fully loaded aircraft passing over him in its decelerating path to oblivion. A proud, lovely, sleek bird turned into a pile of scrap metal destined for the furnace to be turned into neat, aluminum ingots.

Marciano retired undefeated only to be killed in an airplane crash.

There wouldn't be any more heavyweight fights for Ed and me to jab and circle, counter and feint, cross and hook in our jousting preliminary to THE bet. Ed was the victim of a TKO forever more. Another triple headed monster added to the list of Cold War casualties. God rest his soul.

I miss you Ed.

THE COWBIRD FABLE

A small cowbird fluttered gamely in the heavy, chill mist as the dull light of the sun sunk into the gloom of winter. The ice congealed on his wings and he had difficulty flying. He couldn't make it to the naked tree limbs of the tree at the edge of the cow pasture.

"It's so cold. I'll rest here in the pasture for a bit then try for that tree before nightfall," he said to himself. Stiff and weary, he fell over as he hit the hard ground.

Before long his feet were numb and his legs were fast approaching the same state. He huddled near a tuft of weeds—a shelter from the wind. All night long he shuddered and shivered, unable to move off the ground, his body almost without feeling, he was so numb.

Towards morning the cold drizzle slackened. The poor cowbird could barely hold his head up. His wings were covered with ice and he was trapped, destined to freeze to death next to the small tuft of grass…

"If only the sun would rise, I could get warm and fly. Maybe sister Tillie would take me in," he thought.

But he was to be disappointed, the clouds continued to cover the sun and dawn found the little cowbird confused and near death. In his delirium he was flying south again with Tillie, happy and free—and warm.

A cow ambled toward him. He could see those huge hoofs steadily approaching while he lay against the tuft of weeds unable to move. She stopped to graze and he was in her shadow—colder than ever. She chewed off the sparse clumps of fodder encased in ice standing over him, then moved another step reaching for another clump as he felt a rear hoof shake the ground near him. He blinked, his eyelids stiff and heavy, barely moveable. A delusion of warmth swept over him—he and Tillie were snug and warm in the nest with mama. Death was near, one step more and he would be crushed. He was resigned. The wind swirled penetrating his icy feathers, deadening his senses to the inevitable.

A huge glob of brown 'go' splashed over his head, then another and still another in rapid succession. Before he could freeze to death or be crushed, it seemed he would drown in cow shit. Dimly, he thought, "Surely, I am jinxed. My planets are out of alignment. This is REALLY bad Karma."

The cow continued to defecate. Huge globs of dirty, brown waste tumbled down, over and around the little cowbird with a sound of soft slaps, steam rising from the huge pie shaped mound in the cold air. "A miracle, I can still hear!"

As the huge pile of manure threatened to reach the little cowbird's beak he stretched—up, up, higher. Then, a surprise, tingling in his toes. Another effort to stretch up, waaay up—up as far as he could to shake his head. The effort was extreme. He dare not open his beak.

Wonder of wonders, he could move! His mighty effort resulted in a feeble shake of his head and shook some of the manure off. He tried his wings. They were very stiff and beginning to tingle smartly, painfully, but there was some movement—he was almost sure.

The sun peeked out from the heavy clouds making the wings of the sparrow hawk circling lazily above shimmer as if traced in gold. A beautiful sight, the world's daily renewal. This day with promise at last. The hawk began to search for his breakfast.

"I can move!" the cowbird exalted and began to sing. He fluttered his wings, still very stiff, as the cow moved away. Now he felt the warmth of the sun added to that of the huge pile of manure. Wonderful, glorious life, the pain and the ache meant he would soon fly!

"Oh what a beautiful morning! Oh what a joyful day," he sang. "I'm alive! Soon I'll be free, tra-la, tra-la. A drink in the stream and maybe a holly berry or three, tra-la, tra-la. The world is smiling on me, tra-la, tra-la, tra-lee! Oh I can see!"

The hawk flew in a tighter circle and climbed higher in the brightening sky.

The cow mooed, ambling toward the brook. The warmth of her dung was thawing the little cowbird and he wiggled and fluttered and whistled. The little cowbird was happy, it was so good to be alive. Even the pain in his wings was almost gone. Soon he would fly, he was sure as he began to preen his wings.

Above, instead of stretching out to the sun in his lazy circle, the hawk's wings were suddenly drawn in as if hunched against the cold. From the tremendous height of his climb he began to plummet, nose down, beak barely separated. Down, down, the wind a growing hurricane over his close-set wings, his legs—and sharp talons tucked tightly into the soft feathers of his underbelly.

The ground rose at a dizzying rate, the tiniest features growing dramatically. The weathered and bare trees seemed to suddenly leap above the diving hawk. There, there was the little cowbird singing and fluttering, about to take wing from the great pile of cow dung.

A slight adjustment, the wings extended a little, the cowbird enlarged in his sight. Now, too late, the little bird looked up, his eyes wide, his song quit mid trill—"tra-".

A soft thump, the talons extended, the huge wings braked the diving hawk and his scream pierced the air as he lifted from the ground, breakfast securely clutched in his sharp talons.

"And so my little chickadees that's the lesson of your uncle Willie—rest his soul." Three pairs of glistening eyes shown like bright beads from the soft down heads tucked away cozily in the cowbird's nest.

"Lesson?" asked Willie, the most precocious of the three and namesake of his dead uncle. "I don't understand, mama."

"The lesson, my son, is this: Not everyone who poops on you is your enemy and by the same token, not everyone who pulls you out of the poop is your friend. The corollary is even more important: If you make too much noise about either you may find yourself in much deeper poop."

ABOUT THE AUTHOR

The author served in the Vietnam War with the Strategic Air Command and retired after twenty-eight years of service. He is the father of eight children and survived four years in the Pentagon.

0-595-34868-8

CPSIA information can be obtained at www.ICGtesting.com
Printed in the USA
LVOW040756010412

275615LV00002B/25/A